DOMINATION INC.

by

DRUSILLA LEATHER

CHIMERA

Domination Inc. first published in 1999 by
Chimera Publishing Ltd
PO Box 152
Waterlooville
Hants
PO8 9FS

Printed and bound in Great Britain

All Characters in this publication are fictitious. Any resemblance to real persons, living or dead, is purely coincidental.

Copyright Drusilla Leather

The right of Drusilla Leather to be identified as author of this book has been asserted in accordance with section 77 and 78 of the Copyrights Designs and Patents Act 1988

DOMINATION INC.

Drusilla Leather

This novel is fiction – in real life practice safe sex

For Bill – With virtual love from Mrs B

Chapter One

'On your knees and worship me.'

The wording on the card caught Laurel Angell's attention as she waited for Joe to answer the phone. It featured a photograph of a voluptuous dark-haired woman encased in a skin of shiny black leather, brandishing a whip, with a Soho phone number featured prominently beneath the image. It was not the only such card stuck to the phone booth wall, but it was certainly the most striking. Laurel carefully peeled the card from the glass and slipped it in the pocket of her leather jacket, not quite certain why she was doing so. Having agreed to meet Joe in a pub just off Camden High Road, she replaced the receiver and went to wait for a break in the traffic on Shaftesbury Avenue.

As Laurel trudged down the subway steps towards Tottenham Court Road tube station, she reflected that anyone else in her position would have a flash company mobile phone, so they could make a call without breaking their journey. But since Roger had disappeared, there was hardly enough money to pay for a company two-pound phonecard.

Laurel did not consider herself to be a violent woman, but if she ever got her hands on Roger Preston again, murder would almost certainly be committed. The two had been partners in the Moonlight Escort Agency for almost three years, and in that time Laurel had come to know the suave, well-spoken Roger like a brother. Or, at least, she thought she had. Now she realised there was a side to Roger that she had never known. A side which would allow the man to conveniently vanish from the face of the earth when the business had run into trouble.

Everything had seemed so promising, at the start. Running an escort agency had never been the career Laurel had envisaged for herself as she studied for an English degree at university, but when she had graduated it seemed that the only jobs available were in telesales. After nine months of trying to sell advertising space in a technical journal and fighting off the attentions of potential clients who were more interested in the sound of her soft, husky voice than in placing an advert, she'd had enough. If she had to sell anything to earn her living, selling the company of a beautiful woman for the evening seemed easier and infinitely preferable. Roger Preston had a certain smooth charm and a way of hooking in a client, and Laurel had quickly learned from her partner's example. The agency had never made a huge profit, but with its innate discretion and a reputation for providing attractive, intelligent girls, Roger and Laurel had always been comfortable. In the last six months, however, things had gone badly wrong: a rival agency, Promises, had appeared, offering girls at half the price Moonlight was charging. It was not long before the number of clients had fallen off dramatically. They'd had to lay off several of their best girls, a couple of whom had, ironically, begun working for Promises shortly afterwards, and even an attempt to branch out and attract female customers by offering male escorts was not enough to stop the rot.

Laurel would never forget the afternoon she had climbed the flight of stairs to the agency's office, above a travel agent's in a busy Soho street, to find its doors locked and Roger absent. In all her time of working with him she had never arrived at the agency before him, and as she fumbled in her handbag for her own keys to the office, she wondered if he might be ill. She had been out of London for a couple of days, attending the wedding of an old schoolfriend, but there had been no message from Roger on her answerphone when she returned to indicate that anything might be wrong. Certainly nothing to suggest that there would be a pile of what looked suspiciously like bills lying on the floor behind the door, or that the lighting and telephone would not be working.

By working her way through the post, with its increasingly abrupt threats of disconnection unless payment was made, it became obvious to Laurel that Roger had been lying to her over a considerable amount of time regarding the agency's financial state. Both the phone and the electricity supply appeared to have been cut off, and there was also a couple of months' rent on the office outstanding.

She had gone down to the travel agency and persuaded them to let her use their phone. A couple of wheedling calls and the promise of a sum of money in the post had mollified Moonlight's most pressing creditors, and she was assured that everything would be reconnected within the next couple of days. Much as she was loath to do so, Laurel knew she could raise the necessary sums by pawning a couple of pieces of antique jewellery her grandmother had bequeathed her. Then she tried Roger's number, furious with him for letting the business fall into such a perilous state. A recorded voice told her the number had not been recognised. Something was definitely amiss here, and it seemed the only way to find out what was happening was to visit her partner in person.

When she turned up at the house in Notting Hill where Roger rented a self-contained ground floor flat, and peered through the window, the place had the same deserted air as the agency. She tried the intercom and received no reply.

As she walked back down the steps, a middle-aged man came towards her, clutching a brown paper bag full of shopping to his chest. Laurel recognised him as Roger's landlord, who lived on the first floor.

'Excuse me, I'm looking for Roger Preston,' she began, as the man fumbled in his pocket for his door key.

He flashed her a look filled with irritation and distaste. 'Aren't we all, love? You, me, the bailiffs.' He turned the key in the lock. 'If you find the bastard before I do, tell him he owes me three months' rent.'

He shut the door firmly in Laurel's face, leaving her standing impotently on the doorstep as a heavy rain began to fall.

That had been almost a fortnight ago; there had been no word from Roger, and her attempts to track him down via his friends and business associates had come to nothing. No one had seen the man for a couple of weeks, and he had given no forwarding address. Laurel had been left on her own to sort out the mess he had created. The agency was dying on its feet: despite her assurances that she had no intention of closing the business, all bar a couple of the girls who remained on her books had drifted away in search of more secure work, and she was finding it increasingly difficult to cater for the thin trickle of clients who still continued to call. To compound her problems, as she began to look through the muddle of paperwork in the office, it became clear that Roger's duplicity was greater than she had at first believed. His name was entirely absent from every single one of the bank loan forms, rental agreements and contracts of employment in the files. Even though the documents outlining their initial partnership had been drawn up over three years ago, Laurel had a clear memory of Roger putting his signature to everything.

They had been equal partners, but now only Laurel appeared to have a stake in the agency – and, more importantly, the responsibility for settling its debts. Quite when Roger had altered the paperwork she would never know, and she had no way of proving what he had done: it was her word against that of a man who, effectively, had ceased to exist.

She had sought legal advice, but it had become clear that unless she could find a way of paying the money the agency owed its various creditors, she was in serious trouble. The sums involved were such that even selling the family heirlooms would not meet them. Her meeting earlier this afternoon with her solicitor, Peter Greycott, had clarified the situation: unless she did something soon, she was looking at bankruptcy and the prospect of having her flat in West Hampstead repossessed.

Laurel tried to put the gloomy thoughts out of her head as she reached *The McColgan Revived*, Joe's local. She pushed open the door that led into the pub's cosy interior and wandered in. A couple of heads turned at the sight of her tall, curvy figure, even buried as it was in a sloppy fisherman's rib jumper and loose-fitting PVC jeans, but she barely registered their interest. She ran a hand through her shaggy, shoulder-length strawberry-blonde hair and looked round for her friend.

The red-headed Joe was already sitting on one of the high stools at the bar, studying the racing form in the *Evening Standard*, a half-drunk glass of Guinness on the wooden counter in front of him. He looked up as Laurel approached him.

'Hi, Laurel, how's it going? Can I get you a drink?'

'Thanks. A white wine and soda, please.' Laurel smiled at the good-looking blond behind the bar as he reached for a wineglass.

Laurel had liked Joe Gallagher since the first time they had met, a little over two years ago. Then, Joe had been a detective constable who had turned up to investigate a break-in at the travel agency beneath the office where Moonlight Escorts was based. The routine conversation had got friendlier over a couple of drinks when Joe had come off duty, and she had found herself warming to his wicked sense of humour and the grin which perpetually lit up his face. The two had continued to keep in touch, even when Joe had been transferred to a station out in Essex. He had lasted a mere four months there before his career had come to a sudden end after a serious accident. While pursuing a suspect in a stolen car at high speed through Epping Forest on a rainy November night, Joe's squad car had spun out of control and crashed into a tree. It had taken the best part of two hours to cut him and his colleague free from the wreckage, and by the time Joe's mangled, unconscious body had been retrieved and taken to the local intensive care unit, doctors were speculating that he might never walk again. He had proved them wrong, a slight limp and a tracery of scars on his legs bearing the only testimony to his brush with death, but he had never been fit enough to rejoin the police force. Now, he worked in an upmarket sandwich bar in Holborn, catering to the hungry insurance brokers and bankers in the area. Laurel looked at her friend, still studying his newspaper, and wondered if he ever missed his old job. It was a stupid question, of course: how could you not miss something that had been your whole life?

'Have you got a pen?' Joe's words cut into Laurel's reverie. 'I think I've found the little beauty that means I never have to cut another sandwich as long as I live.'

'Sure.' Laurel rummaged in her jacket pocket, searching for the ball-point pen she knew was in there. As she did so, the prostitute's card fell out. Joe picked it up off the floor and looked at it quizzically.

'What's this?'

'I got it from a phone booth.' Laurel felt her cheeks reddening. 'Don't ask me why. It's not like I'm going to make an appointment or anything.'

'Is that because you don't want to, or because you just can't afford it at the moment?' Joe's tone was gently teasing.

'That's not funny,' Laurel replied. 'You know I was seeing my solicitor today? Well, it's worse than I thought. It looks like I'm going to lose the business, my flat – everything.' Unexpectedly, she felt tears pricking the backs of her eyes.

'If there's anything I can do…' Joe said gently, catching her hand with his and giving it a squeeze. 'I've still got some money left from the payout they gave me when I was pensioned off from the force.'

'Thanks, Joe, but I couldn't.' She sighed, and gently disentangled her fingers. 'It's not just a question of settling the debts I've got. I don't want to lose the agency. I need to find some way I can keep it alive.'

'Well, have you considered specialising?'

'Specialising?'

Joe tapped the card where it lay on the table between them. 'Look at this. You've seen how many cards there are offering services, but how many are just for girls giving nothing more than quick hand relief, or maybe a blowjob? And then you get one or two that are aimed at this market. Domination, bondage, the stuff that's more highly sought after – and pays better, too. I tell you, Laurel, there are lots of men looking for a woman who'll dish out a really good spanking, or make them wear a dress and humiliate them; all these straight-as-a-die City types, and judges and

MPs, wanting a good old thrashing just like they used to get at public school.'

'How come you know so much about this?' Laurel asked.

'I had a girlfriend who was into it. Not the heavy stuff so much, but she loved to be spanked.' Joe drained his glass and attracted the barman's attention. 'Same again?'

She nodded. 'So who are we talking about?' There had been so many girls flitting in and out of her friend's life that it was almost impossible to keep track of who he was seeing at any one time.

'You remember Judy?'

Laurel cast around in her memory, finally recalling a petite Scottish girl with a mass of curly dark hair, whom she had met at a Sunday afternoon barbecue party Joe had hosted a couple of months before his accident.

'Well, there was always something about Judy, I don't know if you'd call it feistiness, or what, but I always got the feeling that she was trying to goad me into something. She had this real impudent streak, and she was always trying to see how far she could push me. I could never work out what her game was, until one night when I was trying to watch the football, and she was really annoying me, standing in front of the TV screen to block my view. Eventually I said something like, "If you don't stop that, I'm going to haul you over my knee and give you a bloody good slap."'

Laurel had a sudden suspicion of where this story was heading. Her guess was confirmed when Joe continued, 'Do you know what she did? She just put her hands on her hips, flashed me this wicked little smile and said, "You wouldn't dare." Of course, that was when it hit me that she'd wanted this all the time, she just hadn't known how else to broach the subject. Something about the way she was looking at me, and the thought of having her wriggling on my lap while I tanned her backside really started to turn me on. I forgot all about the match I'd been watching, and I grabbed her by the arm and pulled her over my knees.

'She made a token attempt to get free, but she wasn't serious about it. She just lay there, her bum raised up invitingly towards me. I caught tight hold of both her wrists, and I pulled her skirt up so I could see her little white knickers stretched tight across her bum cheeks. Then I brought the flat of my hand down on her bottom. It was an instinctive thing – I'd never done anything like this before – and I thought I might have hit her too hard and hurt her, the way she gave a little surprised yelp of pain. So I was a bit more gentle with the next couple of slaps, but she kind of pouted and made it obvious that she preferred the rougher stuff. So I obliged, with about a dozen firm blows on her bottom.'

Joe was staring into the middle distance, his drink forgotten and a dreamy expression on his face. 'I was really getting into it by now, and it must have been obvious to Judy that she was lying so that her mound was pressing down hard on my erection. The more she squirmed, the harder I was getting. Part of me wanted to just unzip my flies and thrust my cock into her, but I wanted to tease her a bit first, get my own back for the way she'd manoeuvred me into this situation. So I pulled her knickers down so that they were just below the curve of her bum, and all that gorgeous naked flesh was exposed to me. I don't think she'd reckoned on me taking it quite this far, but I was enjoying the whole situation so much, I didn't want to stop just yet. I carried on spanking those firm little cheeks of hers, fascinated by the way her skin was flushing a deeper and deeper shade of crimson. By now she was making little whimpering noises, partly because her backside must have been really stinging, and partly because she was getting turned on by the whole damn thing. I'd felt the dampness in the gusset of her knickers as I'd yanked them down, and I could see little drops of moisture glistening on the hairs of her pussy. I knew that if I put my hand between her legs she'd be slippery and ready for me.

'I just skimmed a finger down the crack of her arse, very lightly, and she was shivering with anticipation. I slicked that finger in the juices that were flowing from her, and ran it back up, just pressing gently for a moment at her little anal opening, letting her know that her bum could be the focus of our pleasures in more ways than one. We'd never done it like that before, but if I'd told her that night that I wanted to fuck her there, she wouldn't have said no.'

'And did you?' Laurel asked, her voice suddenly constricted in her throat. The thought of being taken anally was not one she had ever consciously entertained, but at this moment she could not help thinking how it would feel to have a cock forcing its way into that tight, untried passage.

Joe stared at her enigmatically. 'Do you think I'm going to let you into all my little secrets? All I'll tell you is that Judy was getting more and more impatient, wanting me to give her an orgasm, so I did, but not quite in the way she was expecting. My hand was starting to get tired, and her backside was glowing a fiery shade of red by now, so I reckoned she'd had more than enough. I laid her carefully on the settee, with her bare bottom still sticking up in the air, and I said to her, "Are you sorry now?"

'There were tears shining in her eyes as she turned her face to me and nodded contritely. I knelt down at the side of her. "That poor little bum of yours looks so red and sore," I told her. "Do you want me to kiss it better?"

'She nodded again, and I pressed my lips to her bottom, gently covering it with little kisses. Then I parted her cheeks, and very slowly licked down the cleft between them, spending a long time lapping at her anal bud, until it relaxed enough that I could just push my tongue a little way inside it. That still wasn't what she really wanted, but when my mouth settled on her pussy she gave a squeal of delight. I'd never licked her out from behind like that, but the novelty value made it more exciting than usual for both of us. She tasted like nectar in my mouth, all sweet and gamy, and I could have happily spent all night with my head buried between her legs. She had an orgasm quicker than I'd ever known her to, but then I suppose she'd been building up to it from the moment that first slap landed on her backside.' Joe smiled, and ran his hands through his short red hair. 'And if you want to know more, tune in tomorrow night for the next exciting episode.'

'You're just a tease, Joe Gallagher,' Laurel replied good-naturedly, not wanting to confess how much the story had turned her on, and how she had unexpectedly found herself wishing that she had been in Judy's position, half-naked and vulnerable, waiting for the touch of Joe's lips and tongue on her chastised and overheating flesh.

'You've given me an idea, though,' she continued, ignoring the pulse of desire that was beating steadily between her legs and forcing her mind back on to business matters. 'It was something you were saying, about how Judy wanted to be spanked but didn't know how to ask you. Well, just consider how many other women secretly fancy being dominated, but their partner isn't into it, or they think they'll get laughed at if they admit to it. I think you're right when you say I could make the agency more specialised, but if I offered domination services aimed purely at women, I think it'd be unique.' The concept was crystallising in her mind as she spoke, and she continued rapidly. 'I could make it work, I know I could. A couple of adverts in the sex magazines that are aimed at women and couples, a little discreet word-of-mouth on the fetish scene... I've just got to bring the agency to the attention of those women who've got a secret fantasy they've never dared act out, or who'd like to go to a fetish club but think they might get hassled if they go on their own. If I got this off the ground you wouldn't fancy sticking some cards up in phone boxes for me, would you, Joe?'

'If you get this off the ground, I want to be a hell of a sight more involved than that,' Joe replied. 'I want to go into partnership with you.'

Laurel looked up at him, surprised. 'You're not serious?'

'Whatever you might say, Laurel, you can't do this without some financial help, and no bank's going to give you a loan with those debts hanging over your head. I told you I've got some money tucked away, and I'm sick to death of making bloody sandwiches. And anyway, getting into the domination game was my idea in the first place.' He pouted at her like a sulky child, making her laugh. Holding out his hand for her to shake, he said, 'Partners?'

She grasped his hand decisively. 'Partners.' As their eyes met he gave her a little wink, and she felt the pit of her stomach lurch unexpectedly. For the briefest of moments she thought about suggesting to Joe that they sealed the deal over a bottle of wine at her flat, with the unspoken certainty that the evening would finish with the pair of them twined together in her queen-sized bed. Then she dismissed the idea. Joe was her best friend; the bond between them ran too deep to be complicated and perhaps ruined by their getting involved sexually. It was better if she went home alone, and tried to forget the images he had stirred of her lying across his lap, her bare backside exposed to him, as his palm came down repeatedly on her vulnerable cheeks, before his fingers sought out her hard, aching clitoris...

She broke his grip on her hand and glanced at her watch. 'I should be going,' she said. 'It's getting late and I've had such a shitty day, I just want to dive into a hot bath and forget everything.'

Joe's expression made it abundantly clear that he would be more than happy to join her in that bath, but he said nothing as she climbed down from her bar stool.

Laurel dropped a light kiss on his smooth-shaven cheek. 'I'll ring Peter Greycott, get him to draw up the paperwork. If we're going to be partners, we'll do it properly. I don't want to wake up one morning and find you've run out on me.'

'You know I'd never do that,' Joe replied, and for a moment Laurel wondered how many other girls had heard such a promise from him. 'Tomorrow I'll go jack in my job. And then…?'

'Then we find out who wants to work for our new agency. Goodbye, Moonlight Escorts, hello Domination Inc.'

Chapter Two

When Laurel rang all the remaining staff on Moonlight's books the following morning and outlined her plans for changing the set-up of the agency, the response was less than promising. Only two of the girls, Elisha Dee and Cindy Beresford, and one male escort, Christian Roscoe, showed any inclination to stay on and offer domination or submission services, and even they were more than a little concerned by the prospect of having to prove their worth at an audition.

'Look, it's nothing to worry about,' Laurel told them as they sat in the office, drinking coffee. 'I just want to know that you're going to be happy doing this kind of stuff.'

'Doesn't bother me at all,' Cindy said chirpily, taking a drag on her cigarette. Laurel was glad the girl had expressed an interest in the agency's new direction. She had always been popular with clients: barely five foot tall and skinny, with peroxide-blonde hair styled into a jaw-length bob, men were attracted to her cheeky personality and gleeful enthusiasm for sex. Laurel suspected that if any of her employees was a natural submissive, it was Cindy.

Elisha, on the other hand, was the dominant type, tall and elegant, with hourglass curves and jet-black hair that she normally kept twisted into a thick plait. She was fiddling with that plait as she spoke, an expression of concern on her strikingly beautiful, high-cheekboned face. 'I just can't get over the fact that the agency's in so much trouble. I mean, Roger never said—'

'Roger never said a lot of things,' Laurel retorted. 'But Roger's not involved with the running of this place any more. That's down to me – oh, and Joe, of course.'

'Yes, where is this mysterious Joe?' Christian asked, pushing aside the stray lock of blond hair that was permanently falling into his green eyes. 'I thought he'd be here, seeing as he's your new business partner and all.'

'He's got a few things to attend to, but he'll be here shortly,' Laurel replied blithely. She did not feel the need to mention that he was handing in his notice at the sandwich bar; the three remaining employees sitting in front of her already seemed sceptical enough about her plans, and telling them that Joe had no experience of running an escort agency could only weaken their confidence and their desire to stay still further. 'So what's really worrying you, Elisha?'

'Well – neither Cindy nor I have ever had a female client before, and I'm not sure how I'm going to react,' the girl replied. 'I mean, I've never really looked at other women in that way.'

'Yeah, well you can't exactly be repulsed by the idea, or you wouldn't still be here, would you, Leesh?' Cindy said. 'If you weren't turned on by the thought of telling some girl what to do, you'd have run off screaming to find another job, just like Marielle and Donna and all those other gutless wonders.' She stubbed the smouldering end of her cigarette into an ashtray shaped like a scallop shell with 'A Present From Margate' embossed on it. It was the only personal effect Roger had left behind on his departure from the office, and Laurel suspected it was because he had always loathed it.

'I bet you were always bossing the other girls around when you were at school, Elisha,' Christian piped up. 'You strike me as the sort who went to boarding school, and when you were in the sixth form they made you head prefect. I can see you now, walking round the dormitory after lights out, looking for stray hands at play under the bedsheets.'

'Is this true, Elisha?' Laurel asked, an idea beginning to form in her brain. If she angled the conversation carefully, she could push the girls and Christian into a scenario which would prove once and for all their aptitude for domination work. 'Did you ever catch one of your friends doing something she shouldn't have been?'

Elisha shook her head. 'Not me. Despite what Chris thinks, I was never a prefect, but my best friend, Amanda, was. She took the role very seriously, and she once told us that if she ever caught any of us playing with our pussies, she would punish us. We were at a convent school, you see, St Agatha's, and we'd all been brought up to believe that sex was sinful unless we were married, and that we should never, ever touch ourselves between our legs unless we were washing ourselves. The nuns and the headmistress, Sister Mary, really were that strict, and we, of course, were too sheltered to know any different.'

She sipped from her mug of coffee before continuing. 'There was one girl who ignored everything the nuns told us, and her name was Geraldine. We'd always been a little envious of her, because she'd been the first girl in our year to develop into a woman. She had large, heavy breasts that pushed against the front of her starched blouse, and when we went for our weekly walks into the village near the school, all the men who we passed couldn't help staring at Geraldine, with her curvy figure squeezed into her little gymslip.

'None of us knew anything about sex, but that didn't stop us from being curious about it, despite all the dire warnings we got from the nuns about the shame that would come upon us if we disobeyed their teachings. There was a boy a year older than us, Tom, who worked in the convent gardens. He was the only male we had any contact at all with on a regular basis, and we all had a terrible crush on him. He was tall and brawny, from digging the vegetable gardens and mowing the lawns, and in the summer he never wore a shirt when he was working, so we could all see his bare, tanned chest, and his muscular arms. I would sit staring at him out of the classroom window, and I had these silly little romantic dreams about how one day he'd fall in love with me. I think some of the other girls did, too. Nothing happened, of course; if we were out in the grounds of the convent and he so much as looked in our direction we'd just blush and run away – all except for Geraldine. I really thought that if any of us was going to be the one who defied the nuns and lost our virginity before we left school it would be her, but it didn't turn out like that.'

'So what happened?' Christian asked, sounding genuinely interested.

Whether Elisha's memories were genuine, or she was embellishing the truth for the benefit of her audience, she seemed to have a gift for storytelling that dragged the audience into the tale, and Laurel was mentally revising her initial impression of the girl's potential usefulness as a member of Domination Inc.'s staff.

'As I told you, Amanda used to make sure that we all behaved ourselves in the dormitories. We weren't bad girls; once we'd put on our nighties and slipped between the starched sheets of our narrow little iron-framed beds, we used to chat to each other and giggle, swapping little secrets, until Amanda came round. She used to carry a torch and shine it at anyone she thought was talking, and we always shut up, because we didn't want her to dish out a punishment. She carried a cane, too, which we all thought was an affectation. As long as I'd been at St Agatha's, no one had ever been on the receiving end of a caning, though I'd heard stories that, a year or so before my time, one girl had been given six of the best by Sister Mary for some misdemeanour that was so awful no one ever talked about it.

'It was one evening in late September, the year I went into the upper sixth; we hadn't been back at school that long after the summer holidays, and it was still warm enough for Tom to have been out in the garden without his shirt. My bed was next to Geraldine's, and we were whispering together about how handsome Tom was, and how it would feel if he put his arms round us and kissed us, and then Geraldine asked me if I ever felt a funny feeling down between my legs when I thought about Tom. I didn't know where the conversation was going, but I had to admit that I did – it was a nice, tingly sort of excitement, and I liked it. Geraldine told me that she knew how to make that feeling a hundred times better; apparently, if you licked your index finger and rubbed it in the forbidden place between your legs, you could get so excited you thought you were going to die. I didn't like the sound of this at all – after all, wasn't that exactly what the nuns had warned us against? But Geraldine told me to ignore the nuns. She said they were all just hypocrites, and they lay in bed and rubbed themselves every night because they knew how good it was, but they didn't want us to find out that was the case because then we might realise that they were telling us other things which weren't true.

'And then I realised that Geraldine's hands had disappeared under the bedsheets. The moon was full that night, and by the pale light that shone through the thin dormitory curtains I could see the sheets were moving slightly, and I knew she had to be touching herself in the way she'd told me about. I don't know why, but at that moment I experienced the feeling I'd told Geraldine I only ever felt when I thought about Tom. For a moment I was incredibly tempted to follow her example, then there was a bright light shining in my face.' She paused. 'There isn't another cup of coffee on the go, is there?'

'I'll sort one out for everyone,' Cindy replied. While she went into the little washroom next door to the office to fill the kettle, Elisha cleared her throat, and then, once the little blonde was back in the room, resumed her story.

'You've probably guessed it was Amanda on her nightly rounds. I was expecting the usual ticking-off from her, but it wasn't me she was interested in. Geraldine tried to pull her hands up above the bedclothes but she wasn't quick enough. Amanda pulled back the counterpane, and there was Geraldine, with her night-dress rucked up round her waist and a guilty expression on her face.

'"Caught you, you little slut!" Amanda exclaimed. She sounded almost gleeful, and I think she'd been waiting for something like this to happen for a while. "You know what happens to filthy girls who play with themselves, don't you?" she asked.

'Geraldine pulled her night-dress back into place, covering herself up. "Sister Mary says they go to hell," she replied dutifully, but it was obvious she didn't believe a word of what she was saying.

'"They do indeed," Amanda replied, "but not in the way you might have thought. Get out of bed, and go and stand in the middle of the room."

'Meekly, Geraldine did as she was told. Amanda switched on the main light, and those girls who had already drifted off to sleep began to stir. The others were already sitting up in bed, aware that Amanda's long-threatened punishment was about to be meted out.

"'Now, Geraldine, lift your night-dress up to your waist," Amanda ordered. Geraldine looked as if she was about to protest, but realised that however humiliating it would be to expose herself to the rest of the girls in the dormitory, it would be even more humiliating to lose face in front of them by refusing. So she took the hem of her nightie and did as she was told, lifting it up so that those girls who were in front of her could see her pussy, covered with its wispy growth of blonde hair, and those behind her, including me, could see her backside. She had a beautiful bottom, plump and creamy-skinned, and I couldn't help staring at it.

'Everyone was waiting to see what Amanda would do next. She put the torch down on the end of one of the beds and went to stand beside Geraldine. Then she unhooked the crook-handled cane from her belt, and tapped the tip of it gently against the palm of her hand. I couldn't believe what was about to happen, and I don't think any of the other girls could, either. Surely no one but Sister Mary had the power to dish out a caning? We were all seniors, we had the power to stop Amanda, but the whole atmosphere in the dormitory had changed; it had become tense and excited, and I think a little part of every girl there was secretly egging Amanda on.

'Her voice was icy when she gave the next order. "Bend over, Geraldine."

"'I shan't. You can't make me," Geraldine replied.

"'Oh, yes I can," Amanda said. "And if you won't do it, I'll get two of the girls to hold you in place."

'That threat was enough. Geraldine let the hem of her nightie drop and bent over so that her hands were on her knees. Her stance didn't please Amanda, who used her feet to nudge Geraldine's ankles until her legs were about a foot apart. Then she raised Geraldine's nightie again, folding it back and letting it rest in the middle of her back, so that her bottom was on show once more, along, this time, with her pussy. Of course, I'd never seen that part of another girl's anatomy before, and I wanted to get closer and study the fleshy, hair-fringed lips, and the little hole between them.

'Amanda positioned herself behind Geraldine and drew her hand back. There was a moment's silence, and then she brought the cane down across Geraldine's buttocks. She couldn't really have hit her that hard, but Geraldine squealed as though she'd been shot and her hands flew round to clutch her smarting bum.

'"Take your hands away," Amanda snapped. "There are five more to come, and I expect you to take them without flinching."

'That was an impossible task, of course. When the second blow followed the first Geraldine yelped again, but she kept her hands where they were. The rest of us looked on in appalled fascination: there was already one line across her bum, red and raised against her pale skin, and now it had been joined by a second, running parallel to the first. To be fair to Amanda, she didn't draw out the punishment as much as she might have done, although it was obvious that she was getting a strange kind of enjoyment from what she was doing, The remaining four strokes were delivered fairly rapidly, Amanda leaving just enough time for Geraldine to recover from each one before renewing the assault. By the time she'd finished Geraldine was sobbing openly, and her bottom was well and truly striped. What seemed more intriguing to me, however, was that the lips of her sex seemed shinier and more open than they had been when her punishment started.

'I can't begin to describe the different emotions that were churning inside me at that moment. I was horrified that Amanda had treated my friend in this way, but I was also excited, and the tingly feelings had started between my legs again, sharper and more insistent than they had ever been. But the really strange thing was that I wasn't so much identifying with Geraldine and her poor bottom, but with Amanda. I wanted to know how it would feel to wield that amount of power, to have another girl cringing in fear and anticipation of what I was about to do to her. I wanted to be the one who dished out punishment, not the one who took it.'

'Told you,' Cindy muttered triumphantly.

'So what happened next?' Christian asked, still wrapped up in Elisha's story.

'Amanda told Geraldine to stand up and straighten her nightie. She said she'd make a note in the punishment book that Geraldine had been caught talking after lights out, and had been given six lines as a result – well, it was partly the truth. I don't know whether Sister Mary ever realised what had happened, though I suspect she probably did. After Amanda had left the dormitory and the lights had gone out once more, I suggested that Geraldine should get into bed with me. I had a tube of hand cream and I used it to rub into the weals on her bottom. Well, at first I did. But soon my hands were moving down lower, until I was touching her between her legs. She didn't try to stop me, but instead she pushed my legs apart gently and began to touch me in return. We explored each other for ages; it felt marvellous as we rubbed away. Geraldine showed me the special spot which she said was guaranteed to make you feel like you were in heaven, and when she touched it, I came for the first time in my life.'

Elisha smiled wickedly. 'It was all downhill from there,

I'm afraid. I got into the habit of playing with myself after lights out, and within six weeks I'd lost my virginity to Tom in one of the greenhouses he looked after. Within ten weeks I'd been caught with him, and expelled, and that was the end of my education. It hacked my parents off no end: I think they had visions that I might go into teaching. If they knew how much more money you could earn just pretending to be a strict headmistress, I think they'd have a fit.'

'So that's what you fancy doing, is it, playing the strict headmistress?' Laurel asked. 'It's just it would be useful for me to know if anyone feels they're suited to any particular rôle.'

Elisha shrugged. 'I'm really not sure. I think I could be the dominant head girl, just like Amanda at St Agatha's.'

'Well, why don't you give it a try?' Laurel said. 'Think of it as an audition piece. You be the head girl, and Cindy can be the naughty one who's been caught playing with herself.' She glanced over at Christian, cast around for inspiration and found it. 'Chris, you're the headmaster. Join in when you feel it's appropriate.'

Cindy and Elisha looked at each other, a little embarrassed, then Cindy sprang to her feet and grabbed her long black coat from where it was hanging on the back of the office door. She perched on the edge of the chair and pulled the coat up to her chin, using it as an impromptu bedsheet. That was the cue Elisha needed. She went and stood over Cindy, catching hold of the coat and twitching it out of Cindy's grasp.

'It's no good hiding,' she said, her voice soft and authoritative. 'I know exactly what you were doing, you wicked little slut. Stand up.'

Meekly, Cindy did as she was told, head bowed, her attitude exactly that of a guilty schoolgirl.

Elisha glared at her, hands on her hips. 'You're a disgrace to the house, Beresford,' she said. 'It's not enough that you've earned demerit points for sloppy schoolwork and for being late for lessons three times this month. Now I catch you with your fingers in your minge. And don't deny it. Everyone knows what a lazy, wanton little bitch you are.'

'I'm sorry, Elisha,' Cindy replied quietly.

'Sorry isn't good enough,' Elisha said. 'I can't ignore your behaviour any longer. I should really report you to the Head, let him sort you out with that long, whippy cane of his. But I'd much rather punish you myself.'

'Please, you can't...'

'Oh, yes, I can.' Elisha positioned herself on the chair Cindy had vacated, and tapped her lap. 'Over my knee, Beresford, or it'll be the worse for you.'

As Laurel and Christian watched, Cindy clambered into place. Laurel watched the tableau that was unfolding before her with a mixture of satisfaction and a strange, unnerving arousal. The two girls were acting their parts so well that she didn't really need Elisha to deliver a spanking in order to convince her she had one potential dominatrix and a confirmed submissive on her books. And yet she couldn't bring herself to ask them to stop. She told herself it was because Christian hadn't yet had a chance to join in the scenario, but part of her longed to see just what would happen when Elisha brought her hand down on Cindy's jeans-covered backside.

'Six for the demerit marks, and six for your slutty behaviour,' Elisha announced. 'I think even you can take a dozen.'

Cindy said nothing, waiting passively for Elisha to begin the punishment. She was not prepared for what happened next, as Elisha reached underneath her prone body to unbutton the fly of her jeans and push them down off her hips. Beneath them, Cindy was wearing a pair of virginal white cotton knickers which stretched tautly over her vulnerable-looking buttocks.

'That's better,' Elisha said, and gave Cindy's bottom a hard smack.

'Hang on!' Cindy exclaimed. 'This is just play-acting, Leesh!'

'Whatever gave you that impression?' Elisha replied. 'Now take the rest without complaining or you'll be in the Head's study for an appointment with his rod.'

'Now that sounds more like it.' Cindy giggled, pouncing on the double meaning in Elisha's words. Her giggle changed abruptly to a squeal as Elisha smartly peppered her backside with hard, stinging slaps.

Though Cindy's bottom was snugly covered by her white knickers, Laurel was certain that it would be starting to turn red, the marks of Elisha's palm visibly imprinted on the flesh. She wanted to see those marks, but could not bring herself to issue the order for Elisha to bare Cindy's backside. Her sex was heating rapidly, the lips swelling, making her black leggings feel uncomfortably tight. It was the same feeling she had experienced when Joe had been telling her the story about his ex-girlfriend goading him into spanking her. Like Elisha, she knew she was turned on by the sight of someone else being punished. Unlike her dominant employee, however, mentally she was placing herself firmly in the position of the one who was on the receiving end.

Laurel shifted in her seat, crossing her legs to try to assuage the throbbing pressure between them, as Elisha ran her hand lovingly over Cindy's cotton-covered backside.

'That wasn't so bad, was it?' Elisha asked.

Cindy shook her head, apparently unable to speak.

Elisha twined her fingers in Cindy's bottle-blonde hair, and pulled her head up gently. 'I can't hear you, Beresford. Aren't you going to thank me?'

'Thank you for giving me the punishment I deserved,' Cindy said obediently.

'Good girl,' Elisha replied, and stroked Cindy's bottom again. This time her hand found its way down into the cleft between Cindy's cheeks, her long-taloned fingers pouching the girl's sex. Cindy moaned appreciatively as Elisha gently rubbed her pussy through the gusset of her knickers. Her legs parted slightly, allowing Elisha easier access to her most private parts. Then, to Laurel's surprise and excitement, Elisha tugged Cindy's knickers down firmly. Cindy made no attempt to protest, or even to close her legs, and Laurel saw clearly that Cindy's pubic hair was the same chemically-assisted blonde as that on her head.

Christian took this moment as his cue to join in. He went to the office door and opened it a little way before slamming it shut hard, the sound designed to make both Elisha and Cindy look in his direction.

'Girls, girls, what are you doing?' he exclaimed, adopting a suitably pompous tone. 'I will not tolerate such shameless, sinful behaviour in my school. You have been warned time and time again that the expression of Sapphic delight is strictly forbidden here.'

Cindy sat bolt upright on Elisha's knee, covering her vulva with her hands, but not before Laurel had been treated to a glimpse of her wet, open furrow.

'Oh, please, Headmaster,' Elisha began, suddenly contrite, 'you won't tell our parents, will you? We don't want to be expelled.'

'You realise the only alternative is six of the best for the pair of you, don't you?' Christian said.

Cindy and Elisha glanced at each other, Elisha clearly discomfited by this turn of events. Her protests were waved away by Christian, who was roaming the room in search of a suitable implement of punishment. He at last alighted on a plant pot on the windowsill, which contained a weedy vine held up by a thin length of bamboo. He unfastened the plant from its supporting cane, which he brandished experimentally.

'Just the thing,' he announced. 'Now, we'll start with you, girl,' he motioned to Elisha. 'Bend over and touch your toes.'

Casting a mutinous glare at Laurel, Elisha did as she was told. Christian positioned himself behind her and flipped up the skirt she was wearing to reveal a beautifully heart-shaped bottom, clad in opaque black tights with red lacy panties just visible beneath them. He flexed his cane, and then tapped Elisha on the bottom with it, measuring out the distance for his strike. The cane swished through the air and landed on its target, firmly enough to make Elisha's buttocks smart, though there was no real venom in Christian's stroke. In truth, this was little more than a token punishment, Elisha's tights and panties protecting her from the real sting of the cane. The remaining five strokes were delivered in quick succession, Christian not even bothering to invoke the time-honoured ritual of asking Elisha to thank him after each one. Laurel sensed that the real performance was to come when Christian turned his attention to Cindy.

Her suspicions seemed well-founded when Cindy was ordered to bend over without being allowed to pull up her knickers and jeans. Elisha stood and rubbed her bottom ruefully, though she seemed well aware that she had been spared any genuine discomfort, and her gaze seemed riveted to Cindy's moist, aromatic sex as it was presented to the onlookers, tucked between her widely-parted legs like some ripe, exotic fruit.

This time, when Christian measured out his swing and brought the cane down, there was no holding back. The cane landed with a satisfying thwack across Cindy's buttocks, leaving a slim red weal in its wake. Her flesh already sensitised by the spanking it had received earlier, Cindy must have felt the stroke all the more keenly, but she said nothing. Stoically, she bit her lip and readied herself for the next one.

Christian took the chastisement at his own pace, making Cindy wait for agonising moments before deciding to lay the cane on once more. Elisha's punishment had been over within a minute, but Cindy's lasted more than twice as long. By the time Christian came to deliver the last stroke there were five distinct, well-spaced tramlines across Cindy's flesh, glowing an angry crimson. He had saved his fiercest blow until the end, and it was aimed squarely at the underhang of Cindy's buttocks, where the flesh was unmarked and sweetly tender. She had remained silent throughout her ordeal, but this time she could not restrain herself from letting out a shriek of pain, and bringing her hands round to cradle her tormented bottom.

Laurel could not help noticing that, despite the discomfort she was in, Cindy's quim was juicier than it had been, and there were silvery trails of excitement trickling down the tops of her thighs. She was suddenly eager to cup Cindy's sex-flesh in her palm and ease a finger into that greedy maw which had been opened by the punishment the girl had taken. She wanted Cindy to writhe beneath her ministrations as she stroked her plump little clitoris and frigged her tight, velvet channel, and then she wanted to feel Christian bring his cane down hard on her own naked backside for having dared to take such liberties with a member of her own staff...

She started guiltily at a knock on the office door. 'Anyone home?' a voice called, and she realised it was Joe.

'Yes, come in!' she replied.

Joe walked in to see Cindy hastily buttoning the fly of her jeans, and Christian replacing the length of bamboo in its pot.

'Everyone, this is Joe Gallagher, my new business partner,' Laurel announced. 'Joe, this is Elisha and Cindy and Christian, our first three full-time members of staff.'

'Nice to meet you all,' Joe said, shaking hands all round, 'but I can't help feeling that I've just missed something.'

'Laurel here's been putting us through our paces,' Cindy replied, smiling at him wickedly. Her hands reached to unfasten her jeans once more, and she began to lower them. 'She just doesn't think I've quite got the hang of this submission lark yet, though, do you Laurel?'

Laurel, knowing that this was far from the truth, but aware of the hunger in Cindy's voice, nodded. 'Why don't you show her how you'd mete out a punishment, Joe? After all, we're likely to be a little short-handed over the next couple of weeks, and you never know when you might have to deputise on an escort job.'

She took the cane Christian had used so recently and handed it to Joe. And when you've shown what you can do to Cindy, why don't you show me what you can do to me? she thought. Hurriedly, she excused herself and went to make more coffee. She had already decided that her own body was not for hire, at any price, and no matter how excited she became at the thought of being firmly chastised, it was a resolution she firmly intended to uphold.

Chapter Three

I need a man, Laurel thought, twisting a beer mat glumly between her fingers. It's all very well planning to offer an escort service for women who like to be dominated, but it's no good if the only men I can provide to dominate them are Joe and Christian. The pair of them will be worn out within a week.

Given their performance in the office, Cindy and Elisha seemed more than capable of catering for those clients who wanted to explore their dominant or submissive tendencies with a woman, and both were eager to begin work as soon as possible. But Laurel didn't feel she could re-launch the agency under its new identity until she had at least one more dedicated male escort on board.

She finished the last mouthful of white wine and soda in her glass and toyed with the idea of ordering another one. There was nothing to go home to, and the prospect of sitting in front of some tedious game show with a Chinese takeaway was less appealing than that of staying a while longer in the friendly warmth of her shabby local pub. Everyone knew her here, and if she wanted to sit in a corner with a book or the crossword in the evening paper, she would not be bothered. She set her empty glass on the table, her mind resolved: just this last one, and then she would be on her way.

As she passed the couple sitting in the alcove next to her own table, she could have sworn she heard the man say to his female companion, 'And when you come back from the ladies', I want you to give me your knickers.

That way I'll know you've taken them off.'

The girl he was with, a porcelain-skinned redhead in her early twenties, was looking at him as though she wanted to protest. Laurel made a show of bending to tie the lace of her ankle boot, listening for the man's next words, not quite able to believe what she thought she had heard. For a moment she suspected that her overburdened brain was finding evidence of domination games everywhere, but then the man said, 'Do it. Or you know what you'll be in for when I get you home.'

The girl gave a shudder, her expression one of fear mingled with anticipation, and left the table, brushing past Laurel as she rose to her feet. Laurel felt her pussy clench with the thought that the girl was about to comply with her partner's bizarre demand.

She hurried to the bar, her eyes scanning the half-empty pub as she did so. She was eager to be back in her seat by the time the girl returned to reveal her newly-knickerless state.

As she passed the neighbouring alcove on the way back with her drink, she took a quick look at the man who sat there. He was dressed in uniform black, like a would-be rock star: battered leather biker's jacket, T-shirt and loose-fitting jeans. His short black hair was gelled back from his face, and he sported a neatly-sculpted goatee beard. He glanced up as Laurel went by, and she was briefly aware of his heavy-lidded grey gaze settling on her and assessing her. There was a dominant, slightly arrogant set to his face, and Laurel knew that if he had demanded she remove her knickers, she would not have dared to disobey him.

She was settling herself into her seat when the redhead pushed open the door of the ladies' and began to make her way back to her table. The girl was wearing a little tartan miniskirt, and Laurel could not help but notice that she was holding the hem surreptitiously, as though afraid that it might ride up as she passed one of the tables. She's done it, Laurel thought. She's really done it.

From where she was sitting, she was not able to see what the couple were doing, but the music from the juke box had faded away, and it was just possible to hear what they were saying if she listened hard.

'So go on, give them to me,' the man was demanding. His voice had a soft Southern Irish lilt, at once insistent and beguiling.

'No, Warren, I – I can't,' the girl replied quietly.

'Oh, yes you can. Or do you want me to haul you over my knee and tan your bare backside in front of everyone here?'

'You wouldn't.' There was a quality to the girl's voice which suggested that was exactly what she was hoping he would do.

'I'm waiting, Sara,' was all he said.

There was a long pause, during which Laurel realised she was holding her breath. She could not resist edging round quietly until she was in a position from which the dark-haired man was partially visible, though his companion's back was still turned to her. At last the girl muttered, 'Here you are.' Laurel thought she caught a glimpse of something white being passed across the table in Sara's fist.

The man the redhead had called Warren took the scrap of fabric from her and held it to his face, as though it was a handkerchief. 'No wonder you didn't want to give them to me, you little slut,' he said. 'These are wet.'

The girl muttered something under her breath which Laurel guessed to be words of contrition.

'It's no good playing the little Miss Innocent with me,

when I know the truth, Sara,' Warren sneered. 'It gets you horny, doesn't it, walking past all the men in here with your arse and your pussy bare to the world, and nobody knowing except me and you.'

That's what you think, sunshine, Laurel thought, wondering how the scene was about to unfold. Would they go home and finish their game in private, or would he cause the girl to undergo the humiliation she so obviously craved right here...?

Her reverie was interrupted by a voice at her elbow. 'Excuse me, do you have a light?' She almost jumped out of her skin at the realisation that the man who was addressing her was the dark-haired Warren.

'No, I don't smoke,' she replied, flustered. 'I'm sorry, I was miles away.'

'I can see that.' He was regarding her again, but there was a different quality to his gaze now, almost as if he thought he was looking at a kindred spirit. 'You've been listening in to what I've been saying, haven't you?'

Laurel could not prevent a guilty blush from rising to her cheeks. 'Some of it, yes. I'm sorry, I couldn't help myself.'

He brushed her apology aside. 'And you're not shocked?'

Quite the opposite, Laurel wanted to tell him, aware of a tell-tale pulse beating between her legs, signalling her growing excitement, an excitement which was being stoked by the man's persuasive voice and dominant aura. She shook her head. 'I've got what you might call a professional interest.'

Warren laughed, a low, feral sound. 'Is that a fancy way of telling me you're a voyeur? And you such a classy-looking girl, too. Well, it takes all sorts, I suppose.'

Laurel, her mind fuddled by his powerful self-assurance,

briefly wondered whether to be insulted or flattered by his comments.

'Look, join us for a moment,' he urged. 'I've been threatening Sara that I'd invite an audience if she didn't behave, but I didn't know when I'd meet the right person – until now.'

As if in a daze, Laurel stood up and followed the stranger back to his table. The red-haired girl's eyes widened at the sight of her.

'Sara, this is...'

'Laurel,' Laurel supplied quickly, smiling at the girl.

'She knows what you've been asked to do,' Warren continued. 'And she's as eager as I am to see that you do as you're told, aren't you, Laurel?'

'Oh, yes,' Laurel replied fervently, slipping into what she sensed was the required rôle. 'If you've been as bad as Warren tells me you have, then I think you deserve everything that's coming to you.' She had no idea what the hapless Sara was being required to do, but she sensed it would be much more humiliating for the girl if an audience was involved.

'But I've been good,' Sara protested. 'Honestly, Warren, you know I have.'

'Giving the glad eye to the barman when you think I'm not looking, refusing to do what you're told when I make a perfectly reasonable request...' Warren sighed. 'I don't call that being a good girl, Sara.'

'But...' The girl's voice trailed into nothing, and she glanced nervously from Warren to Laurel and back. Laurel could not help comparing her attitude to that of the feisty Cindy. Where the little blonde would fight back against a potential punishment with cheek and defiance, Sara already seemed resigned to her fate.

'Lift your top up, Sara,' Warren ordered.

'But someone might be looking,' Sara replied half-heartedly.

'Ah, well, you should have thought of that,' Warren replied.

Laurel cast a quick glance over her shoulder. No one seemed to be looking in their direction, and if they had been, she suspected that she was shielding Sara from immediate view. Don, the barman, was shambling from table to table on the other side of the room, collecting empty glasses, but he seemed more engrossed in that task than anything which might be happening elsewhere in the bar.

'Do as you're told, Sara,' Warren said.

The girl was wearing a cropped jumper in fluffy white wool. She caught hold of the hem where it rested against her bare midriff, her eyes pleading silently with Warren not to make her go any further. He stared back, enigmatic as a carved Buddha, but obviously in control of this particular battle of wills. Sara caved in, and pulled up her top. Two firm, creamy breasts, topped with nipples of the palest rose, were revealed to Laurel's gaze. Laurel could not help but notice that the girl's aureoles were already taut and crinkled, the teats standing proud from those barely-pink surrounds. The sight made her pussy clench with anticipation.

'What do you think, Laurel?' Warren asked, his tone almost proprietorial.

'Oh, she's got beautiful breasts,' Laurel replied sincerely.

'Hasn't she just?' Warren said. 'The rest of her is pretty special, too. Watch.' He turned his attention to Sara once more. 'Lift your legs up, knees apart. I want the heels of your shoes resting on the seat.'

'Please, Warren, don't make me do this,' Sara pleaded. 'I haven't got any knickers on, remember?'

'How could I forget?' Warren murmured.

'Won't that position be uncomfortable?' Laurel asked.

'She's got to learn,' Warren retorted. 'Anyway, she goes to dance classes. She's so supple she could lick her own pussy if she wanted to.'

As Laurel watched, Sara raised her long legs, resting her feet on the worn plush banquette. It was a movement she could not make without giving Laurel a good flash of her wet, puffy sex, crowned with a blaze of flame-red hair. Laurel shifted in her seat, feeling the seam of her jeans cutting into her own quim, which felt hot and damp against the faded blue denim. The sensations intensified as Sara slowly let her thighs spread wide, as Warren had demanded. Laurel could imagine how shameful it would feel to have to present herself in such a way, every fold of her most intimate flesh exposed to a scrutinising gaze, with the possibility of being observed by complete strangers who would no doubt take the image home to form the basis of their own masturbatory fantasies.

Satisfied that Sara was in the required position, Warren was busily planning the next stage in her humiliation. He gestured to the empty glass on the table in front of her. It had contained tomato juice, a glutinous red residue still clinging to the sides of the glass, and a couple of partially-melted ice cubes sat in the bottom.

'Take one of those ice cubes out of that glass,' Warren instructed Sara, 'but don't let your top drop down.'

Mutely, Sara did as she was told, clutching the hem of the jumper in her left fist as she fished one of the sticky ice cubes out of the liquid that remained in the bottom of the glass.

'Now, lick it clean.'

Sara parted her lips, letting her pointed pink tongue peep between them, and obediently licked the ice cube. With her breasts and sex so brazenly on display, the girl was a marvellously erotic sight, Laurel thought. She had already guessed what Warren intended Sara to do with that ice cube, but she still wanted to see the redhead's reaction as he delivered the order.

'Okay, rub your right nipple with the ice cube,' Warren said.

Sara's eyes opened widely in surprise. Surely she must have known what Warren was leading up to? Laurel thought. Perhaps she had expected Warren to take the ice from her and apply it to her flesh himself. In other circumstances, Laurel suspected, he might well have done. But how much more degrading it was for Sara if she had to do it.

The girl closed her eyes and let the ice cube brush lightly against her nipple. She whimpered, and began to move it in small, languorous circles. The little nub of flesh, already stiff, peaked even further as the ice chilled it.

'And the left,' Warren said. Sara followed his command automatically, pressing the slowly-melting ice to her other nipple.

Laurel looked round to see if there was any chance of their being interrupted, but Don was busy serving a customer, and the bar itself seemed to have emptied somewhat over the last few minutes. Perhaps Sara's performance had been spotted and the tables had been vacated by men eager to pile into the gents' and relieve their suddenly swelling cocks, spending their seed in a tribute to the redhead's beauty and submissive nature.

'You're enjoying that, you slut,' Warren said. Laurel started guiltily, wondering which of them he was referring to. 'Let's see how you feel once you've cooled that hot little cunt of yours. Come on, Sara, I want to see that ice cube sliding into your hole.'

Warren's words were almost needlessly crude, but from the way Sara whimpered, Laurel realised the girl found such earthy language a powerful turn-on. Sara needed no further encouragement to insinuate the ice cube into the opening of her sex, working it in and out of the tight, juicy orifice. Her breathing was rapid and shallow, and when the lump of ice skittered down her slippery crease and settled on her clitoris, her agonised shudders indicated that she was likely to reach orgasm within seconds.

'That's it, Sara,' Warren crooned. 'Come for me, you little tart.'

Sara's only answer was a low, guttural groan, as she pushed the ice cube deep into her vagina and left it there, while her middle finger rubbed frantically at her clit. Her cries as her body arched in climax were drowned by the sound of the juke box kicking into life with the opening bars of a raucous heavy metal track. Within seconds, she was subdued and still once more.

Warren reached over and planted a delicate kiss on the top of Sara's tousled red hair, the first sign of tenderness Laurel had seen him show towards the girl. Then he turned to Laurel, his eyes glittering with satisfaction.

'So, do you fancy a turn?' he asked.

Laurel glanced at Sara's glass, registering that it still contained one ice cube. Was he wanting her to tell Sara what to do with it, or – her quim spasmed at the thought – did he want her to bare her breasts and use the ice on herself? An image flashed vividly into her mind, of Warren's fingers opening the fly of her jeans, slipping the ice down the front of her knickers, and pressing it firmly against the crevices of her sex.

'Come back with us,' Warren urged, putting his arm round her and stroking the soft inside of her wrist with his thumb. 'Sara's place is just round the corner. You can find out just how good she is at licking pussy. She loves that, and she loves being made to suck my cock after I've fucked another woman with it.'

For a moment Laurel leaned into his caress, severely tempted, then she shook her head. If she wanted Warren to work for her, then she had to dismiss any thoughts of becoming involved with him sexually. It just wasn't professional.

'I'm sorry, I don't think it's a very good idea,' she told him.

'Come on,' he said, 'you're giving me every indication that you want my body.'

The arrogance of the man was breathtaking, Laurel thought, but she kept her tone civil as she replied, 'I do, but not in the way you're thinking.' She pulled away from him and pressed a business card into his hand, one of a batch she'd made up herself at a vending machine on the concourse of Charing Cross station the day before. 'I'm recruiting for my escort agency, and I thought you'd be just the man to join my staff. You're a very accomplished master, Warren, and I could put a lot of work your way. But I want you to understand that our relationship would be strictly professional. I don't mix business with pleasure.'

'It sounds like you don't mix anything with pleasure,' he retorted, but she noticed that he slipped the card into the pocket of his leather jacket before ushering Sara out of the pub.

'I'll wait to hear from you,' Laurel said to Warren's disappearing back, but she could not help feeling that, perfect for the agency as he would have been, she would hear nothing more from the man.

'He was ideal, Joe, and I blew it,' Laurel sighed, as the two of them sat in the office the following morning. Her desk was covered with duotone images of women in submissive postures, courtesy of a photographer friend of Cindy's, which they were looking through in an attempt to find one that would be suitable for their publicity material. They needed cards to put up in the phone boxes throughout the West End – even though such flyposting was strictly illegal, it was a risk they were willing to take in their attempt to get the agency off the ground – and flyers to be distributed in clubs and the fetish clothing shops that were clustered largely around Old Compton Street.

'So who was this bloke?' Joe asked.

'I don't know. All I know is he's called Warren, and his girlfriend lives fairly close to me. I suppose I could keep going back to the pub, on the off-chance I'll see him again, but I doubt it.' She ran her hands through her shaggy strawberry-blonde locks. 'I know I did the right thing by not sleeping with the guy, but—'

'You were tempted, weren't you?' There was an edge to Joe's voice that made Laurel look up sharply.

'How long have you known me, Joe? Am I the sort of woman who'd contemplate a threesome with a couple I'd been friendly with for ages, let alone one I'd only met five minutes earlier? But he just had something – I don't know, call it sex appeal – that I found incredibly hard to resist. And that's the sort of man we need working for us.' She slumped in her chair, suddenly eager to change the subject. 'He's history, though. Forget him. We need to get these flyers sorted out and down to the printers' as soon as possible.'

Joe's reply was cut off by a knock at the office door. 'Shall I get that?' he asked, aware that they were not expecting visitors.

Laurel nodded. 'If it's the bailiffs, tell them we haven't got anything worth taking.'

She looked back at the photographs on the desk, but her concentration was broken by the sound of a familiar voice asking, 'Is this Domination Inc?'

'Yes, it is,' Joe replied. 'How can I help you?'

'Actually, it's your friend I've come to see.' The Irishman strode past Joe, and came to a halt in front of Laurel's desk. He seemed to be relishing the height advantage as he looked down on her, smiling. 'So you weren't spinning me a line, then.'

'What are you doing here?' Laurel asked, her throat suddenly dry. She was uncomfortably aware that her nipples were peaking beneath the soft cotton of her bra.

'You said you could put some work my way, if I was interested. Well, I'm interested.'

He must know he'd caught her off-balance, Laurel thought. She had wanted to be in control of the situation if they had met again, and yet here she was, her quim moistening even as her brain cursed him for his overbearing self-confidence.

'Can I get you a coffee?' Joe asked.

'Black, please,' Warren said, 'and the stronger the better.'

'I should introduce the two of you,' Laurel said. 'Warren, this is my business partner, Joe Gallagher. Joe, this is Warren—' She paused. As she had said, that was all she knew about him.

'Keating,' Warren told her.

As Joe bustled around, busying himself with mugs and coffee powder, Laurel said, 'So tell me about yourself, Warren. What line of work are you in – if you're in work, that is?'

'I'm an actor,' Warren replied, 'and I'm good at what I do, but work's a little precarious at the moment. I get two lines in a soap commercial here, a walk-on part there, but nothing steady. And I thought, well, what you're offering me, it's just another sort of acting, after all. And I like sex, and most of all I like sex where I'm dominant. What I wanted to ask you was what the money was like.'

Which you could have done with a simple phone call, Laurel thought. But no, you had to come here in person and make your presence felt. 'Well, we negotiate a rate with a client, and you take seventy-five per cent of the fee. Everything's decided up front – no extras. The women who are going to come to us will be in potentially a very vulnerable position: they're taking us on trust, and we are going to do nothing to abuse that trust. It's their scenario, and we have to stick to it.'

'I don't have a problem with that,' Warren declared, taking the mug of coffee Joe offered him. He drank from it deeply, and signalled his approval with a nod to Joe.

'And we'll need to do some checks on your background,' Laurel continued. 'We need to know you haven't got a criminal record, that sort of thing.'

'I've done nothing wrong in my life,' Warren said, 'except maybe break a few more hearts than I should.' He grinned, registering Laurel's wince. 'Ah, come on, Laurel, you want me to be the rogue, don't you?'

'I just want you not to let the agency down,' Laurel said. She rose to her feet. 'Would you mind if I had a quick word with Joe, in private?'

'Sure, I'll just wait outside,' Warren said easily.

When he had left the room, Laurel turned to Joe. 'What do you think?'

'You're right. He's full of himself, but he's certainly got charisma. If his background checks out, we can't afford to turn him away. Are you going to break the good news to him, or am I?'

'I'll do it,' Laurel said, and went to fetch Warren back into the office. With this last piece of the jigsaw in place, she could begin advertising the agency's services with impunity. She only hoped that by the time she was dealing with Warren on a daily basis she would be able to keep under better control the surge of submissive desire his presence seemed guaranteed to inspire in her.

Chapter Four

The card was lying on the mat when Joanna Morrison came in from work, among a litter of flyers for her local curry house and boiler repair specialists, and her personal selection of numbers for the *Readers' Digest* prize draw.

The image caught her eye: a woman, pictured from behind but obviously topless, head bowed and hands cuffed behind her back. Intrigued, she studied the wording on the reverse. 'Domination Inc. We know what you want.' Underneath the central London phone number, it added, 'No need too great, no desire too dark.'

Joanna studied the card for a moment, wondering which of her friends might have mocked it up and left it with her post as a prank, then crumpled it up with the rest of the junk mail and threw it in the bin. She poured herself a glass of white wine from the fridge and flicked on the radio. It had been a rough day at work, and a blast of something loud and energetic was what she needed to help her forget the impossible deadline she was struggling to meet. But the combination of music and alcohol failed to work its usual magic; she was still aware of a nagging feeling in the back of her brain, a feeling that somehow, somewhere, she was missing out on something.

She took a sip of her wine, savouring its icy chill. If she was honest, the only thing she was missing right now was sex. It had been eight months since Pete had left her for a temp in his office typing pool; eight long months in which to be bitter about his betrayal, to declare herself defiantly celibate and, finally, to decide that what she needed, more than anything, was a good hard fuck. However, that was proving to be more than a little elusive; she had no desire to get involved in another flirtatious series of dates which would eventually lead to the bedroom, but neither did she want to hunt the singles bars and find nothing better than an instantly forgettable one-night stand. London was not an easy place to find a new lover; single available men who were intelligent, attractive, witty and not gay were incredibly thin on the ground, and they could have their pick of the city's women. Joanna's standards were high, and she was reluctant to lower them simply in an attempt to ease the void between her legs.

In the kitchen, on her way for a refill, she reached into the bin and pulled out the crumpled flyer. 'No need too great, no desire too dark...' The words were tantalisingly full of promise. Even if it was just a joke, it was still tempting to think that someone out there might be able to reach into her psyche, discover what she really wanted, and provide it for her. No hearts-and-flowers romance, no soppy sentimentality. Just raw, straightforward sex.

Joanna curled up on the settee and glanced at the illustration on the flyer again. In her mind's eye it was she who stood, cuffed and half-naked, waiting to be punished for some unspecified misdemeanour. Absent-mindedly, her fingers moved to touch her breasts, rubbing at her nipples and hardening them. Yes, she was awaiting her master. She could almost see him now: not overly tall, but powerfully-built, his dark hair short and spikily-cut, his eyes a piercing grey that saw into her soul and had no mercy for what they found there. She would keep her head down as he approached her, only raising her eyes on his command, knowing she could not speak without his permission.

Her hands were straying lower now, raising the hem of

her short, businesslike checked skirt as she imagined him easing down her knickers, leaving her utterly naked and vulnerable. With her hands restrained, she would have no way of shielding her pussy from his gaze. If he came to inspect her he would find she was already wet, her juices flowing in anticipation of the punishment she was about to receive.

His palm was broad and slightly calloused, and she tensed herself for the feel of it against her soft, unprotected backside. And when she had taken the required number of strokes, he would push her to her knees without ceremony, unzip the fly of his tight black jeans and order her to suck his thick, straining cock.

As she imagined taking that solid length deep into her mouth, Joanna touched her fingers lightly against her clitoris, and came...

Joanna waited until the other girls in the office had gone to the sandwich bar across the road for lunch before she picked up the phone. There was no way she could make the call if there was even the slightest chance she would be overheard. She dialled the number with trembling fingers, and waited while it rang at the other end. Half-expecting to be greeted by the laughter of a friend, she was surprised when a soft, educated female voice said, 'Good afternoon, Domination Inc. This is Laurel. How may I help you?'

'Well, I saw your leaflet and I... er...' She stopped, unsure of how to continue.

'And you have a fantasy you'd like us to fulfil.' The woman on the other end of the line sounded as matter-of-fact as if she was taking an order for a takeaway pizza. 'Why don't you tell me about it?'

Hesitantly at first, Joanna began to outline the thoughts

that had crystallised when she had seen the flyer: how she wanted to be taken out of her everyday existence and made to kneel in homage to a cruel but just master. She was not about to tell her that the scenario she had created had been so powerful she had frigged herself stupid over it, but she suspected this Laurel was astute enough to realise that had been the case.

When she had finished, the woman quoted her what seemed a surprisingly reasonable price for providing such a service. Not that money was a problem, Joanna thought, as Laurel took her payment via credit card: eight months of staying in on her own and refusing dates had been considerably cheaper than eight months of going out with Pete, or whoever might have otherwise replaced him.

'So what happens now?' she asked.

'We'll collect you, tonight,' Laurel told her.

'When?' she asked, amazed at the efficiency with which this mysterious outfit seemed to operate, but the woman refused to give her any further details. She simply told Joanna the code word that would be used, and wished her good day, then hung up, leaving her in a state of nervous, excited anticipation. She was still wondering whether she had done the right thing when the girls returned from lunch.

It was raining when Joanna left the office that evening, and she turned her coat collar up against the downpour. The city's taxis always seemed to disappear with the onset of unpleasant weather, and she began to make her way towards the nearest tube station. Perhaps the man Laurel had promised to provide was already waiting at the flat for her to arrive. Perhaps her lateness would increase the length of her punishment.

She did not notice the squat, black four-wheel drive as

it came to a halt by the side of the road; the first she knew that she had company was a hand grabbing her from behind, and its twin being placed over her eyes.

'What the...?' she began, and then a voice hissed the code word in her ear, and she knew she was being collected. There was a second man driving, Joanna realised, and the four-wheel drive was pulling away even as she was bundled onto its back seat. Any number of people had been around to witness her apparent abduction, but she knew that no one who had noticed anything would be likely to raise the alarm. It was just as well, she supposed; this was hardly a matter for the police to investigate.

She hoped the man who had hold of her would release his grip, but he clung on to her tightly as they sped through the city streets, still blocking her vision. She was trying to relax, confident that the mysterious Laurel would not have placed her in a potentially dangerous situation, but adrenaline was coursing through her body and she was finding it difficult to stay calm and quiet. The driver seemed to be taking left and right turns entirely at random, and within a couple of minutes she was completely lost and disorientated. A strange prickle of foreboding ran down her spine as she thought of what was to come.

They eventually came to a halt and she was dragged out of the vehicle. Joanna had the briefest glimpse of the façade of what appeared to be a deserted, boarded-up warehouse, and then she was ushered through the door and down a flight of steps. Her captor pushed her into a small, cold, brick-walled room, and locked the door behind him.

For the first time she got a good look at him. Average height and slender, with blond hair falling over one eye. Good-looking, admittedly, in a boyish way, but not the dark fantasy man she had described over the phone at all. She felt a deep pang of disappointment, which was immediately banished by his words.

'You've got to prepare for him, you know.'

'How…?' she began.

'Strip,' he ordered her bluntly, his tone quiet and oddly polite. If he was not the cruel master she had hired, did that mean the driver would be…?

His voice cut into her thoughts, all politeness gone. 'I told you to strip. And when I tell you to do something, I don't mean do it tomorrow. You're simply earning yourself a couple of extra strokes, you know.'

She felt a sudden, unexpected fluttering in her pussy as he mentioned her impending punishment. Shivering slightly, she shrugged off her coat and looked around for a chair, a hook, anything to hang it from. Finding nothing, she let it drop to the floor. It was swiftly followed by the charcoal-grey, box-cut jacket of her business suit, then she unzipped her smart pencil skirt, which slithered in a heap around her ankles. The blond watched her every movement, his silence indicating that he was not yet happy with her performance. Taking a deep breath, she grasped the top button on her cream blouse and unfastened it, repeating the procedure till the garment gaped open, revealing her heavy breasts in their plain white cotton bra.

'That, too,' he ordered her.

Joanna demurred for the merest second, knowing that her hesitation would be reported to her unknown master. That would no doubt count as another slap or three on her backside, and she wondered whether a part of her secretly wanted to increase the severity of her paid-for chastisement. Her hands fumbled behind her back, then her bra joined the discarded blouse in the pile of her clothes that was forming on the floor. She was aware that her large, chocolate-coloured nipples were already stiff and heavy, announcing her obvious arousal. The blond's eyes never left them; she felt humiliated beneath his impartial gaze, but found herself welcoming the sensation. He was not allowed to admire her; his duty was simply to prepare her for her master, and in this he was as much a chattel as she.

She slipped her fingers beneath the waistband of her knickers, prepared to remove those, too, but he shook his head. Instead, he removed a set of handcuffs from his jeans pocket, and ordered her to place her hands behind her. Grasping her by the wrists, he slipped on the cuffs. He gave her one last, not entirely unsympathetic appraisal, then pushed her through the door and marched her down a dingy corridor to the next room.

'Wait here,' he said, and left her.

The room was as bare and functional as the first. There was no furniture, no way in which she could make herself comfortable. She had no idea how long she stood there. Perhaps twenty minutes passed while she contemplated what was to happen next. Her breasts ached with anticipation, and there was a dull throbbing between her thighs.

Suddenly the door flew open, and he entered. He was dressed as she had requested, in a battered biker's jacket over a dark plain T-shirt and skin-tight black jeans. His short black hair was gelled into fashionable spikes and he had a neatly-trimmed goatee beard. His eyes were cold and hard and unforgiving, and she dropped her head before his gaze.

He circled her slowly, taking in every inch of her bound, shapely form. She gave a gasp as he grabbed hold of her hair and yanked her face up to meet his own.

'Not bad – for a wanton, idle slut,' he conceded finally.

'Christian tells me you need to be punished for your tardiness. Is that true?'

So Christian must be the blond, Joanna thought to herself. 'I – I don't know,' she stammered.

'I don't know – what?' His tone was harsh.

'Master.' The unfamiliar word burned on her tongue.

'That's better.' He circled her again as he spoke. 'Yes, you certainly are in need of punishment. You know I'll make you beg, don't you, slut? When that first blow lands on that pert little backside of yours, you'll beg me to stop, and yet, in your heart, you'll be begging me to carry on, to give you the treatment you know you deserve.'

His hand roamed over the cheeks of her arse, caressing the soft flesh through the thin cotton of her knickers. Without another word, he inserted his thumbs into the waistband and yanked the flimsy garment down around her ankles. Contemptuously, he pushed her legs slightly apart, and ran an inquisitive finger over her tufty blonde pubic hair and into her cleft. As they had both expected, it came away slick with her viscous, musky juices.

'Bend over.'

Quickly she obeyed, anxious to avoid any extra strokes. Her position was slightly precarious, with her hands still bound behind her back and her breasts stretched out like taut cylinders of flesh. He fondled her hanging nipples, squeezing them roughly between finger and thumb. The unexpected pain made her gasp at the same time as her pussy twitched and moistened further.

'Perfect,' he muttered, and for the first time she thought she detected a hint of approval in his voice. She had no further time to think of anything as the first slap landed, hard and stinging, on her left buttock. A second followed with alarming rapidity, this time on her right. She wanted to cry out, but she thought that might anger him and earn her a couple more blows. Her fantasies had not prepared her for the shocking pain of her initiation into spanking, nor for its twin attendant, the throbbing undercurrent of pleasure that was making a furnace of her sex.

He was thorough in his attentions; whoever he was, this was not the first time he had doled out a spanking. His palm was covering the taut flesh of her cheeks, never seeming to settle on the same place twice, so that every centimetre of her skin was reddened and smarting.

At last his hand was still. 'Very good, slut,' he muttered. 'I never thought you'd take all that without a sound.' He sounded almost admiring, and she wanted to turn her head and flash him a smile of gratitude. His next words pushed that thought from her mind. 'I haven't heard you beg, yet, have I?'

His palm smacked hard against her buttocks again. His earlier attentions had sensitised her nerve-endings, so that now she felt each blow with increased severity. When his hand moved down to tan the soft crease where the flesh of her bottom met the tops of her thighs, she could not prevent a squeal of anguish from escaping her lips. She thought that might earn her a reprieve, but the reverse seemed to be true. She shuddered, fearing she might lose her balance, but he was holding her steady, his arm around her waist and the flat of his hand pressing against her pubic mound, making her want to squirm and press herself against it. Despite the ache in her buttocks, which she was finding impossible to ignore, she was almost unbearably aroused.

She lost count of how many slaps landed on her unprotected backside, and wondered how she looked to him, her creamy flesh mottling with a tracery of vicious scarlet prints. God only knew how she would manage to sit down in the office the following day. At last she cried out, 'Please, I'm sorry, Master.' Tears welled in her eyes, born as much of frustration as pain.

And then she was aware that the spanking had stopped for a second time, and his fingers were tracing a path over his handiwork, circling her flaming buttocks and coming to rest in the crease between them. One finger moved lightly over her weeping sex and she wriggled beneath his touch, desperate to feel it inside her. But it was merely gathering her juices and smearing them, she realised with shocking clarity, over her other, forbidden entrance.

His index finger penetrated deeply into her rosy arsehole. She tightened against the unexpected intrusion, before relaxing, realising that this was her ultimate humiliation. His thumb pressed hard against her clit, but he did not rub her, and she knew instinctively that if she wanted to come, she was going to have to do the work. She thrust against him, humping his hand, making mewling noises as she sought her release, while all the time his finger probed relentlessly inside her arse. Mere seconds later, a dizzying spasm exploded in her gut and she came, slumping against him.

He brought her gaze up to meet his own once more. His expression was unfathomable. 'Very good, slut,' he smiled, 'but you aren't finished yet.'

She watched as he slowly unzipped his jeans, bringing his cock out into the light. It was not as long as her fantasy might have willed it, but it was thick, with a taut, glistening head and a lengthy foreskin that was already beginning to retract.

'Suck it, slut,' he ordered.

Obediently, she dropped to her knees, and took its purplish tip between her lips. Her hands still cuffed, she was unable to cradle his taut balls as she might have liked, and she concentrated on taking his length deeper into her gullet. He tasted clean and masculine, and she licked with relish at his swollen glans. Risking a glance upwards, she saw that his eyes were half-closed in pleasure, and he was making low crooning noises in his throat.

She lapped and nibbled at his penis, running her tongue in intricate patterns over his cock-head. A ring of her pale pink lipstick, which seemed so demure and functional in the office, was smeared around the base of his shaft, in lewd contrast to the dark, blood-engorged flesh. She felt as though she could have gone on sucking him all night.

As his climax approached he took hold of her hair once more, so she could not pull her mouth away. He grunted and came, and deposited a wad of thick spunk into her mouth. She swallowed most of it, but a small trickle escaped from her lips and ran down her chin.

He released his grip on her and zipped himself up once more, before taking a tiny key from his jeans pocket and unlocking her handcuffs.

'Well done, slut,' was all he said as she rubbed the feeling back into her tired wrists.

'Thank you, Master,' she replied, and then he was gone.

Half an hour later she was standing, dressed once more in her respectable business clothes, outside a subway station a couple of stops from home, watching the four-wheel drive recede into the thinning flow of evening traffic. She thought again of her master, or the man who had played him. He had been excellent, everything she could have wanted, and yet she didn't even know his name.

Joanna's sore bottom ached pleasurably as she slipped her travel pass into the slot and made her way through the barrier. She tried to analyse the feeling, knowing she would need to be in a situation like that again soon.

There was a tatty flyer on the seat of the train when she

went to sit down. All it had on it was a drawing of a set of handcuffs, the address of a club in the west of the city and the coming Friday's date. She tucked it surreptitiously into her coat pocket, aware there was a contented smile on her face as she began her short journey home. Domination Inc. had opened the door for her, and now she was ready to step inside the secret world of submission and mastery, and explore her sexuality to the full. Joanna gave a silent thank you to Laurel, and to Christian and his dominant companion, and wondered whether, somewhere close by, someone else was receiving as fulfilling an experience as she had so recently enjoyed.

In a small, freshly-painted office over a travel agency in Soho, three people sat round a desk, toasting each other with sparkling wine in polystyrene cups.

'I can't believe how well that went,' Warren said, lounging back in his chair to rest his legs, crossed at the ankles, on the cluttered desktop. His grey eyes shone with self-satisfaction. 'We gave her exactly what she asked for, and she loved it.'

'It's all right for you,' Christian replied, reaching for the wine bottle and topping up his companions' cups. 'You were the one who got to spank that incredible arse of hers, while I was stuck in the next room, listening. Next time, Laurel, can you take a booking from someone who wants to be watched while they're being punished, or preferably someone who likes blonds.'

'So you think there'll be a next time?' Laurel asked.

'Definitely,' Warren assured her. 'There are plenty more where Ms Morrison came from, just dying to have someone tell them what to do.' He took a swallow of his wine, and fixed Laurel with a hard stare. 'I've never found a woman who didn't want to submit, deep down. Even the ones like Elisha, who reckon they're pure dominants, just sometimes they feel the need to switch.'

'And what about dominant men?' Laurel replied. 'Do they ever want to switch, too?'

Warren shook his head. 'I never have.' He drained the last of his wine, crushed the cup in his fist and tossed it, without looking, towards the waste-bin. Laurel waited for it to miss its target. The fact that it didn't increased her irritation with the man all the more.

'And so, suddenly, you've got the authority to speak for dominant men everywhere?' she shot back.

'Come on, Laurel, if you had all the power in a situation, would you want to give it up?'

'I thought it was the submissive who had all the power,' she said. 'I mean, look at Joanna Morrison. You might have been spanking her, but she set all the rules. She told you what her limits were, and she made you stop when she wanted to. I think that makes her pretty powerful, don't you?'

'You think so?' Warren replied, coming to stand by her, so she had to look up at him from her seated position. 'She set the rules because she was paying for it. And every submissive woman thinks she knows what her limits are, but I've never met one who wouldn't let you bend those limits. They all love it when you push them that little bit further than they've ever gone before.' He grinned, sure in the knowledge of what he was saying. 'And if I have no power, how come Sara, or any one of a dozen girls, would drop everything and come running if I clicked my fingers and told them they deserved a good hiding?'

'You don't half fancy yourself,' Laurel snapped.

'Yeah, well, you can't deny that you fancy me, too.' Warren took hold of her arm and dragged her to her feet. Christian was watching the two of them with undisguised interest, wondering where this little scene was leading.

'Warren, please...' Laurel knew her response was half-hearted, but put it down to the fact that it had been a long day, and she had expended a lot of energy worrying about the success of their first job.

'Please what?' His tone was mocking. He stood behind her, pulling her on to him, so that she could feel his erection pressing into the small of her back. 'Don't tell me, you'll put this down to the power of a woman, too. Oh, Christian will agree with me, you women have got the power to get us hard, sometimes without even knowing you're doing it, but it works both ways.' He lowered his voice, whispering sensually into her ear, 'What would happen if I slid my hand into your little knickers now and found you were wet? Who'd be responsible for that, eh?'

His hand rested on the swell of her stomach, the warmth of his palm radiating through her cotton dress, and for a moment she wanted him to act on his words, to lift the hem of her dress and push her knickers down, baring her fleecy mound to his and Christian's gaze. Her sex felt red-hot and swollen with need, and she knew that if Warren were to touch her, his fingertips would indeed come away coated with her juices.

As abruptly as he had caught her, Warren let her go. 'Ah, but you're not interested in that sort of thing, are you? You should be getting home, so you can have your cocoa and sit up in bed with an improving book. Because that's what passes for fun in the Angell household, isn't it?' He glanced over at Christian. 'Can I give you a lift, Chris?'

Christian shook his head. 'Thanks, but I'm going south of the river.'

'I'll see you around, then.' He paused in the doorway. 'Laurel?' When she merely glared at him, he shrugged.

'Perhaps some other time, then. I'll be waiting for your call – for my next assignment, naturally.'

Laurel could have screamed. The man was nothing more than an arrogant, over-confident jerk, so why did she have the urge to run after him and continue their argument until the only way it could be settled was by his hand imprinting its will on her backside? The frustration she felt at his behaviour was largely sexual, and she hated him for knowing that fact.

She felt a hand on her shoulder, and turned round to see Christian looking at her sympathetically. 'Don't let him get to you,' he said.

Laurel said nothing. How could she explain to him that Warren already had?

Chapter Five

Alice Marber almost rang twice to cancel the appointment. Even as she waited for the fast Thameslink train to London at Harpenden station, she thought about turning back and phoning to say it had all been a terrible mistake. The idea that a respectably married forty-five-year-old woman should even be considering going to see a sex therapist was ludicrous, and yet she felt that if she did not speak to someone about her problem soon, she would surely go mad. If she had been like most of the other middle-aged housewives in this part of Hertfordshire, quietly bingeing on sherry and daytime talk shows to escape from the monotony of their daily lives, her addiction would not have been remarked upon. But if she admitted to the dark fuel of her obsessive fantasies, her behaviour would be treated with revulsion and incomprehension. However nervous she felt about seeking it, discreet professional help was the only answer.

The best part of an hour later, she was lying on a couch in a small white-painted consulting room in Harley Street, her shoes on the floor, her stomach churning in sick anticipation of the therapist's arrival. When the door finally swung open, Alice did a double-take. Instead of the sympathetic woman of her own age she had been hoping for, she was confronted by a girl who seemed barely old enough to have completed her studies, tall and stunningly pretty, with lustrous black hair hanging in a braid that reached almost to her waist. Glancing at the girl's svelte figure, which was hinted at by the clinical white coat she wore, Alice was more conscious than usual of her pendulous breasts and the rolls of fat around her stomach and hips which no amount of dieting had ever seemed to shift. The therapist smiled, acknowledging Alice, and drew a chair up to the couch. She perched on it, and consulted the manila folder she was carrying.

'Alice Marber,' she murmured, almost to herself. 'Thank you for coming to see me, Alice. I want you to relax and feel completely comfortable. I promise you nothing that's said will go any further than this room. Now, according to my notes, you believe you're suffering from some kind of compulsive disorder, is that right?'

Alice tried to answer, but her voice came out as nothing more than a squeak. She was aware that the button at the waistband of her navy skirt was cutting into her flesh, and wished she had thought to wear something more comfortable. She cleared her throat, and tried again. 'I... I don't really know how else to describe it. I don't have to wash my hands a hundred times a day, or keep going back to check the front door's locked every time I leave the house – if I did, I wouldn't be seeing someone with your... specialist knowledge. Oh, I know you're going to think I'm crazy, but I have this one particular fantasy, and if I don't use it, then I can't have an orgasm.'

'I don't think you're crazy at all, Mrs Marber. This fantasy you use – is this when you masturbate?' The word sounded shocking to Alice's ears, coming from such young lips. She looked up to see if there was any amusement or contempt on the therapist's face, but the girl's expression was studied and neutral.

'Not just then,' Alice confessed, 'although I have been doing that every day over the past few months, sometimes more than once if the truth be told. No, I use it when my husband makes love to me, too. Keith – that's his name –

well, he doesn't realise. He doesn't know what I'm thinking about, and he puts it down to his own skills as a lover. Though if I had to rely on those—' Alice was aware of a sudden bitterness creeping into her tone '—I doubt if I'd have another orgasm from here to Doomsday.'

'So does your husband not feature in this fantasy?' the therapist asked.

Alice shook her head. 'No. And he'd be horrified if he knew I had any fantasies at all. He thinks that if a man and woman love each other, that's all that's needed, even after twenty-three years.'

'Why don't you tell me about it? My notes are very sketchy, I'm afraid.'

Taking a deep breath, Alice began to unburden the scenario she had been acting out in her head for months. 'It all started when Keith brought his latest golf partner home. His name's Richard, and he's the new head of the marketing department at Keith's firm. He's in his late twenties, about half the age of the man he replaced, and he fast-tracked his way to that position. I didn't like him when I first met him – he's very arrogant, a little bit too sure of himself, and from what Keith's told me, half the women in the firm were in love with him after he'd been there a couple of weeks. Richard is very good-looking, admittedly, with thick dark hair and long eyelashes, and his suits are all Italian – very flash. The problem is that he knows it; Keith said he expects women to be falling at his feet, and he goes through them very quickly. Apparently he doesn't treat them particularly well, either.

'After he'd been round to our house a couple of times, however, I found I just couldn't stop thinking about him. For all his arrogance, he has a certain charm, and I started casting him in fantasy situations where he was in charge, and I was having to do as he told me. For instance, he'd tell me that when he next came round to the house I'd have to wear stockings and suspenders and no panties, and that he would come into the kitchen when I was making a snack for him and Keith, and feel me up to check that I'd done as he'd asked.'

'So, would you say you have a submissive streak?' the therapist asked, making a note on a sheet of paper that was stapled into the folder.

'I've never really thought about it until now, but I think I must have,' Alice replied, 'especially the way the fantasy has progressed. I've refined it over the months, until it's become like a little film that I screen in my own head, for my own pleasure. What happens is that Richard makes it more and more obvious that he wants to have sex with me, and he becomes very good at touching me surreptitiously, and working me up to a state with his voice and his fingers where I think I'll burst if nothing happens between us. He tells me I have to find an excuse to go away for the weekend with him. He also makes it clear that if I do come away with him, it's on the understanding that I will have to do exactly what he tells me the whole time we're together. So I tell Keith I've been invited to stay with my sister, Gillian, in Leeds, and he seems quite happy with that.

'Keith drops me off at Harpenden station on the Saturday morning. What he doesn't know is that, as Richard has requested, I'm wearing stockings and suspenders, and no knickers. He kisses me and waves me off on the train, telling me to have a good time, and I smile because that's exactly what I intend to do. I get off the train at the next stop down the line, where Richard is waiting for me in his silver Mercedes. The first thing he does is put his hand straight up my skirt to check that I'm dressed the way he requested. When he finds my bare sex he tells me I'm a good girl, which sounds ridiculous coming from a man who's so much younger than I am, but I still glow with pleasure at having earned his praise.

'As we drive off he tells me he's taking me to this discreet bed and breakfast place he knows in the country. Apparently it's run by a couple who are close friends of his, and there will be two other guests staying there besides us. That's all he'll say on the subject, but I sense he has something planned for me, and that these other people are somehow involved.

'When we arrive at the cottage we're shown to our room. It's small, but very beautifully decorated, with sloping eaves and an en suite bathroom. Richard tells me to go and shower, and says that when I come back the clothes I have to wear for the rest of the weekend will be lying on the bed. He adds that if I don't like what I find, I have the option to leave then and there, but that he will never have anything to do with me again.

'I've waited so long for this moment that I have no intention of refusing – until I walk out of the little bathroom dressed in nothing but a towel, and see what's on the bed. All he's given me to wear is a black lycra minidress, a pair of sheer black hold-up stockings, three-inch stilettos and what appears to be a thick silver collar. Nothing else. It's a completely unsuitable outfit for a woman of my age and build, and I'm sure Richard is totally aware of that fact.

'I look at those skimpy little things lying waiting for me, and then I look at Richard. Part of me wants to leave, but I know I've come so far that I can't. At last I reach out and pick up the dress. I make to take it into the bathroom and try it on, but he stops me. I have to drop the towel and get dressed in front of him. It's so humiliating to have him staring at my pale, flabby body, but he's in charge and I have to do as he asks.

'When I'm dressed, the result isn't quite as bad as I feared. The dress is so very clingy, and so short it barely covers my bottom, but it has underwired cups which lift my breasts, and the high heels make my legs look longer and more shapely. If I was just wearing the outfit for Richard's eyes in the bedroom I'd be completely happy with it, but I know that won't be the case.

'The last thing I have to do is fasten the collar around my neck. As I do I realise this is the symbol of my submission. I've become Richard's slave for the rest of the weekend. It's a frightening thought, but it excites me, too.

'Richard tells me I look just as he'd hoped. While I'm trying to work out what he means by that remark, he orders me to get down on my knees. It's difficult in the stilettos, but I manage it. Before I realise quite what's happened, he's unzipped his fly and pulled out his cock, which looks long even though it isn't erect yet. He tells me to suck it, and obediently I reach out and take the end between my lips. As I begin to lap at it with my tongue it starts to grow and swell; it's thicker than I first thought, and I find I have to stretch my jaws really wide as Richard pushes more of its length into my mouth. I'm trying to take my time and give him pleasure, but he's impatient. He grabs hold of my head and holds it still, so that now he's thrusting hard, using my mouth as a receptacle. I can't do anything, and yet the fact that he's treating me so roughly is exciting. Though my jaw is aching I can feel myself getting wet, and know I'm turned on by what he's doing to me.

'It's all over in a few minutes. He grunts and deposits his semen at the back of my throat in a series of salty, convulsive jerks. Then he just withdraws from my mouth, wipes his wilting cock with a tissue and zips himself up once more. All the time I've been sucking him I've been looking forward to some pleasure in return, but nothing is forthcoming.

'Richard tells me that he's going downstairs to see his friends, as he has some arrangements to sort out, and that I'm to stay in the room. To make sure I don't masturbate in his absence he ties my hands behind my back with my own scarf and leaves me lying on the bed. He's only gone for half an hour, but it seems like a lifetime. I'm so aroused I end up rubbing my thighs together, trying to stimulate myself, but it's no good. He wants me to be frustrated and horny – and I don't know why.

'When he comes back he tells me everything's ready, and dinner will be served in a few minutes. I'm hoping he'll unfasten my hands, but he doesn't, and when we go down together he has to guide me down the stairs. He warns that I am not allowed to speak without being given permission, and that I must remember I have agreed to do everything he tells me. The first thing I notice when I see the dining table is that it's set for five places, and that the other couple who are staying here are already seated. Like Richard, they're much younger than me, and they're casually dressed in jeans and T-shirts, which makes me feel even more out of place in my tarty dress and high heels.

'I'm about to go and sit at the table, but Richard restrains me, and I suddenly realise that the other seats must be for the owner and his wife. Just as I work this out she comes in with a covered tureen, followed by her husband, who takes his place at the table.

'As she's dishing up the starter, which I quickly realise is asparagus spears in butter, Richard announces, "This is my slave, Alice. Alice has agreed that she is to be the property of everyone here for the evening. She likes to be treated quite roughly, so don't be shy about how you use her."

'I'm sure they can all see the alarm in my face, but when I try to say something Richard asks, "Have I given you permission, Alice?" and I have to bite my lip. "Now," he orders me, "take your place at my feet."

'In front of the others I have to kneel at the side of his chair, my hands still tied behind my back. Everyone begins to eat, but because my hands aren't free, I can do nothing. So Richard feeds me, holding the buttery asparagus out for me to nibble. It's delicious, but the juices are running messily down my chin and onto the tops of my breasts, and I can't wipe them away.

'As the others eat they chat amongst themselves, and I realise that the other young couple know Richard quite well. From what they say it soon becomes obvious that I'm not the first middle-aged woman Richard has brought here for this treatment. He describes it as "charity work", and the fact that he's dismissing me and my feelings so contemptuously hurts me, and makes me want to do everything he might ask to his satisfaction, so he can't find fault with me.

'When the first course has been cleared away, the owner's wife, Marion, serves everyone with rare roast beef, Lyonnaise potatoes and beautifully-prepared vegetables. I wonder if Richard will feed me again, but this time a plate is placed on the floor by me. All the food has been cut up into bite-sized pieces, and it's obvious that I'm intended to eat from the floor, like a pet. It's so humiliating, and I can hear them all commenting on my efforts not to overbalance as I kneel and feed myself.

'My head is down over my plate as I hear the cottage's owner say, "So, tell me, Richard, what are you letting them wear underneath their dress these days?"

'Richard is laughing as he replies, "Why don't you find out for yourself, Michael?" The next thing I know the owner is crouching down beside me, and his hand is lifting the hem of my dress.

'"Hmm," he says, "a good ample arse there. How does it colour when you punish her?"

'"I haven't had that pleasure yet," Richard admits. I want to protest at the way this Michael's hand is now roaming over my bum cheeks and down into the cleft that divides them, as if he, and not Richard, owns me. And then I realise that I've used the word "owns", even if it's only in my own head, and I know I'm in further over my head than I ever imagined, and I don't have any idea where this is all going to end. I think of Keith, blissfully unaware of what's happening to me. He thinks I'll be sitting in Gillian's lounge, swapping gossip over a glass of white wine, instead of kneeling here, indecently clad, with a man I've never seen until today stroking me between my legs.

'Suddenly a voice pipes up, "So, what are her tits like, then?" It's the other young man, whose name I believe to be James.

'"I'll show you them, if you like," Richard tells them. I look up at him, gaping stupidly. "Hurry up," he says. "Stand up."

'I scramble awkwardly to my feet, and stand there. I can't raise my head to meet the gaze of anyone in that room. I'm so ashamed of having placed myself in this position, where I'm at the mercy of these cruel, thoughtless strangers, and yet I can't deny that part of me is excited by the thought that Richard is about to bare my breasts for them.

'He tugs at the cups that are built into the dress, and I feel cool air on my suddenly naked breasts, which sag down under their own weight. I realise, too, that Michael hasn't bothered to hike the hem down, and they can see the tangle of hair at the fork of my thighs as well.

"'So, shall we make the slut play with herself?" the girl who's come with James asks. "I love it when they have to do that. It's so undignified for them."

'All the frustrations I've had to endure so far have aroused me to the point where, much as it would humiliate me to do so, I'd rub my clit and stick my fingers inside myself while they watched, if only it would put out the fire that's burning in my sex. Richard shakes his head. "I've got a better idea. Didn't you say it was banana split for dessert, Marion? Would you like to go and get it for us?"

'She smiles, and hurries out of the room. I wait, dreading to think what might be about to happen. When Marion returns she has with her a can of that cream you can spray on to things, and a banana, thick, green and barely ripe. There's an air of anticipation in the room as she sets them down on the table.

'Richard asks her if she would like to do the honours while he unties my wrists. The relief I feel at having my hands free at last is tempered by the sight of Marion peeling the skin off the banana, before garnishing it with a coating of cream. Then she hands it to me.

"'I don't really need to tell you where that's going, do I, Alice?" Richard says. "Quickly now, bring yourself off."

'This is the most demeaning thing I've ever been asked to do in my life, and yet I can feel myself getting even wetter, my sex lips peeling apart in readiness. As the other guests watch I guide the banana to the opening of my pussy, and very gently push it home. It's colder than I expected, the cream liquefying slightly in the heat of my channel, but it feels so good to have it inside me. With five pairs of eyes looking on, I start to furiously thrust that banana in and out of myself, and that's the moment that triggers my orgasm – every time.'

Alice stopped, aware that the therapist had put her pen down and was listening intently. She didn't believe she had ever talked for so long, uninterrupted, in her entire life. She shifted on the couch. 'That's it. That's where the fantasy ends. Tell me – am I abnormal?'

'Oh no, not at all,' the therapist reassured her. 'There are lots of women who come to me with submissive fantasies. They're so anxious about them when they arrive, and when they leave they feel nothing but relief.'

'Now you mention it,' Alice said, 'I do feel better for having talked to you.'

'I'm sure you do, but that's only part of it.' The therapist rose to her feet as she spoke. 'You remember when you first booked this appointment, it was stressed that our techniques here are somewhat unorthodox? Well, we believe in making sure the treatment is tailored exactly to the patient's needs. And it's become clear to me while you've been telling your story exactly what you need, Mrs Marber.'

'And what is that?' Alice asked, a little alarmed by the growing severity she could detect in the therapist's tone.

The therapist quickly unbuttoned her white coat and shrugged it off her shoulders. Underneath, she was dressed in a high-necked bodysuit of shiny black PVC that clung to the curves of her breasts and hips. A cruel smile flickered across her lips. 'You need a good hiding.'

'But...' Alice spluttered. 'There must be some mistake.'

'None at all. This way, we will find out whether you secretly crave your desires to be translated into reality. Now, come on, off with that skirt, and your tights.'

Alice, stunned, reached obediently for the waistband of her skirt. She unbuttoned it and pulled down the zip, before dragging down the skirt and her tights in one swift movement. Beneath them she wore a pair of white cotton briefs, comfortable and functional.

The therapist had settled herself back on her chair, one hand behind her back. Alice suspected she was holding something, but could not see what it was. 'Now, over my knee,' the therapist said.

Alice complied nervously. She had to admit the position she was being placed in was similar to her fantasy in that she was being ordered around by someone half her age. She waited for what seemed an eternity, conscious of her bare toes pressing against the cold, polished floorboards and her breasts hanging heavily, her nipples thrusting unexpectedly against the plain cotton.

'Now, I think a dozen is necessary in a case like this,' the therapist said.

The first blow came down hard and fast on her right buttock, catching Alice off-guard. The pain was like nothing she had anticipated, and she jerked upright, clutching at her abused flesh.

'Please, Mrs Marber, it's for your own good.' The therapist made it sound as though she was dealing with a naughty child. 'And I do have other clients to see. Clients who aren't quite so problematical.'

As Alice was pushed forcibly back into place, she twisted her head just far enough to see that what the therapist was holding was a thick rubber paddle, roughly the size of a table tennis bat. She could not believe that such an innocuous-looking implement could be so painful. Mentally, she steeled herself for another blow. This time her right buttock was the target. She let out a yowl as the rubber seemed to imprint itself deeply on her flesh.

'Think yourself fortunate, Mrs Marber,' the therapist said. 'The really severe cases have to be punished with a caning, or maybe a round half-dozen with the birch. I assure you this is nothing in comparison.'

It might have been nothing to the therapist, Alice thought in anguish, as the paddle fell again, but it was everything to her. By the time the sixth of the allotted strokes had been dispensed, her whole bottom felt as though it was ablaze, her nerve-endings shrieking for the punishment to come to an end.

However, it seemed as though the therapist was determined to string the dozen strokes out a little longer. She ran her hand soothingly over Alice's cotton-covered bottom. Alice, lying passively in place, thought for a moment that she felt the lightest of touches down the cleft of her buttocks and over the gusset of her knickers, then dismissed it. Such treatment would be thoroughly unprofessional. But then, she asked herself, what was professional about being made to haul herself over this woman's knee and submit to a paddling? Or was she alarmed that if the therapist did touch her there, she would discover that Alice's underwear was damp from the excitement she had experienced while describing her fantasy, and that the strokes she had already taken had done nothing to diminish this excitement?

'Halfway there, Mrs Marber,' the therapist said. 'But I don't think we've quite got to the bottom of your submissive feelings, if you'll pardon the pun. You see, almost anyone could take a dozen strokes of this paddle, and not all of them would derive pleasure from it.'

So she does know I'm wet, Alice thought with a shiver. She barely had time to wonder where the conversation was leading before the therapist continued smoothly, 'The true test of whether you are submissive – whether you do indeed derive pleasure from pain and humiliation – is if you allow me to continue your punishment after I've done this...'

As she spoke, she hooked her fingers into the waistband of Alice's knickers and began to pull. 'Oh, no...' Alice murmured, but she did not attempt to stop the other woman from removing the garment. I must be submissive, she thought, feeling a rush of heat to her sex at the thought of taking the remaining six strokes on her naked backside. As in her fantasy, her soft pale buttocks were being bared to the gaze of a stranger, and it was not an unpleasant sensation.

'Six more on the bare,' the therapist said. 'Oh, I know it's going to hurt, Alice, but then the truth always does, doesn't it?'

Alice said nothing, waiting for the punishment to resume. This time there was nothing to shield her flesh, however ineffectually, from the force of the blows, and she whimpered and began to sob as the paddle slammed down repeatedly on her reddening cheeks. The therapist spaced the strokes evenly, but each one seemed to mount pain upon pain, until her backside felt swollen to twice its normal size.

When it was over she lay where she was, unable to move. She wanted to soothe the stinging heat away. She wanted a mirror, so she could see how her skin had blotched and reddened. But most of all, she wanted to reach down between her thighs and bring herself to orgasm.

'Well done, Mrs Marber,' the therapist said, and her hand stroked over Alice's heated skin once more. 'Very well done indeed.'

This time there was no mistaking it; her finger was skimming along the crease between Alice's bottom cheeks, and into the liquid well of her sex. She had never imagined that another woman might want to touch her there, and touch her so expertly. The finger had settled on her clitoris, flicking it with butterfly lightness, and Alice was conscious that she was wriggling on the therapist's lap, thrusting her hips in little movements that were subtly increasing the pre-orgasmic excitement she was feeling.

Now there was no more pain, only pleasure, as the therapist's finger moved faster, pushing Alice to the very brink. Her sobs were ones of ecstasy as she felt the tension in her loins build until it was almost unbearable, then break in a spiralling rush of sensation.

Embarrassed at having reacted quite so forcefully under the stimulation she had received, she shuffled off the therapist's lap and began to tug her briefs back into place.

'I think you needed that just as much as you needed to be spanked,' the therapist observed.

Alice said nothing.

'There's no reason to feel ashamed,' the therapist said. 'It's quite a normal reaction, I can assure you. I'd be surprised if you didn't feel better for having unburdened yourself like that.'

Alice nodded fervently. She could not deny that she did feel much better. Not only was she experiencing the glow of well-being which followed orgasm, but she had also been given the chance to come to terms with her sexuality. The therapist was right: there was no shame in her submission, only a sense of having learned something important about herself.

Only one thing remained: the matter of payment. Alice reached into her handbag and took out her purse, counting from it a number of twenty-pound notes, drawn from her private building society account. It was not conventional to pay the therapist in person, rather than a receptionist, but then nothing about this particular therapist was conventional, it seemed.

'I can't thank you enough, Miss—' Alice hesitated. At

no point had the therapist actually introduced herself formally.

'Oh, just call me Elisha,' came the reply. 'That way, if you feel the need for any further treatment, when you ring Domination Inc. you'll know who to ask for.'

Alice rubbed her still-glowing bottom absent-mindedly. 'Thank you, Elisha. I might just do that.'

The two women walked together to the door of the office that had been acting as Elisha's consulting room. 'So, it's on the train and back to the suburbs then, Mrs Marber?' Elisha asked conversationally.

Alice shook her head. 'No, I thought I'd go and look round the shops. I – well, I don't fancy doing anything which involves sitting down for a little while. I'm sure you understand.' She paused at the top of the stairs. 'And when you speak to that nice girl who takes the bookings, tell her that she can safely class me as a very satisfied customer.'

Chapter Six

Cindy was applying a second coat of lip colour when the doorbell rang. From the way a heavy finger was stabbing on it rhythmically, she guessed it was the taxi driver. She capped the lipstick and dropped it into her bag, casting a final glance at herself in the dressing table mirror before heading for the door. Her progress was slower than usual in the four-inch heels which were a requisite part of her outfit, and she called out, 'Just coming!' for the benefit of the cabbie as she teetered down the hall. The shoes were blood-red, with spindle heels that pushed her insteps up artificially high and made her small feet look even daintier and more vulnerable. Fuck-me shoes, Cindy thought, made all the more provocative by the wide straps that encircled her ankles, and from which little padlocks hung. A thin length of chain between those padlocks, and Cindy's progress would be slowed to a hobble, should a demanding mistress require it.

And tonight, Cindy was escorting the most demanding of mistresses. Sheena Thorn, the editor of *Sappho* magazine; the woman who had turned sadomasochistic lesbian erotica into an art form. She was holding a women-only party at *The Cage*, a regular fetish club that occupied what had once been a cinema in Stoke Newington, to celebrate *Sappho's* fifth birthday, and Cindy was to be her paid-for partner for the night. Hence the outfit, and the hideously impractical shoes.

Sheena had been incredibly specific about the clothes Cindy was to wear when she had made the booking with

Domination Inc., and the whole effect had been to turn the little blonde into one of the submissive playthings from a *Sappho* centrespread. She looked every inch the willing slut, from the black roots of her peroxide hair, which Sheena had been most insistent she should not touch up for several days before the party, to the tips of her ankle-strap stilettos. Her make-up was whorishly heavy; thick black kohl circled her eyes, and her lips and cheeks were painted a vivid carmine. She was dressed in a black rubber bra top, cut so low that her pale pink nipples threatened to spill from its clinging restraint at any moment, and a matching waspie that cinched her trim waist, and to which sheer black stockings were clipped by wide suspenders. The little rubber G-string which covered her mound was so small she might as well not have been wearing it at all. The thong back snaked between her taut round buttocks, and the cotton gusset pouched her naked sex. Sheena liked her women shaved smooth, and Cindy was to be no exception.

If she had been visiting *The Cage* as a paying customer, which she had been known to do on occasions, she would have thrown her old fawn mackintosh over the skimpy outfit and hopped on public transport. Tonight, Sheena had booked her a cab to take her to North London and bring her back home, but the trade-off for this was that Cindy was not allowed to wear a coat. As she opened the front door to the taxi driver, she was aware of his eyes roaming over her barely-clad body, lingering on the tops of her breasts and the expanse of uncovered flesh between the tops of her stockings and the bottom of her waspie.

'Cab to Stoke Newington, right?' the man said.

Cindy nodded, and followed him slowly down the path. She gave grateful thanks that at least she was behind him; if the positions had been reversed, he would have had a wonderful view of her naked backside, thrown into jutting prominence by her high heels.

As she settled herself on the back seat the cabbie asked conversationally, 'So where are you off to?'

'It's a friend's party,' Cindy replied, as non-committally as she could, hoping he would not press her for details.

'Shame I don't have a few friends like yours,' he said. 'I like parties where you get to dress up for the occasion.' She was aware of him glancing surreptitiously at her reflection in his rear-view mirror, and she studied him in return. He was, she guessed, about thirty, with streaky blond hair pushed back from his forehead in short wings. His eyes were small and blue beneath a heavy brow, and there was a light dusting of fair stubble on his chin. His plain white T-shirt was stretched tightly across a muscular chest, and his faded blue jeans drew attention to the bulge at his crotch. Good-looking enough if you liked them on the rough side, Cindy supposed, but not her type.

He turned the dial on the stereo, filling the car with pumping techno music. 'Would you mind turning that down, please?' Cindy asked, aware that she would have to listen to the same monotonous beat for three or four hours in the club.

The driver shrugged, and lowered the volume. For a while he kept silent, content to ogle Cindy in his mirror. She, in turn, was happy to sit wrapped up in her own thoughts, subliminally aware of the car's fabric seat against her naked bottom, and the growing sense of anticipation in her lower body as she contemplated what was about to happen to her at *The Cage*.

Eventually, the cabbie asked, 'So, does your boyfriend mind you going out dressed like that?'

It's none of your business, Cindy wanted to tell him. The only man in her life who might have qualified as her boyfriend, Tom, would more than likely be sitting at home with his wife, a woman who wouldn't even have known what a rubber waspie was, let alone how it felt to have the garment fitting snugly around your waist, the suspender straps stretching along your thighs. The cabbie was waiting eagerly for Cindy's reply: noticing the gold wedding band that circled his ring finger, she decided to tease him a little. 'He prefers it when I stay in and wear it,' she said.

'I'm sure he does,' the cabbie murmured. 'And... er... what exactly happens when you stay in and wear it?' He aimed for a certain nonchalance in his tone, and missed.

'Well, if you want to know the truth, he actually thinks that only a slut would dress up in rubber and high heels. And if I dress like a slut, then he treats me like one.' Cindy closed her eyes and settled back on the seat, an impish smile forming on her lips as she mentally created a scenario that was guaranteed to turn the taxi driver on. 'He'll take me into the bedroom, and he'll push me down onto the bed, on my hands and knees. Then he'll get the silk rope he keeps in the bedside cabinet, and he'll tie my wrists and ankles to the bedposts – not so tightly that it hurts me, but securely enough so, no matter how much I wriggle and squirm, I just won't be able to free myself. There I am, my bottom sticking up in the air towards him, waiting for him to decide what to do with me.'

'Does it take him long to decide?' the cabbie asked. 'I'd have thought it would have been obvious.'

'It can do. You see, he's got what he calls his box of tricks, and I never know what he's going to take out of it. Sometimes it's a feather, and he uses that to tickle every inch of my body – and I mean every inch. I'm incredibly ticklish, and I'll plead and I'll beg him not to tickle me, but he just keeps on and on and on. He'll even use the feather on my clit. That's the worst, because it drives me completely hysterical, until I don't know if I'm going to wet myself, or come, or both.

'He's got a little bottle of oil in there, too,' Cindy added, eyes open now so she could watch the cabbie's reaction to her confession in his mirror. 'When he gets the oil out and pours it over the crack of my bum, I know exactly what's going to happen. He'll spend ages smoothing it into my pussy and my other hole with his fingers until I'm absolutely wide open and dripping wet, and then he'll take me in the arse. He's got a nice sized cock for that, and he takes his time so he doesn't hurt me, and then, just before he comes, he'll pull out so he can shoot his load all over my bum cheeks.' She smiled to herself at how the strait-laced Tom would react to the picture she was painting of their sex life. Though their lovemaking together was, he claimed, kinkier than that he enjoyed with his wife, he'd only ever tied her up on one occasion, and the thought of buggering her had probably never even entered his mind. However, it suited her needs to let the taxi driver think she was telling the gospel truth. From the flush that was creeping up the man's cheeks, her tales were having the desired effect.

'My absolute favourite thing, though, is this carved wooden dildo he's got,' she continued. 'It's really old, and it's been worn shiny and smooth through use. It's a good ten inches long, I would have thought, and as thick round as your wrist. When that's inside you, you really know you're being stretched – especially when you're as small and tight down there as I am. I never think I'm going to be able to take it, and if I wasn't tied up I wouldn't let him near me with it. But when I can't move, and I can't do anything about it, that's when I relax enough to let him ease that obscenely fat phallus into me.'

She stopped her story, aware that the taxi had pulled up

outside their destination and feeling she had teased him enough. The cabbie swivelled round in his seat. 'Here you go. That'll be eleven pounds, please.'

Cindy gaped at him. 'But I was told this was on Sheena Thorn's account...'

The taxi driver shrugged. 'Sorry, darlin', if it'd been paid for they would have told me back at the office.'

'Well, I don't have enough money on me.' There was a five-pound note nestling at the bottom of Cindy's bag, enough to pay for a couple of drinks and nothing more. 'I don't suppose you'd let me go inside and find Sheena, ask her if she can sort this out?'

He shook his head. 'How do I know you're not going to do a runner once you get out of the cab?'

Dressed like this? Cindy wanted to reply. Try and run down the street, I'll probably trip over a paving stone and break my neck. She looked helplessly at the cabbie, aware that he was gazing at her hungrily.

'I'd take something else in lieu of payment,' he said, and his tone made it obvious what he was asking of her. Cindy suddenly began to regret the stories she'd spun to turn him on.

'How about my phone number?' Cindy asked. 'I can think of a few men who'd pay quite highly for that.'

'Yeah, I'm sure they would, but that's not what I want. I want you up on that seat on your hands and knees. I want to see what that boyfriend of yours sees when he's got you tied up on the bed.'

'You can't make me do this,' Cindy said, aware of a sudden traitorous dampness in her G-string as she realised that a part of her wanted desperately to do what the cabbie ordered.

'Oh, no?' He was unbuckling his seat belt as he spoke. 'The way you've carried on, I ought to use my belt on your backside, leading me on with those saucy stories of yours and thinking you could get away without paying your fare. Now get up on that seat.'

Meekly, Cindy unfastened her own seat belt and did as she was told, facing away from the cabbie. Her head was pressed against the padded back of the seat and the heels of her stilettos were digging slightly into the cheeks of her backside as she knelt there, waiting for whatever he might choose to do. She could imagine how she looked to him, with the tiny G-string bisecting the cheeks of her bottom and moulding to the contours of her sex-lips. And what view might she be presenting to any curious passer-by who might choose to glance in the car window? The thought brought a wave of shameful heat rushing to her pussy.

'Part your legs more. And push the gusset of that thing to one side,' the cabbie ordered. 'I want to see everything.'

Her fingers trembled slightly as she moved to obey him. Now he would be able to see that her labia had been denuded of hair, and that they were glistening with a telltale coating of slick moisture, the evidence of her rising excitement.

For a moment he said nothing. The car door opened, almost too quietly for Cindy to hear it, and then she felt a hand on her bottom, work-calloused fingers tentatively touching her naked flesh. She sensed that, for all the man's bluster, he was unsure of himself and how to proceed in this erotically-charged situation. Cindy made his task easier by moving under his touch, thrusting her pelvis back towards him. She was finding the humiliating position he had placed her in so arousing that she wanted him to touch her pussy and discover how wet she was.

His hands were moving with more assurance now; he cupped her buttocks in his hands, spreading them apart to give him a better view of her puckered little anus. She'd told him she loved to be fucked there; it had been no lie, and she wondered if he would dare to breach the tight, forbidden hole.

Cindy's sex was pulsing with need, and when she felt his thumbs running down the crack between her cheeks, she could not prevent herself from whimpering. 'Please,' she whispered, wanting his touch to go lower, into the molten wetness of her cunt.

'Your boyfriend's right, you are a slut,' the cabbie commented. 'No respectable woman would be begging some stranger to touch her up in the back of his car.'

'I'm sorry,' Cindy replied, using the contrite tone she knew was guaranteed to turn the man on further. 'I know it's a bad thing to do, but I can't help it.'

'Oh, you'll be able to help it all right by the time I've finished with you.' The cabbie's voice was thick with lust. She heard him fumbling with his belt, and wondered if he was going to keep his promise to use it on her backside. That would be a pretty present to give Sheena Thorn, she thought, turning up at the party with red stripes already marking her bottom...

The sound of his zip coming down brought her back to reality.

'Look at me, slut,' the cabbie ordered, and she turned her head to see him looming over her, his jeans and boxer shorts round his knees and his cock clasped firmly in his right hand. She moaned as she saw it; what must have been eight inches of blood-engorged flesh, the foreskin already pulled back to reveal the fat shiny head.

'Stroke it,' he said, and she complied eagerly, reaching behind her to fondle the veined length. As she played with it the cabbie eased her G-string down off her hips. She wriggled her bottom to help him in his task, and he pulled the little garment down further till it was around her ankles. Obediently, she kicked it off her left foot, leaving it dangling around her right ankle like some erotic pennant.

At last the cabbie's hand settled in her slit, parting her inner lips and stretching them open. Cindy needed no encouragement to guide the head of his cock to her entrance. She braced herself for the moment of entry, crying out as she felt the swollen glans nudging into her. The man had a firm hold of her hips, and she relaxed back against him as he gradually fed his shaft into her moist channel. He stretched her as the imaginary wooden dildo had stretched her in her fantasy, and by the time she was solidly impaled on his cock, she was as full as she could ever remember having been.

His breath was warm on her neck as he began to thrust, and one hand came up to free a nipple from the confines of her rubber top and roll it between finger and thumb. When he gave the stiff little bud a hard pinch, Cindy squealed, caught between pain and pleasure. He was fucking her with surprising finesse. Unlike a lot of the well-endowed men she'd been with, he realised that just possessing a big cock wasn't enough – he had to know how to use it, too. And using it he was, Cindy thought blissfully, as the gyration of his hips and the pressure of her own finger on her clit forced her into a swift orgasm which had barely faded before a second, more powerful one rocked her slight body.

The cabbie kept on pumping into her, his breath growing increasingly hoarse and ragged and his movements speeding up as he approached his own climax. He cried out suddenly and gave one last, powerful jerk of his hips, slamming even deeper into her as his semen jetted against the neck of her womb. He held her for a long moment, his stubbled cheek pressed against hers in a surprisingly affectionate gesture, and then he withdrew. Taking a tissue from a box on the rear windowsill, he wiped the traces of their lovemaking from his cock, then pulled out another and wiped it delicately over Cindy's saturated sex.

He shrugged as she settled herself into a sitting position on the seat and pulled her G-string back into place. 'Just 'cos you drive a cab for a living, doesn't mean you can't have a bit of class, darling,' he told her.

She opened the door and slid her feet out onto the pavement. 'Thanks for the ride,' she said, grinning.

'I thought that was my line,' the cabbie replied, and drove off in the direction of his next fare.

The foyer of *The Cage* still bore the plush damson drapes and carpets that had once marked it as the gateway to a picture palace. However, no film which had ever flickered across the screen in the small auditorium could have possessed the visual impact of the women who already thronged the building, in their fantastic creations of latex and PVC, leather and lace. Cindy's eyes scanned the crowd, searching for Sheena Thorn. She was more than half-convinced that the editor had set her up to be fucked by the taxi driver; the woman had been so precise about making the arrangements for this evening, even ringing the agency the day before to double-check that Cindy had been given the correct instructions regarding her outfit and the preparations she needed to make, that Cindy could not believe she would neglect as fundamental a detail as a cab fare. Not that she hadn't enjoyed what the cabbie had done to her, she thought, acknowledging the slight soreness in her pussy where his thick cock had stretched her delicate flesh, but Cindy was sure it had all been arranged for a purpose.

'Ah, you must be Cindy.' She spun round on hearing a

soft Scottish voice behind her, to be confronted by a tall woman with hair dyed a vivid burgundy and a voluptuous figure squeezed into a high-necked dress of the softest black leather. So this was the famous Sheena Thorn.

'Hi, Sheena,' Cindy replied, feeling unaccountably nervous.

'You're a little late, Cindy.' There was the merest hint of reproach in Sheena's voice. 'Did you have a problem finding us?'

'Well, the taxi driver didn't have any record of the fare being paid in advance, so we... we took a while sorting that out.'

'Come down to the playroom with me,' Sheena said. 'We can talk about it there.'

The playroom was a box-like, low-ceilinged room that ran beneath the main auditorium. When this had been a functioning cinema, it had housed the huge Wurlitzer organ which would rise up in front of the screen between the B-picture and the main feature. Cindy had read somewhere that the instrument had been sold to a collector in Colorado or Utah. Its absence suited her fine; the cabbie had already provided her with the only massive organ she would need this evening.

The room had been painted a monotone black, as befitted a dungeon, and it had been kitted out with a variety of customised pieces of equipment. There was a wooden pillory, a couple of whipping stools of varying heights and a free-standing frame which housed a St Andrew's cross to which a willing victim could be tied spread-eagled. Cindy had become familiar with all these toys during her previous visits to *The Cage*, and she knew that before much longer she would be fastened to one for Sheena's benefit.

There was another woman in the room, Cindy realised,

as her eyes became accustomed to the dim lighting. She was a little above average height, with long tousled dark hair and an olive complexion.

'I'd like you to meet my art editor, Consuela,' Sheena said.

If Cindy's outfit was on the daring side, Consuela's was positively indecent. She wore a sheer bodystocking of fine mesh, and a leather corset belt that was fastened in front with four large buckles. Crosses of black gaffer tape covered Consuela's nipples, but she wore no panties, and the thick, jet-black bush of hair that covered her mound was clearly visible through the bodystocking.

'I am pleased to meet you,' Consuela said, with a heavy Spanish accent. She held out a hand for Cindy to shake, but when Cindy went to exchange the pleasantry she found herself being thrown through the air, to land in a heap on the playroom floor.

'I must stop her from doing that,' Sheena told Cindy. 'She's not only a talented designer and a very beautiful woman, but she's an expert in judo as well.'

'Thanks for warning me,' Cindy said, rubbing her backside.

'So we tie her up now?' Consuela asked, a wicked smile on her face.

'You're very eager tonight,' Sheena chided her. 'Don't we have time for a few social niceties? After all, we've got a birthday to celebrate, and I do like to unwrap my presents before I play with them...'

Sheena helped Cindy to her feet, and pressed her lips to the bottle-blonde's in a deep, lingering kiss. Her mouth was soft, so different in feel from a man's, and Cindy tasted cigarettes and red wine as she returned the kiss. Consuela, despite her apparent impatience to see Cindy tied up and thrashed, could not resist joining in the embrace, her hands roaming over Cindy's gentle curves and the fuller contours of Sheena's body, before moving down to unfasten the waspie Cindy was wearing, and to roll the stockings down her legs.

It was Sheena's finger, however, that finally snaked down under the edge of Cindy's rubber G-string, seeking the soft warmth of her vagina.

'You're incredibly wet,' Sheena murmured. 'You must really want this, Cindy.'

She removed her probing finger and put it to her lips, wanting to taste Cindy's juices. An expression of surprise crossed her face as she licked it clean. Instantly, she pulled away from the three-way clinch.

'You've been with a man!' she exclaimed.

'W-well—' Cindy stammered. 'I told you, the cab hadn't been paid for, so I had to give the driver something to cover the fare.'

'So you used your body,' Sheena sneered. 'It's not the most imaginative solution, is it, Cindy? You knew tonight was all about the pleasures that only a woman can bestow on another, and yet you choose to – to defile yourself with a man's spunk.'

'I'd hardly say I'd been defiled,' Cindy replied, her quim muscles clutching involuntarily as she thought how the blond taxi driver had thrust so pleasurably into her. More than ever, she was sure that Sheena Thorn had intended this to happen. Even though the immediate traces of their lovemaking had been wiped away by the cabbie, the remnants of his spunk were bound to leak from her. It was all the excuse Sheena needed to administer a good beating.

'What you have to say isn't important any more,' Sheena told her. 'Consuela, help me, will you?'

The Spanish girl required no second bidding. She aided

Sheena in dragging a struggling Cindy over to the St Andrew's cross and pressing her firmly against it, her front flush against the smooth dark wood, while Sheena strapped Cindy's wrists and ankles to the frame. The whole movement was effected within seconds, leaving Cindy securely bound and helpless. As a final touch, Consuela unclipped the fastening of Cindy's bra top, leaving the little garment to dangle uselessly from Cindy's shoulders.

With the back of her body completely naked, apart from the thin rubber strip of the G-string, she knew she presented a tempting target. She had no idea what Sheena intended to use to punish her, until the woman came to stand before her. The cross had been designed to leave the victim's face visible, and Cindy was also aware that a semi-circle had been cut out from the bottom of the X, squarely at crotch level. Her mind was still reeling with the implications of that refinement as she realised what implement Sheena was brandishing. It was a cat o'nine tails, the thin leather thongs about a foot long and shiny from use.

'I did think about gagging you,' Sheena said, 'but I want to hear you beg for mercy.'

She disappeared out of Cindy's line of sight. The next thing Cindy knew was the impact as the cat cut into her flesh, points of fire scattering across the surface of her buttocks. She shrieked, knowing her cry would be inaudible to anyone outside the room. Above them, dance music continued to play at high volume, muted to a rhythmic thud by the thickness of the playroom's ceiling.

The cat fell again and again, Sheena wielding it expertly. After half a dozen strokes Cindy felt as though her whole bottom was ablaze and she was, as Sheena had predicted, begging for her punishment to stop. Her pleas were futile, however: the next stroke fell hard across the tops of

Cindy's widely-spread thighs, and she jerked in her bonds, her eyes smarting with tears.

'Consuela, I think you may need to take Cindy's mind off things,' Sheena suggested.

'*Claro.*' With that word signalling her assent, Consuela dropped to her knees before the St Andrew's cross. Now the reason for the cutaway section of wood became clear; it gave the Spanish girl unrestricted access to Cindy's shaven sex. She pushed the gusset of Cindy's G-string to one side and pressed her lips to Cindy's labia. Her tongue snaked out, laving the length of Cindy's juicy furrow. Cindy moaned as Consuela began to lick her in earnest, the point of her tongue flicking at Cindy's clitoris.

Distracted by the pleasurable sensations Consuela's oral ministrations were creating between her legs, Cindy had forgotten that Sheena was still holding the cat o'nine tails. She was suddenly, shockingly reminded of that fact as it fell hard against her back, striping the soft skin. Consuela kept licking, even as Cindy bucked and howled.

'Nearly there, Cindy, nearly there,' Sheena crooned, and as Consuela's busy tongue attacked Cindy's clitoris, the underlying meaning in her words became evident. An orgasm was building, unstoppable, low down in Cindy's body, and when the cat landed again, scoring Cindy's back for a second time, the messages her brain was receiving from her nerve-endings fused in a mixture of pain and exquisite pleasure, and when Cindy cried out this time, it announced to the others in the room that she had reached her climax.

As her quim pulsed and contracted, Consuela's tongue was moving away. Something was replacing it; something hard and warm. As it slid into Cindy's sopping channel she realised it was the handle of the cat o'nine tails. Cindy hung in her bonds, grateful that she was securely held in place, as Sheena used the implement as a makeshift phallus, thrusting it in and out of Cindy's body.

The pumping motion pushed Cindy rapidly towards a second orgasm. Her inner muscles clasped the leather handle of the whip as greedily as they had embraced the cab driver's cock earlier in the evening. She wondered what the man would say if he could see her now, being brought to a climax in this fashion. She wanted him to be here, watching, stroking his thick shaft with his fist. He would time his orgasm so that he came at the same time as she did, his creamy seed splattering over the weals on her back and buttocks, violating her body and yet worshipping it. She could almost taste the thick salty fluid as he wiped it from her skin and pressed it to her lips, ordering her to lick her fingers clean...

But this was Sheena's night, she reminded herself, and no men were allowed to enter her Sapphic sanctum. As if to press this point home, she had pulled the cat from Cindy's shuddering body, and instead of seminal fluid, it was her own juices Cindy was ordered to lick from the handle of the whip.

Once the smooth leather had been cleaned to Sheena's satisfaction, Cindy was released from the cross and helped to stand upright. Sheena took Cindy in an embrace, fastening her bra top for her.

'Thank you; you were everything the agency promised,' she said, kissing Cindy tenderly on the lips. 'I think you deserve a drink after that. Come on, let's go upstairs. I want to introduce you to a few people.'

Two hours later Cindy was standing in the foyer, bidding Sheena goodnight. Half a dozen business cards had been stuffed into her little handbag, all bar one from women who, impressed by Sheena's enthusiastic account of

Cindy's performance in the playroom, were eager to engage her professional services for themselves. The last card was Sheena's. 'You've got just what it takes to be in a *Sappho* photo-set,' Sheena had told her. 'I can just see you now, in nothing but high heels and a blindfold, sprawled on black satin sheets...'

I'm sure you can, Cindy had thought, but what are you going to want me to do for the photographs?

Sheena gave Cindy one last peck on the cheek. 'Your taxi should be here any second. I'm sorry about the mix-up on the way here, but I'm sure I told them to put the fare on my account. Let me give you some money; I wouldn't want you to have the same problem going home.'

Cindy glanced across the foyer, and spotted a familiar blond figure standing by the door, his eyes widening at the sight of so much scantily-clad female flesh. She shook her head, remembering the feel of his thick cock, and guessing how he would react when he saw the stripes that marked her punished backside. 'It's okay, Sheena. If you don't mind, I'd like to come to my own arrangement...'

Chapter Seven

'He wants me to do *what* while he watches?' Warren asked incredulously.

Laurel slipped on her wire-framed glasses and looked at the notes she had taken in the course of her conversation with Alan Wesley. 'It seems Mr Wesley and his wife have got this fantasy where he comes home from work unexpectedly and catches his wife in bed with some young stud. The wife and her lover make the guy strip off, tie him to a chair, laugh at the size of his cock, and then she lets this bloke do all the things to her that she's never let her husband do while the husband is forced to watch them at it.'

'But I thought we were only catering for submissive women,' Warren said. 'This guy sounds like the biggest wimp on the planet, if you ask me.'

'Well, they've planned it as a fortieth birthday treat for the wife, Carol, and they'd be paying us for an overnight stay, so I don't really want to turn them down. Anyway, I don't see why we shouldn't cater for the odd couple now and again, if there's a demand. And I've never known you to have any qualms about performing in front of an audience before.' Her hazel eyes flashed with mischief behind the lenses of her glasses. 'Or is it that you're worried you're not going to match up to Mr Wesley's idea of a stud?'

She rested her chin on her cupped hand, and slipped her little finger between her pink-painted lips as she did so. Warren realised her gesture was purely intentional in its symbolism, and fought not to rise to the bait, even as his cock twitched treacherously in his boxer shorts. The only thing he wanted to see sliding into Laurel Angell's mouth was his rigid erection, and he was sure she knew it as well as he did. And you didn't need to have a nine-inch monster lurking in your underwear to convince a woman you were the best lover she'd ever experienced, not if you were an expert in using what you actually had. If Laurel's wet little pussy or tight, unplundered arse were ever available to him, she'd learn that lesson remarkably quickly. One day he'd have her over that desk and give her backside the skelping she deserved for being such a blatant tease, boss or no boss...

He realised Laurel was staring at him, an amused expression on her face. He stared back, giving every impression of having been completely unruffled by her actions.

'There'll be no complaints on that score, don't you worry,' he told her. 'No point in just giving a woman a little something for her birthday, now is there?'

Warren was still grinning with self-satisfaction as Laurel reached for the phone to confirm the booking.

The Wesleys lived in an anonymous-looking tree-lined avenue in Ruislip. Strictly commuter country, Warren thought, walking down past identical houses where television sets flickered behind net curtains and front gardens were dotted with ornamental gnomes and miniature stone wishing wells. Just the sort of neighbourhood where dull suburban couples spiced up their lives with polite wife-swapping sessions at the weekends, passing their partners around like canapés at a cocktail party.

When Laurel had filled Warren in on Alan Wesley's

background, it had not surprised him to learn that the man worked for a firm of accountants in the City; a dreary job for a dreary-sounding individual. The picture of middle-class respectability had been completed with the information that Wesley was high up in the local Round Table, and played golf off a low handicap on Sundays. No wonder his idea of sexual excitement involved ridicule and humiliation.

Warren pushed open the front gate of the Wesleys' semi and walked up the path to the white, double-glazed front door, conscious that in his battered leather jacket he probably looked more like a potential burglar than a houseguest. Carol Wesley opened the door on his knock, as though she'd been watching for his arrival, and ushered him quickly inside. She was a mousy-haired woman, visibly approaching middle age; Warren suspected that twenty years ago she would have been a stunner, but time and the monotony of being a housewife had given her a careworn look which made her seem older than her years. Her hair was piled on top of her head, ringlets framing her face, and she wore a plain black cocktail dress with spaghetti straps that emphasised a surprisingly good figure with small, high breasts and long, slim legs. She giggled, and Warren wondered whether she had fortified her resolve to go through this scenario with the aid of a little alcohol; his suspicion was confirmed when he followed her through to the lounge and spotted an almost empty glass of red wine standing on a fussy lace coaster on the coffee table.

He kissed her on the cheek, and handed her the bottle of champagne he had brought as a present. 'Happy birthday, Carol. You're looking great tonight,' he said, slipping into the rôle of attentive lover.

'Thank you,' she replied, blushing slightly at the compliment. 'Should I put this in the fridge?' she asked, gesturing to the champagne. She sounded slightly nervous, and eager to please.

'Sure,' Warren replied easily, 'we can drink it after...'

Carol chattered on as she walked down the hall. 'Look at the time. Typical of Alan, can't even leave the office early on my birthday.'

'Gives us more time to spend together, though.' Warren dropped his jacket over the arm of the sofa and wandered into the kitchen. As Carol was busy finding a space in the overloaded refrigerator for the bottle, he came up behind her and began to nuzzle her neck. She smelt of a floral, slightly powdery perfume, and wriggled half-heartedly in his grasp.

'Not here, Alan might be back at any minute.'

'Ah, come on, Carol, wouldn't you like him to see you like this? In the arms of the man who makes you feel the way he's forgotten how to? Or would you prefer him to see you like this?'

As he spoke, Warren pushed the straps of the dress down over her shoulders. As he had guessed, she wore no bra beneath it, and he turned her to face the big picture window over the sink, so they could see their own reflections against the glass, the small brown aureoles of Carol's breasts already stiffening with excitement. Warren cupped the soft mounds and began to squeeze them roughly, summoning a moan from between Carol's lips. His cock had already begun to stir, and the feel of her firm breasts in his hands made it twitch with excitement and lengthen further.

'Look at yourself, Carol,' he murmured, pinching harder at her nipples. 'Really look at yourself. You've been with Alan so long all you see is the little drudge he's turned you into, but deep down inside is the sexy slip of a thing he married. Sex is a chore with him, now, isn't it? A couple of minutes of humping and heaving on a Sunday morning, and him not caring whether you come or not.' He caught her hair, pulling it loose from the clips that held it, so it spilled down onto her bare shoulders. 'When was the last time your husband had you like this, half-naked in the kitchen and panting like a bitch on heat?'

He was rucking up the hem of her dress as Carol hung limp in his arms, lulled by the hypnotic tone of his voice and the images he was planting in her head. She made no protest as he took hold of her hand and guided it beneath the bunched-up fabric, to rest on her peach-coloured French panties. Her best underwear, saved for a special occasion, he suspected.

'Go on, Carol, touch yourself,' he urged. 'I want to watch you play with your pussy.'

Hesitantly at first, Carol began to comply, running her fingers lightly over the silky material. As she continued to stroke her mound Warren bit her throat, bruising her skin.

'What are you doing?' Carol whispered, startled back to awareness by the sudden pain.

'As soon as I saw the creamy skin on that neck of yours I wanted to mark it,' he replied. 'It'll let that wimp of a husband know you've been with a real man.' Warren lowered his voice. 'I'm going to mark those lovely tits of yours, too.'

He noticed that Carol's fingers moved lower as he spoke, cupping her fleshy labia where they were cradled in the gusset of the French panties.

'Do you want that, Carol?' he asked. 'Do you want me to bite your tits? Do you want me to do it while your husband watches?'

She moaned again, a noise he took as assent, and her fingers slipped below the leg of her panties as she widened her stance slightly. Warren fought the urge to rip the flimsy garment off her; that would come later, but he was working to his own internal script of how this scene should be played out.

'You know I'm going to make him watch me fucking you, don't you?' Warren said, as Carol began to rub at her sex in earnest. 'He's going to see my cock sliding up into you, and know that for the first time in your life you'll be really filled. Didn't you tell me he's got nothing between his legs that's worth writing home about?'

Carol Wesley had thrown her head back, and her eyes were half-closed as she masturbated herself. 'Yes,' she muttered, 'I want a big fat cock inside me. Warren, I want to feel it when you thrust into me...'

'Come on, let's go upstairs,' Warren urged, anxious to undress and relieve the pressure of his penis as it pressed against his button fly. They made it as far as the bottom of the stairs before Warren was tugging her dress down off her hips, so that all she stood in was her panties, stockings and suspenders. Again, he took her in his arms, kissing her passionately and coaxing her to stroke the aching bulge in his jeans. Her breasts were crushed against his chest, the nipples hard points that he wanted to twist until she cried out in pleasurable pain.

Halfway up the stairs he finally tugged down her French knickers. He made a show of raising them to his nose and sniffing at the gusset before he tossed them away. 'Gorgeous,' he said with approval, and the shocked look Carol gave him made him realise that her husband was probably no fan of the natural female aroma unless it was buried under the artificial scents of soap, deodorant and perfume.

Warren strode with assurance to what he took to be the master bedroom, and was rewarded with the sight of a double bed with a frilly floral counterpane, a pink nightdress lying neatly folded on one side, and a pair of striped pyjamas on the other. Contemptuously, he pushed the pyjamas off the bed to land in a crumpled heap on the floor, and threw Carol down on the bed. She lay looking up at him as he began to strip off. He took his time, pulling his T-shirt slowly over his head so that she could watch the play of muscles on his chest and arms as he stretched. He stooped to pull off his boots and socks, then turned his attention to his belt buckle. Once his jeans were unfastened, he pushed them down and off. Carol was watching him attentively, but he noticed that her eyes were increasingly drawn to his crotch. He had eschewed his usual boxers in favour of a pair of hip-hugging designer briefs which had been a present from an old girlfriend, and which clung to his cock and balls, presenting them in a way which was practically making Mrs Wesley salivate. Perhaps the game he was playing with the woman wasn't that far divorced from reality, he thought. Perhaps she really wasn't used to being screwed by a man with a decent-sized dick.

'You want this, Carol, don't you?' he said, stroking his erection through the white cotton.

She nodded, helplessly. He noticed that her thighs had lolled open slightly as she lay on the bed, revealing the hairy lips of her pussy, and a hint of the glistening, salmon-pink flesh they usually concealed.

'Well, you're going to have to beg for it,' Warren told her.

'Please...' she whispered, her words barely audible. 'Please, Warren, make love to me.'

'Make love?' Warren sounded contemptuous. There was a pile of paperback romances on the bedside table, and he gestured towards them. 'That might be what they call it in that sort of trash, but I want to hear it called what it really is. Come on, Carol, say it. Say what you really want me to do to you.'

'I want you... I want to fuck me,' she said, finally.

'Good girl,' Warren said, coming to lie on the bed beside her. He put her hand on the waistband of his briefs, and obediently she pulled them down. His cock bobbed slightly as it was released from the constricting pants, and Carol Wesley reached out a hand towards it.

She stroked a tentative finger along its veined length. 'It's much bigger than my husband's,' she said. Those words alone were enough to make it twitch and extend even further.

'It'll probably get even bigger if you suck it,' Warren told her.

'Oh, I don't think I could do that,' she replied quickly.

'Why ever not? I mean, just think how Alan will feel if he comes in and sees his wife with her lips wrapped around another man's cock, her mouth stretching to cope with something that's fatter than she's been used to.'

'That's just it,' Carol said. 'I'm not used to sucking Alan's. I don't lick him... and he doesn't lick me.' There was a sudden, regretful tone to her voice.

'Doesn't he now? Well, it's about time you found out what you've been missing, then, isn't it?' As he spoke, Warren was positioning himself between Carol's legs. He lowered his face towards her moist sex.

'You're not... You can't be... Oh...' Carol's protests faded and died as Warren's mouth settled on her vulva. His tongue laved the length of her swollen crease, moving slowly over the slippery flesh. He glanced up at the woman's face as his tongue reached the apex of its journey; her expression was one of mortification mixed with rapidly-dawning pleasure. How could Carol Wesley have reached the age of forty without ever having her pussy licked? he wondered, as he made the tip of his tongue into a hard point and used it to flick at her clitoris. She wriggled and writhed beneath him, pushing her hips up towards his face as she moved closer to her crisis.

Somewhere in the distance, a door slammed, and a voice called out, 'Carol, darling, I'm home...'

'It's Alan,' Carol gasped. 'Oh, Warren, it's really going to happen, isn't it?'

Warren couldn't work out whether Carol was referring to the enactment of her fantasy, or to her impending orgasm. He didn't have time to think about it. As Carol grabbed a fistful of his dark hair and cried out in ecstasy, her salty juices flooding into Warren's mouth, the bedroom door burst open and a voice exclaimed, 'Carol, what the hell is going on here?'

Carol, fighting to recover, said nothing. Warren turned his face, smeared with the evidence of Carol's orgasm, towards the man who stood in the doorway. Alan Wesley was exactly as Warren had pictured him: in his early forties, with receding sandy hair and thick, horn-rimmed glasses. He was staring at his wife's flushed body, naked but for stockings and suspenders, and the play of emotions was visible on his face: excitement that his cherished fantasy was about to come true, mixed with jealousy and humiliation. It looked as though the latter feelings were winning. If he had called a halt to the paid-for proceedings and thrown Warren out of the house now, it would not have been a surprise: it was one thing to dream about your wife having an orgasm courtesy of another man's lips and tongue, enjoying a pleasure which you had been quite happy to deny her throughout your marriage, but quite another to stand in your own chintzy bedroom and be confronted with the reality of the situation.

Warren pounced on the man's indecision and took control of the situation. 'I'm about to give your wife the fucking of her life – show her what it's like to have a real man's cock inside her for once. Have you got a problem with that?'

'I... er...' Alan Wesley stammered. There was a pronounced bulge in the crotch of his dark suit trousers, which Warren gestured to contemptuously.

'Obviously there's no problem, otherwise that pathetic little dick of yours wouldn't be getting so hard.' He sat up on the bed, giving Wesley a good view of his own erection, standing proud from its dark bush of hair. To Warren's surprise, the man seemed as impressed by it as his wife had been. 'Carol told me just how small it is, you know. Said she could hardly feel it when it's up her. Come on, get your trousers off; I want to see that miserable excuse for a penis so I can commiserate with her properly.'

Wesley dropped the briefcase he'd been holding, and hurried to comply with Warren's demand. Soon his trousers and underpants were round his ankles, and his cock was tenting out the front of his white nylon shirt.

'That as well,' Warren said, pointing to the shirt. Wesley quickly stripped off the rest of his clothes and stood nervously in front of Warren. His skin was pale, his body hair sparse and fair, and he had the beginnings of a paunch. His much-derided cock stood stubbily erect, and Warren had the satisfaction of realising it was indeed a good couple of inches shorter than his own. The fantasy, like his ego, remained unpunctured.

Warren shook his head and sighed. 'Truly, truly pathetic.' He noticed that the man's penis twitched slightly as he spoke, and realised that Wesley was revelling in the situation. What kind of man got off on being told that he was seriously lacking when it came to his wedding tackle?

Warren wondered. Still, he was paying handsomely for the privilege, and the night was still in its infancy. There was a good deal more humiliation to come for Mr Wesley, if he only knew it.

'It's no wonder Carol needs someone like me in her bed,' Warren said. 'I can see you need a lesson in how to satisfy a woman properly, judging by the way she came off on my tongue just now. Yes, Alan–' Warren got up and went over to clap the man on his shoulder '–she got licked out for the first time in her life, and she loved it. Shame you've never wanted to do it to her, considering a good tonguing can make up for any deficiency in the dick department.'

As he spoke, he was steering Wesley over to the wicker chair that stood in front of the dressing table. He turned it round so it was facing the bed, no more than a foot away from the frilled edge of the counterpane, and ordered the man to bend over and hold on to its low back.

Warren tugged the belt out of Wesley's trousers and flexed it between his hands, looking at Wesley sadly. 'Oh, Alan, if you'd given your wife the sex she wanted, when she wanted it, we wouldn't be in this position now, would we? I'm going to have to give you something to remind you not to deprive her in future.'

Before Wesley was aware of what was happening, the end of his own belt had cracked down on his buttocks. He yelled and made to rise, but Warren pushed him back into place.

'Stay where you are, you're getting another five of those,' he said. Five times in rapid succession, the belt landed on Alan Wesley's buttocks, supple leather branding a series of red tramlines on the white flesh. When Warren had finished, Wesley's eyes looked suspiciously wet, and he was rubbing his punished cheeks vigorously, trying to soothe them. Despite the shock of his unexpected chastisement, his cock was as hard as it had been at any point since he'd walked into the bedroom.

Warren ignored Wesley's obvious discomfort, and turned to Carol. 'Darling, I'm going to need your stockings,' he ordered. Carol unclipped her stockings from her suspender belt and rolled them down and off her legs, before handing them to Warren. He pushed Wesley down onto the chair, Wesley wincing as his sore buttocks pressed against the coarse wicker seat, then used the stockings to secure his ankles to the front legs of the chair, taking care that the nylon would not bite into the man's skin if he wriggled and tried to free himself. He picked up Alan's discarded tie next, and twisted it between his fingers. Both the Wesleys appeared to be surprised when he looked quizzically at Carol and asked, 'So, which hand does he use to wank with? Because I take it that's what he's going to want to do while he watches.'

He waited while Carol considered the question. By ignoring Wesley and letting his wife make the decisions, Warren knew he was increasing the impotence – no, he checked himself mentally, noting the strength of Wesley's bloated erection, make that powerlessness – the man must be feeling. But even Warren was taken aback when Carol replied, 'I don't think I want him to be able to. Tie both his hands.'

The tie was looped round a protesting Wesley's right wrist and knotted in place, fastening his arm to the chair. His left followed quickly, held in place by the belt from Wesley's trousers. Now the show could begin.

Carol Wesley settled back on the bed, cupping her breasts in her hands as if to offer them to Warren. He went to lie beside her and pressed his mouth to hers. Her lips opened beneath the pressure of his, allowing him to possess her mouth with his tongue. They kissed long and noisily, Carol leaving her husband in no doubt as to how much she was enjoying Warren's ministrations.

Warren let his tongue snake in a slow, wet trail down Carol's neck and over the plane of her collarbone, before using it to circle the crinkled aureole of her left breast. He caught the nipple between his teeth and bit at it gently, then, remembering his words in the kitchen, he turned his attentions to the soft white breast itself. The sucking pressure of his mouth changed to a sudden nip, hard enough to bruise, and Carol cried out.

'Told you I'd do it, didn't I?' he said. 'I told you I'd mark those gorgeous tits of yours.'

Carol's only answer was to groan in pleasure and present her other breast to Warren for the same treatment.

As Warren's mouth worked on her breasts, his hand reached down between her legs. Her inner lips had peeled apart, and he slipped a finger into the entrance of her vagina, following it quickly with a second, and a third. He spread the fingers slightly, feeling the strong ribbed walls of her channel pushing against him. She bit her lip to stifle a moan. 'Stretching you a bit, is it, darling?' he enquired. 'You'll need to get used to it, because that's what it'll feel like when my cock's inside you.'

He worked his hand back and forth for a few moments, finger-fucking her. His thumb had settled on her clitoris and was rubbing the little button of flesh. Wesley was more than close enough to smell his wife's briny, excited aroma, and see how the shiny crimson mouth of her sex was stretched taut to accommodate Warren's fingers. She was beginning to build towards another orgasm, and Warren increased the pressure of his thumb until she bucked and gasped beneath him, her sheath gripping tightly at his fingers.

'Was that good?' he asked, when her breathing had subsided to something close to normal. She nodded, as he stroked wisps of hair away from her forehead.

'Are you ready for me?' he asked. She nodded again. He looked over to where Alan Wesley was sitting, bound securely to the chair. The frustration in the man's body language was evident as he writhed in his seat. His cock was jutting upwards, darkly swollen with blood; Warren could imagine how it must feel to want to relieve the tension in that throbbing column of flesh, and to be unable to do so. Just one touch would be more than enough to bring the man shuddering to a climax, but that would come later, when the speed of Wesley's ejaculation could be used to ridicule him further, as the man had expressly asked.

Warren turned his attention back to Carol, motioning to her that she should get up on all fours. She did as he asked, kneeling so that she was directly alongside her husband. Warren positioned himself behind her and let his erection rest in the crease between her buttocks. For a moment its slick head pressed against her tight, puckered rosebud.

'Well, if he never licks you out, I'm damn sure he's never taken you up the arse either, has he, Carol?' Warren murmured. 'Would you like him to watch that? You know he can't do anything to stop me.' He coated a finger in the juice that was running freely from her vaginal opening, and used it to push against her anal hole. There was a brief resistance, then it slipped inside her. Carol groaned and squirmed against the unfamiliar intrusion, then relaxed as the finger began to work back and forth. Her husband was watching with appalled fascination.

'Yes, I'll definitely have you there later,' Warren told her, withdrawing the finger, 'but I just can't wait any longer before I sample that lovely cunt of yours.'

With that, he guided his cock inside her, feeling the warm velvet channel clasp him possessively. He grasped her hips tightly, pulling her back onto his erection. In this position, not only would Alan have a compelling side-on view of the action, as Warren's cock powered in and out of Carol's pussy, but he would also know that the penetration was deeper, enabling his wife to fully appreciate the fact that she was being screwed by a man with a larger tool than his own.

Warren's movements were slow and leisurely at first, setting up a gentle rhythm which Carol matched, pushing back eagerly onto his shaft. Gradually, though, he upped the tempo until it was almost frenetic, his balls slapping against Carol's buttocks. Carol's head was down, her long wispy hair falling into her eyes, and her breasts hung like two cones. Wesley seemed mesmerised by the scene before him, unable to tear his gaze from the point at which his wife's body and Warren's were conjoined.

At last, Warren felt the familiar roiling in his balls which indicated he was on the verge of coming. He gave a final fierce thrust and spent his seed deep inside Carol Wesley's body. Her fleshy sheath rippled in the spasms of her own orgasm, squeezing him and milking the last drops of his viscous emission.

Warren pulled out of her and rolled onto his back, enjoying the smug afterglow of sex with another man's wife. Carol turned and looked at her husband; her skin was flushed and gleaming with sweat, and her eyes shone with a vitality which had been completely absent when Warren had first met her.

'There's champagne in the fridge,' she said, when her breathing had slowed to normal. 'Warren brought it. I'll fetch it.' She slipped off the bed and padded to the door, not bothering to find anything to cover her nakedness.

'And Alan, you look pathetic sitting there like that.' She gestured to the items of clothing that bound him to the chair, and the erection which still thrust upwards. 'Warren, sort him out, can't you?'

Warren shrugged and went to untie Wesley as Carol made her way downstairs. He bent and loosened the stockings around Wesley's ankles, then rose and was about to free his wrists when he noticed the other man staring raptly at his groin. Warren glanced down, realising that his cock was more than half-erect – due to the thrill he got from exercising control over Alan and his wife, he supposed. The shaft was glistening with a mixture of his own spunk and Carol's juices.

'That's it,' he said to Wesley. 'Take a good look. Admire it, why don't you? After all, it's given your wife a better time than you seem to manage.'

Wesley licked his lips, and nodded. 'She's never said anything, but I do sometimes feel that I can't really satisfy Carol with what I've got.'

Warren said nothing. If Wesley had as little knowledge of what constituted good sex as he suspected, then the man could have had a cock the size of a baguette and still left his wife unsatisfied.

'I always wondered what it would be like to have a big cock like that,' Wesley continued, gazing wistfully at Warren's erection.

Warren would never know what made him say what he did. Perhaps it was the intoxication of completing another successful job for the agency, or perhaps it was the image of Laurel Angell sitting at her desk, sucking meaningfully on her little finger. Whatever, the words that came out of his mouth surprised even him. 'Why don't you find out?' he asked.

'What?' Wesley replied.

'You've never tasted your wife's cunt juices, and you've never had a big dick. So why don't you take my cock in your mouth and find out what it's like to do both? Come on, Wesley, clean me up.'

'I couldn't,' Wesley replied, even as he was craning forward in his bonds, trying to get closer to Warren's groin.

'You'll do as I tell you, otherwise I may just leave you tied to that chair all night while I fuck your wife's arse in the spare bedroom. How would you like that, Alan, hearing every moment of what we're doing, knowing exactly where this cock's going, and not being able to watch? Maybe I'll wait until afterwards and then make you suck me clean.'

Wesley said nothing, but the fact that his erection had not diminished in its intensity spoke volumes on his behalf. Warren took his own cock in his hand and rubbed the juice-slick shaft, feeling it thicken and grow to its full length. Then he positioned himself squarely between Wesley's legs and presented the head to Wesley's mouth. There was a moment's hesitation, then Wesley's lips encircled Warren's glans and he began, nervously, to suck. The sensation was so different to that of being in Carol's soft mouth, the warm wet pressure Wesley was applying heightened by the knowledge that, by letting another man pleasure him in this way Warren was breaking one of his own taboos.

'Come on, Alan, suck me harder,' Warren ordered, and the man hastened to comply, his head bobbing up and down more rapidly. By the way his eyes had closed and the way he was taking more of Warren's length into his gullet, Wesley was giving every indication of enjoying what he had been compelled to do. As the sensation mounted, Warren caught hold of Alan's sparse fair hair and pulled the man's head harder onto his cock. Instead of complaining at having his mouth used in this way, or attempting to pull away, Wesley submissively allowed Warren to dictate the speed of his thrusts. Having come once already, Warren expected to last longer, but the novelty of the situation was too much for him, and it seemed all too short a time before he was pumping his come to the back of Wesley's throat, the man swallowing every drop. He groaned, and swore on the lives of all the saints he could remember.

He finally opened his eyes, aware that Wesley was staring at him meekly. 'So, what's it like to have a big cock, then, Alan?' he enquired.

'Amazing,' Wesley replied.

'Good man,' Warren said, and reached down. Wesley, expecting to have his wrists untied, relaxed. Instead, Warren's hand caught hold of Wesley's cock and began to wank him without ceremony. Wesley's breathing speeded up and he began to whimper with pleasure as Warren's fingers quickly and methodically brought him to climax. It was over within seconds, Wesley's stringy come oozing down over Warren's fist.

As he raised his fingers to Wesley's mouth, ordering him to lick them clean, Carol came through the door, carrying a tray on which stood the bottle of champagne and three glasses. If she registered her husband's flaccid member, and the trace of semen at one corner of his mouth, she said nothing. She poured the champagne as Warren finally released her husband from his impromptu bondage.

Warren took the proffered glass and drank from it deeply, relishing the way the bubbles popped against his tongue. The night had barely started; there was still a lot he had to show the Wesleys about the joys of submission. A smile crossed his face as he wondered just how far he would be able to push them. He thought of the hungry look on Alan's face as he had watched his wife being shafted, and the relish the couple had expressed every time the subject of anal sex had been mentioned, and suspected it would be quite a long way. He settled back, glass in hand, and silently toasted the beautiful, absent Laurel for the pleasures yet to come.

Chapter Eight

Joe Gallagher completed the last of twenty repetitions on the pec deck and stared at his reflection in the mirror that ran the length of the gym wall. A light sheen of sweat coated his upper body, and his sleeveless grey marl vest was stained with dark patches where it clung to his pectoral muscles. Still, it had not been a bad workout, and the best part of it was that he was being paid to sit here and exercise.

He still felt slightly self-conscious about being in such an exclusive health hydro. Normally his exercise sessions took place in his local gym, which was frequented mostly by amateur boxers and serious fitness freaks. This was a place for posers, he thought disdainfully; the equipment here was the most up-to-date he had ever used, and yet the other clients seemed to be more concerned with the cut of their designer leotards than with putting some proper training in.

Then again, he had to admit that the leotard-clad girls he had seen going through their aerobic paces in the dance studio would be a welcome sight in old man Greenwood's gym. Joe could quite happily have stood for ever and watched that array of firm breasts and toned buttocks, accentuated by clinging lycra in all colours of the rainbow, as the girls stretched and gyrated and thrust their pelvises in an almost indecently explicit routine. He could also have made himself very much at home in the inviting-looking spa complex, with its sauna, steam room, bubbling jacuzzi and aqua-tiled swimming pool. When he had first begun the process of recovering from his accident, trying to regain the strength in his damaged left leg, he had swum for hours almost every day. It was the best way to build up the muscle tone, the hospital's physiotherapist had informed him, and even now he preferred swimming to working out on the treadmill or exercise bike.

However, a relaxing swim was definitely not on the agenda today. The client he was waiting for, a Natalie Wolf, had asked for a scenario which revolved around the gym, and that was what she was going to get.

Joe was surprised to have been asked to take part in this session. The bulk of female clients requesting a dominant male were still serviced by Warren Keating. It was something to do with the man's air of dark, brooding menace, enhanced by the beard which emphasised the contemptuous set of his mouth, and the condescending, masterful look he achieved by narrowing his heavy-lidded gaze. Joe practised the look himself, half-closing his eyes and staring scornfully through his long, sandy lashes. 'Not bad, sunshine, but you need a bit more practice,' he told his reflection wryly.

Natalie Wolf was not paying for dark menace, though; she wanted a fit firm young hunk to play the rôle she had requested, and in that respect at least, Joe fitted the bill. He still felt slightly less confident in his ability to act the part of the dominant master. Unlike Warren, he had never seriously experimented with sadomasochistic sex until he'd joined forces with Laurel to run Domination Inc., and with no regular partner in his life, he had little chance to practise the skills he hoped he was honing on his agency call-outs.

He would not have been comparing himself to Warren, he knew, if it had not been so obvious that Laurel was sexually attracted to the man. For all that they affected to dislike each other, Joe knew that the tension which was growing between Warren and Laurel was the sort which could only be dispelled by means of a good hard fuck, presumably after Laurel had had her backside tanned a deep cherry red by Warren's palm. Joe had never classed himself as the jealous type, but the thought that she might one day end up in Warren's bed provoked envious feelings that were almost impossible to ignore. If Laurel ever broke her self-imposed rule about not having a relationship with someone she worked with, he wanted it to be him, and not Warren, who slid his cock into her velvet depths and pressed his groin against the warmth of her just-punished arse. Perhaps it was just as well Laurel had declared herself off-limits; at least Joe currently had the satisfaction that if he wasn't getting anywhere with her, then neither was Warren.

His reverie was disturbed by the sound of the gym door opening and shutting behind him. Joe stared straight ahead, apparently still lost in thought, but watching Natalie Wolf's mirror image walk towards him. Warren would be disappointed at missing out on this assignment: Miss Wolf was one hundred per cent babe. Joe felt his cock stiffening just watching the slow, sinuous movements of her hips as she approached him. She had mentioned to Laurel that she was originally from California, where everyone was a workout freak, and that she had competed in the Stateside version of *Gladiators*, but nothing could have prepared Joe for the perfection of her body. Her crow-black hair, mahogany skin and prominent cheekbones marked her out as being of Native American extraction, and her tall lithe body was perfectly proportioned. She wore a sawn-off black T-shirt that barely covered her large firm breasts, and her black lycra cycling shorts clung indecently to the V of her sex, her plump labia outlined in minutest detail. She looked like an X-rated version of Pocahontas, and she was Joe's to command. Hitting the Lottery jackpot could not have felt sweeter.

'I hope I'm not late,' she said, her voice sounding to Joe's instantly besotted ears like honey being poured over gravel.

He swung round lazily, climbing down from the pec deck, and made a show of looking at his watch. 'Just on time,' he told her. 'Luckily for you.'

There was a thin towelling band around Natalie's left wrist, and she used it to twist her hair up into a high ponytail. 'You won't make me work too hard, will you?' she asked, sticking to the scenario she had discussed with Laurel. 'I like to keep in shape, but I don't want to torture myself.'

'We'll see,' Joe said. 'I want you to do five circuits of the gym, just as a warm-up.'

Natalie nodded, and began to jog slowly round the room. Joe watched as she moved, admiring her easy grace. Apparently, she was an investment banker, putting in six months' secondment to the London arm of the operation, and it was obvious to him that she invested pretty heavily in her appearance, too.

Once she had completed her circuits, Joe asked Natalie to do some simple stretches, loosening her hamstrings and the muscles in her shoulders and back. That done, the hard work could begin.

'Okay, we'll start with the treadmill,' he said. Natalie went to stand on the rubber conveyor belt, and Joe turned the machine to its lowest setting. Having accustomed her to walking pace, he began to gradually turn up the speed, so that soon she was trotting gently, then running, staring confidently into the middle distance, her impressive chest rising and falling as she took deep breaths. He could have watched her forever, but that was not in his plan. He increased the tempo notch after notch until she was practically sprinting. Supremely fit as Natalie was, there was no way she could keep pace with the rapidly-moving treadmill for very long. She stumbled a couple of times as she attempted to carry on running, and caught hold of the handrails to help her keep her balance, glancing round at Joe anxiously. Aware that he did not want her to hurt herself, Joe turned the speed control until Natalie was moving at a jog once more.

'I thought you told me you were fit,' Joe sneered, silencing Natalie's immediate protests with a curt, 'You need a lesson in how to maintain a steady pace. Keep jogging, hands on the handrail, and look straight ahead.'

He knew that as Natalie gazed stonily forward, she would be able to watch in the mirror as he went over to the kit bag he had left by the far wall and took out of it the implement she had specified for her chastisement – a long, supple leather belt about two inches wide. Joe flexed it thoughtfully as he walked back to the treadmill.

'Okay,' he said, 'a decent athlete keeps going at all times, whatever the distractions. So let's see if you're a decent athlete.' As he spoke he wrapped the end of the belt around his hand, cradling the buckle in his palm. He positioned himself behind the jogging Natalie, raised his arm and brought the belt down smartly. It cracked against Natalie's taut arse cheeks, the sound magnified by the tight lycra of her shorts. She yelped, but kept running.

'Good, that's better,' Joe said. His wrist flicked and the belt snaked out again, catching Natalie full on the crown of her buttocks. 'Now one more for luck, and we can move on,' he said, surprised by his own dexterity. This time the belt hit Natalie across the softer underhang of her bottom, and her howl of complaint was the loudest yet.

Joe was as good as his word, switching off the treadmill

and allowing Natalie to climb down from it. She bent over, hands on her knees. Tendrils of her dark hair clung to her perspiring forehead, and her damp T-shirt was moulded to the contours of her breasts, revealing clearly that despite the fullness of her breasts, she was not wearing a bra.

Joe allowed her to recover for a couple of moments in that position, then issued his next command. He pointed to a free-standing frame which supported a single metal bar at roughly head height. 'You can do chin-ups, can't you?'

'Sure I can,' Natalie replied nonchalantly.

'Right, show me.'

Joe stood, arms folded impassively, as Natalie caught hold of the bar and used the strength in her arms to haul herself up. Once her chin was above the bar she dipped gently back down again, repeating the movement a dozen or more times without too many signs of effort or discomfort. As she moved, her T-shirt rode up slightly, offering Joe tantalising glimpses of the undersides of her breasts. His cock was almost painfully hard as he watched her, chafing against the fleecy lining of the baggy jogging bottoms he was wearing.

He waited till her feet were dangling a good foot off the floor once more, and then he said, 'Hold it there.'

'Wh-what?' Natalie said, startled. 'I can't – at least, not for very long.'

'There's no such word as "can't" when you're training with me,' Joe replied. 'Do as you're told.'

Natalie obediently dangled in mid-air, knowing what was to follow. Joe obliged her, by using the belt on her bottom once more. The length of leather sliced repeatedly across her buttocks and the tops of her thighs, and she could not prevent her legs from jerking convulsively as she fought against the pain Joe was inflicting.

'Please, no more,' she begged, but for the moment Joe seemed oblivious to her entreaties. The belt whistled in the air and fell hard against her burning cheeks time and again. Though he could not have given her more than a dozen strokes in total, it must have felt to her throbbing flesh as though the punishment was continuing for an eternity.

At last he permitted her to drop gently back to the floor. By now her air of cool composure had been shattered, and tears sparkled in her dark eyes. Joe looked her up and down levelly.

'I expected you to take those with much less fuss,' he said. 'You've forfeited the right to wear that T-shirt. Take it off.'

Natalie hesitated for a moment, then her fingers went to the tattered hem of the sweat-soaked garment. She peeled it off and over her head, baring her upper torso to Joe's delighted gaze. Her nipples were large and dark, surrounded by soft chocolate-brown aureoles. Little droplets of sweat had gathered on her skin, and Joe longed to lick them away.

Instead, he motioned to the pec deck, anxious to see the muscles beneath those impressive breasts at work. While Natalie positioned herself, he adjusted the weights. He was not requiring her to lift as much as he had been doing before she arrived, but it was still an impressive poundage for a woman to deal with, however fit.

'Twenty repetitions,' he ordered.

'Sure thing.' The first ten were easy for Natalie, and Joe wondered if he had misjudged her remaining strength. By the time she had completed fifteen, however, she was visibly struggling, the sweat forming in beads on her collar bone and trickling down the valley of her cleavage. She could still have managed the last five, he was sure, but with three to go, she gave up, her bare breasts heaving as she fought for breath.

Joe shook his head and tutted in displeasure. 'Only seventeen, Natalie. You know that's not good enough, don't you?'

'I'm sorry. I – I tried,' Natalie replied.

'It's earned you three more stripes with the belt. On the bare, this time.'

'On the—?' The terminology was unfamiliar to Natalie, but she quickly twigged what Joe meant. 'You mean I have to take my shorts off, right.'

'Right,' Joe confirmed.

'And if I refuse?' Natalie asked.

'Then you'll have the chance to know what it feels like when this belt slices into those tits of yours,' Joe replied.

For an anxious moment Natalie stared back at him, calling his bluff. He responded by slapping the end of the belt meaningfully and dropping his gaze to her stiff nipples. The implied threat was enough; she shrugged out of the cycling shorts, pulling them off over her trainer-clad feet. She was not, as he had hoped, naked beneath them, but the little G-string she wore did almost nothing to conceal her bush of dark hair, and when she turned round on his command and bent over, there was nothing to protect her buttocks from the sting of the belt. He could see how the dark skin was already well-marked from previous lashes, and could not resist running his fingers over the weals he had raised. Natalie moaned as he stroked the tender flesh.

'It's what you wanted, don't forget,' he reminded her.

'I know, but...' She broke off as his finger skated along the barely-covered crease between her cheeks, settling in the depression of her anus and rubbing gently until he elicited a guilty groan from her. He knew in that moment that she was entirely his.

'Steady yourself, Natalie,' Joe said.

He spaced the three strokes out for what must have been, to Natalie, an interminable length of time. The belt seared her naked buttocks, making her sob as it caught skin which had already been striped. Her ponytail hung down limply, and the remaining fight seemed to have been beaten out of her.

Joe was not quite finished, however. There was one last exercise Natalie had asked to perform, and he was more than happy to oblige. Though first came the small matter of her G-string.

'I want you completely naked for this one,' Joe told her, and meekly she complied, tossing the scrap of fabric to the floor. Joe wanted to pick it up and bury his nose in it, sure that it would be fragrant with her spicy, feminine aroma.

'Leg curls,' he said simply, and Natalie went to lie on the padded bench which had leg weights attached. She hooked her ankles round the back of the weights, and began to lift them. As she moved, Joe had a perfect view of her sex from behind, flexing and opening rhythmically. The sight was such a powerful turn-on that he wanted to push her flat to the bench and slide his cock deep into her moist channel then and there.

He let her raise the weights a couple of dozen times, before judging that he had finally exhausted her. Once more he ordered her to bend and touch her toes. She clasped her ankles and waited patiently for him to use the belt on her arse again, but Joe felt he had punished her enough. He quickly stripped off his vest and jogging bottoms, and then went to hunt in his kit bag. Among the tangle of clothes and toiletries in the bottom of the bag was a jar of petroleum jelly. He snatched it up and went to stand behind Natalie.

Taking a generous dollop of the greasy jelly from the jar, he reached between Natalie's legs and began to smooth it over her puffy labia. She was already wet there, with a mixture of sweat and her own natural juices, and as his fingers explored her intricate, hidden crevices, she began to lubricate more freely, and widened her stance to offer him easier access. He dipped his finger into the jelly once more. This time he bypassed her sex, rubbing it instead into her dark anal rosebud. She whimpered as his finger pushed at the tight ring of muscle, seeking entry; whimpered more vigorously when he pushed past the resistance of her sphincter.

'Not there…' she whispered. 'No one's ever touched me there.'

'There's a first time for everything,' Joe told her. 'Relax, Natalie. Go with the feeling.'

'I know what you're doing,' she gasped, as Joe's finger started to move gently in and out of her virgin hole. 'You're getting me ready so you can fuck me there, aren't you?'

As he heard that word coming from Natalie's full, sensual lips, it took all Joe's self-control not to come on the spot. He let the jar of petroleum jelly fall to the floor, and pressed his body tightly to hers, so that his erect cock lay snugly in the valley between her bottom cheeks. She groaned at the feel of his hot, rigid length.

Joe wanted to tell her how beautiful she was, his lips aching to shape a paean to the perfection of her body, but that was not how Warren, his rôle model, would behave. Warren would call her a slut and a whore, and with every cruel, deliberately unfeeling word, he would push her closer to orgasm. He sighed inwardly, and settled for reaching round to fondle Natalie's magnificent breasts. His touch was intentionally rough, grasping and twisting her hard nipples, and she writhed against him, her shudders more of pleasure than pain.

At last he turned his attentions back to her bottom, the mouth of the little hole pouting at him where his finger had penetrated it. He stopped playing with her nipples and used his hands to part her arse cheeks more widely, opening her up her further, and causing her to moan as he pressed against flesh that was tender from prolonged punishment. Then he took hold of his cock and guided its blunt head until it was resting against that expectant hole. Infinitesimally slowly, he pushed into her, breaching what remained of her resistance. He took his time, moving inch by steady inch into the untried passage. Natalie cried out as she was stretched painfully, wanting to fight against the unfamiliar intrusion that she seemed to both fear and welcome.

'Touch yourself,' Joe ordered. 'I want you to slide two fingers into that wet cunt of yours.'

Natalie did as she was told, and as Joe's cock rubbed against the thin wall of muscle that divided her anal and vaginal passages, he could feel her fingers moving in tandem. Natalie cooed in wonderment as she experienced the full sensation of this dual penetration, and when the pace of Joe's strokes began to rise inexorably, she matched him with her own hand.

It was impossible for Joe to hold out as his dick was milked by the tight embrace of Natalie's anus, and he cried out as the spunk shot up from his balls, gushing deep into Natalie's bowels. Realising what had happened, Natalie screamed in shocked pleasure as her own orgasm hit her.

Joe held her until her body stilled, and then he withdrew from her. She said nothing, and he knew he'd fulfilled the demand she'd made when she booked his services – to bring her lower than she had ever been, and yet take her to heights of ecstasy like she had never experienced.

'Come on, let's go and clean up,' he said. There was a private suite of offices adjoining the gym for the instructors who normally worked there, and Joe helped Natalie into her discarded T-shirt and shorts before pulling on his own jogging bottoms and ushering her out of the room. Unlocking the office door, he took her through to the little shower room where they could change in privacy.

He stripped as quickly as he had dressed, and stepped into the shower. Adjusting the temperature of the water until it was pleasantly hot, he beckoned for Natalie to join him. She did not hesitate to undress and free her hair from its sweaty ponytail, happy for Joe to command her.

Now his touch was tender, rather than cruel. There was grapefruit-scented shower gel, and he used it to shampoo her hair and wash every inch of her body, lathering away the traces of the workout and their lovemaking. She made no protest as his soapy hands lingered on the full curves of her breasts, then snaked down between her legs to touch her sex. Natalie responded by reaching for the shower gel and smoothing it into Joe's chest, back and buttocks.

Soon they were kissing, wet bodies twined together as the steamy spray pounded down on them. When Natalie reached for Joe's cock, it stiffened under her caress, and he sighed as she soaped his balls and the sensitive flesh between them. Her touch was greedy and demanding, wanting him hard and ready for her again, and as soon as he was fully erect she guided him to the entrance of her vagina, moaning as he slipped easily inside.

Their lovemaking was as urgent this time round, with Joe pressing her against the tiled wall of the shower as she thrust back at him.

'W-when I spoke to your boss, she said you d-didn't do extras,' Natalie said between gasps.

'Oh, this one's on the house,' Joe replied, groaning as he came inside Natalie for the second time in half an hour.

'And what's your boss going to say about that?' Natalie asked, her last coherent utterance before her own orgasm hit her and she slumped against Joe, unable to speak for the shudders of ecstasy that were running through her body.

Laurel, to Joe's surprise, said very little when he told her that his encounter with Natalie Wolf had overstepped the bounds of the specified scenario.

'You can't blame me, though,' Joe told her, as they sat in the office. 'She's probably the most gorgeous woman I've ever seen. Present company excepted, of course.'

'Flattery won't get you anywhere, Joe,' Laurel replied.

'Perhaps not, but you can't tell me you don't appreciate it,' Joe retorted. 'And anyway, I felt like I needed a little treat, seeing as these days my sex life seems to end as soon as I stop working for this place.' He shot a meaningful look at Laurel. 'You ought to try it, too. Treat yourself to a night of passion with someone you're never going to see again. Get rid of some of that pent-up tension.'

'You know that isn't my style.' Laurel sounded annoyed. 'And what do you mean, pent-up tension? Joe, we've been mates for a long time. I don't expect to get a lecture on my private life from you, of all people.'

'All I'm trying to do is get you to let your hair down a bit. I'm concerned about you, if you want the truth.' Joe went to stand behind her, and dropped his hands to her shoulders, massaging them through her white wraparound top. 'This is the tension I'm talking about,' he said, as his fingers worked on the knotted muscles. 'You spend all day in this office, you put in stupid hours, and you seem to have forgotten how to have fun. And I know for a fact you haven't slept with anyone since we took over the agency. Warren's started calling you the Born-again Virgin.'

Laurel, who had been relaxing under Joe's ministrations, stiffened in her seat. 'Warren can go fuck himself.'

'I think he'd rather fuck you, given the choice,' Joe said. He was aware he was tormenting both of them by bringing up the subject of Warren Keating, but he needed to know how Laurel felt about the man.

'In his dreams,' Laurel replied vehemently, but she had hesitated for long enough to suggest to Joe that, on a subconscious level at least, she had thought seriously about such a scenario. 'I'm sorry, Joe,' she said, slumping back against the chair, 'but everything's going so well at the moment. The agency's started turning a profit, we're getting repeat bookings and we've had some great write-ups in *Forum* and on a couple of the American fetish web sites. I'll take a few days off in a couple of weeks, I promise, but I just need to know that the agency will be able to run okay in my absence.'

'Well, I think it'll run itself long enough for us to slope off to the pub for a while, so why don't we have a couple of drinks and then some dinner at that pasta place you like?' Joe suggested. 'My treat.'

Eventually, Laurel nodded. 'You're right. I've done everything I can for tonight. Why don't you go on ahead and get the drinks in, and I'll join you when I've locked up here and put some lipstick on.'

'No problem,' Joe said, pleased that for once he seemed to have talked some sense into Laurel. He left the office and took the stairs down to ground level two at a time, already tasting the creamy, bitter tang of Guinness at the back of his throat.

Laurel stood at the window and watched Joe head out into the busy street below. She had powered down her computer, but instead of heading for the little washroom to freshen up as she had suggested, she went back to her chair and put her feet up on the desk. Joe's tale of his exploits with Natalie Wolf, combined with the suggestion that Warren was keen to get her into bed, had left a buzzing sensation in Laurel's sex.

It was an itch that needed scratching, and without being consciously aware of what she was doing, she hitched up her skirt with her right hand, her left stroking gently over her panty-clad pubis as her mind began to drift.

She imagined that Joe and Warren were standing before the desk, as she gave the two of them their assignments for the following day. Joe was scratching the back of his neck, apparently eager to head off to the pub, while Warren stared down at her impassively, his arms folded. She had chosen not to wear a bra beneath her ballet top, and was aware that the white cotton did not do all it might to conceal her disproportionately large apricot nipples.

'Any questions?' Laurel asked. When neither man answered, she continued, 'Well, if there's nothing more to say, we might as well all go home.'

'But there is something to say.' It was Warren who spoke. 'I think there are questions that should have been asked by you a long time ago, Laurel.'

'Questions?' Laurel said, wondering where the conversation was heading.

'Well, it seems to me that for someone who spends all day dealing with the needs of submissive women, you're singularly lacking in the experience of what those needs entail,' Warren replied. 'I mean, when a client tells you she wants to be spanked till her bottom's all red and glowing, how can you be certain she's getting what she asks for? Joe and I seem to be doing a good job, the clients tell you they're satisfied, but you don't really know, do you, not for sure? And we think it's time you found out just how good a job we're doing. Grab her, Joe.'

Laurel had not realised until too late that as Warren had been speaking, Joe had been moving stealthily behind her. Now he caught hold of her arms and hauled her out of the chair, his strong grip ensuring that she did not fall.

She fought to free herself from Joe's grasp, but he held her firm as she wriggled. 'What are the two of you playing at?' she asked, as Warren came to stand before her, sandwiching her between himself and Joe.

'We're not playing at anything,' Warren replied. 'We're deadly serious. We think it's finally time you got a good spanking – just so you're completely sure of what it entails, you understand.'

As Warren pressed her against the front of Joe's body, Laurel was aware that both men were already hard, Joe's cock snug in the small of her back and Warren's twitching and lengthening, as though it was seeking out the haven of her sex through the layers of clothing which separated them.

'I think I know what a spanking involves,' Laurel said.

Warren shook his head. 'I don't think so. Are you going to do the honours, or am I?' he asked Joe conversationally, ignoring Laurel's complaints.

'You start, I can always join in later,' Joe replied.

While Joe continued to hold Laurel, Warren pulled her chair away from behind the desk, and placed it in the centre of the room. Then he sat down and motioned to Joe, who took Laurel over to him. Together they arranged her over Warren's knee.

She was still fighting them, trying to prevent whatever might be about to happen to her, but she was growing increasingly aware that she was only raising a token protest. At a subconscious level, she did want to know what it would feel like when Warren's hand came down on her backside. She knew that the victim was usually required to bare her bottom for this treatment, and her quim began to moisten at the thought that either he or Joe would strip her of her underwear before much longer.

What she did not expect was that Joe's hands would reach for the tie fastening of her top, loosening it and pulling it apart so that her naked breasts were visible to both men.

'You've been hiding those beautiful tits of yours from us for too long,' Warren told her, as his hands caressed the full, creamy globes lovingly. 'I think you should be made to go topless in the office every day. Just imagine that, Laurel, having to deal with everyone from Elisha and Cindy to any customers who might call in to the postman, with those big, juicy nipples of yours on display to whoever might want to touch or fondle them. What do you think, Joe?'

She had not believed Joe would collude so fully in Warren's schemes until her friend chipped in with, 'I know she likes to order in sandwiches at lunchtime. I'd make her get them from the Italian deli round the corner, the one with the delivery boy who's just out of school. Imagine him coming up the stairs to be confronted with a luscious pair of boobs like Laurel's on show. I bet he'd come in his pants.'

'Speaking of pants,' Warren said. 'Do we let Laurel keep hers on?'

'Yeah, if we don't want to give the lad a heart attack when she bends over to get her purse out of her handbag.'

Warren laughed, his fingers never leaving off the teasing games they were playing with Laurel's nipples. 'I meant now, while I'm tanning her arse. Do we let her keep them on to get her used to the feel, or do I spank her on the bare right from the start?'

'Oh, take them off, definitely,' Joe replied. 'She hasn't earned any privileges.'

Without ceremony, Warren flipped up the hem of Laurel's skirt, turned it over on itself and tucked it into the waistband. Then, keeping hold of her wrists with one hand, he tugged her lacy white knickers down firmly with the other.

Warren raised them to his nose, and sniffed at them approvingly. 'I'm going to keep these,' he told her, 'and the next time I have a wank, I'm going to wrap them round my cock.'

Laurel could not stifle a moan at the thought of Warren lying on his bed, naked, running her knickers up and down the length of an erection which she had as yet not seen, only felt. She imagined his semen ultimately soaking the flimsy fabric in a tribute to her femininity, and shuddered.

Warren's palm stroked the soft curves of Laurel's bottom, his touch encouraging her to spread her legs despite herself. She knew he would be able to see her pussy in close detail, and felt a mixture of shame and wantonness as she imagined his reaction to the sight.

'If only you knew how long I've wanted to have you like this, that gorgeous arse of yours naked and vulnerable. You've teased me for far too long, Laurel, flaunting yourself, coming on to me and never letting me touch you. Now it's time you paid for that teasing.'

The next thing she felt was a stunningly hard slap on her left cheek. She had thought he would only give her some light taps, and prove this was nothing more than play-acting, but his touch was fierce and determined. She made a vain attempt to slide off Warren's lap, appalled by the unfairness of what was happening to her.

'No you don't, sweetheart,' Warren said. 'You're taking your punishment like a woman.'

'You can't do this to me,' Laurel replied, her words punctuated by slaps, each successively harder than the last. She yelped as the pain began to build deep in her buttocks, pain like nothing she had known. She was certain that if she could see the reflection of her backside in a mirror, it would be deep scarlet, the marks of Warren's hand burning into the previously pale flesh.

'I can do what I want, and you know it,' was Warren's phlegmatic reply. 'Admit it, Laurel, you've always known it. This is the only thing you've wanted since the moment we met.'

'No... no,' Laurel said repeatedly, shaking her head. She was sobbing now, unable to believe that she had let Warren humiliate her in this way, and that Joe, her closest friend, had done nothing to stop him. As she glanced over at Joe, she realised he was stroking his erection through his jeans, an expression of dreamy pleasure on his face. Like Warren, he was turned on by seeing her like this, practically naked, her bottom a sore, blotchy mess where it had been punished.

She was suddenly aware that the pain she felt was no longer all-consuming. It had become the low bass note that balanced a delicate melody of pleasure, the music of her submission. Her mind struggled to encompass the knowledge that, deep down, she was no different to Cindy, or the woman who paid for the male members of her staff to chastise and humiliate them. It was a revelation that could break her utterly – or set her free.

Warren seemed to have realised that her reaction had changed, for his hand was no longer beating a relentless tattoo on her backside. Instead, it was probing between her cheeks, seeking out the liquid core of her sex.

'Well, that tells me all I need to know.' There was a note of triumph in Warren's voice. 'She's ready for us, Joe.'

Warren pushed her off his lap, letting her land on her hands and knees on the floor. Laurel looked up again, to see that Joe was unbuckling the belt of his jeans. Behind her, Warren was shrugging off his leather jacket. Once the two of them had stripped, they dealt with Laurel's top and skirt, leaving her as naked as they were. She stared from one man to the other, her eyes widening at the sight of Warren's thick penis rising from the dark mat of hair at his groin and Joe's longer, more slender erection bobbing as he moved towards her.

She was too dazed to resist as they manoeuvred her so that her head was at Joe's crotch and her rump sticking out, ready for Warren's attentions. She felt Warren's glans nudging at the entrance to her sex, and parted her legs more widely, suddenly eager to feel him inserted into her. With a swift movement his cock lodged itself in her juicy cunt, making her cry out with the sheer joy of that initial penetration.

Now it was Joe's turn. He presented the head of his dick to her lips, and she swallowed it gratefully, savouring the fresh male tang of his cock-flesh. The two men began to thrust into her, seeking and then finding a rhythm which suited all three. As Warren pushed into her moist channel, his groin pressing against her aching bottom, the forward movement compelled her to take more of Joe's manhood into her mouth and lave its length with her tongue.

Warren's finger settled on her clitoris, flicking over the little bud. The sensation was too much for her, and she shuddered in the throes of a climax more powerful than she could remember. Her greedy internal muscles gripped and milked Warren's shaft, triggering his own orgasm. Joe, enthralled by the sight before him, followed within seconds, spending his load of come in Laurel's eager mouth...

Laurel snapped back to the present, aware that one hand had snaked inside her top and was twisting her nipples, while the other was down the front of her knickers, two fingers buried deep in her vagina as her thumb rubbed her clit and brought her the relief she had craved.

She sat for a moment, trying to clear her head before she went to catch up with Joe. She felt infinitely better for having masturbated, but she was concerned that it was the fantasy of being dominated by Joe and, more particularly, Warren, which had caused her to reach orgasm. She could no longer deny to herself that a part of her really wanted to be treated like that, but she knew that if she got involved with either of them, it would complicate the harmonious working relationship she had worked so hard to cultivate. When everything at the agency was going so well, why should she do anything to jeopardise it? At last she felt she had exorcised the ghost of Roger Preston. Domination Inc. was a success on her terms, and she was determined that nothing should stop her from keeping it that way.

Chapter Nine

Roger Preston smiled and accepted a gin and tonic from the blonde, heavy-breasted air stewardess. The gin might be contained in a small plastic miniature, and the tonic in a tiny ring-pull can, but at that moment it was more welcome than a drink from any high-class cocktail bar. He would never have thought he would be happy to leave the unbroken Californian sunshine for a miserable English winter, but after six months on the West Coast, he'd had enough. It was no fun living in a part of the world that treated anyone who drank, smoked or liked the taste of red meat as a social pariah. Not for him endless alfalfa salads, herbal elixirs and therapists who wanted him to explore his chakras. Next time circumstances compelled him to lie low for a while, he would go to Amsterdam, where people knew how to have a good time.

He noticed that the stewardess had turned her attention to the girl at his side, handing her a screw-top bottle of Chardonnay. The girl at least looked as though she might make this wretched air journey a little more pleasurable. She was incredibly slender and fine-boned, with black hair that fell in a shining wave to her waist and eyes like twin chips of emerald. If it was not for the fact that she was travelling economy, rather than business class, he would have suspected that she was a supermodel en route to some photographic assignment.

She caught him staring at her, and he smiled. 'I'm sorry, you look so familiar I was trying to place you. The cover of January's Vogue, right?'

It was bullshit, and both of them knew it, but he suspected she'd be unable to respond to such a blatant compliment. 'Not me,' she replied, in a voice which had just enough of a drawl to suggest that though she was originally English, she had spent several years in the States. 'I'm not a model. I work in information technology.'

Roger might have been tempted to add, 'Clever as well as beautiful,' but that would have been pushing his luck. There was a secret to seducing a woman – and after only a couple of moments in her company, he was certain he wanted to seduce her – and too many corny chat-up lines were not part of that secret. Instead, he said, 'Do you know much about setting up a database?'

'That's easy,' the girl replied. 'You learn that in Software 101. Why do you ask?'

'Well, I'm going back into business, and I'm going to need to keep records of my clients' details. If I was in luck, you'd be travelling back to England permanently, rather than just going for a couple of weeks' holiday, and you'd be looking for some piece work to tide you over until you found something steady. At which point, I'd offer you this—'

He'd put the business cards together in the departure lounge of Los Angeles Airport. The address was temporary, the home of a friend who owed him a favour, and the account for the mobile phone had been surprisingly easy to set up. The girl took it and gave it a cursory glance, but did not immediately hand it back.

'Roger,' she mused. 'Well, hello Roger, I'm Nina.' They shook hands briefly before she continued, 'So – this business of yours. What would it involve? If I were to need some piece work, as you put it?'

Hooked, Roger thought triumphantly. 'You might say you'd be working in the service industry,' he replied cautiously. He itched to tell the girl the whole story – how he had left Laurel with the ruins of a failing escort agency, expecting her to sink under the debts she had unwittingly inherited. How, instead, the buzz was that Laurel had turned the agency round beyond all expectations, taking it in a direction which, if he was honest, he had never considered, and how he was now about to reclaim his half-share of the flourishing business – but he was not sure of her attitude towards what might be considered a sleazy profession.

'That could mean anything,' Nina replied. 'I've had guys who work in burger restaurants telling me they're in the service industry.'

'In which case, I'll be frank with you,' Roger said. 'How do you feel about escort work?'

Nina glared at him suspiciously. 'Is this some kind of a come-on?'

He shook his head. 'Not at all. Before I left London I was running an escort agency.'

'That is so weird,' Nina said. 'Would you believe my sister does exactly the same thing?'

'Your sister?' Roger was intrigued. 'Is this in California?'

'No, London. And though I say sister, she's really my stepsister. Her mom married my dad when I was about thirteen. We're not exactly close.'

Roger's brain was racing ahead of the conversation. 'And what's your sister's name, if you don't mind my asking?'

'Not at all. It's Laurel. Laurel Angell. She has an agency called Moonshine, or some dumb name like that. You might have come across her, seeing as how you're both in the same line of work.'

It was an answer Roger had half-expected, but it still

stunned him. The chances of meeting a relative of his erstwhile business partner on a Transatlantic airline were almost infinitesimal. That the girl should have no idea of the relationship between himself and Laurel was even more unlikely. For a moment he felt as though he had stepped into the in-flight movie. Then he recovered his composure.

'You're going to think I'm making this up, but I know Laurel very well. In fact, we used to run the agency together. I can't believe she's never mentioned me.'

'Like I said, we don't really get on.' Nina's voice took on a bitter edge. 'If you want the truth, I hate the tight-assed bitch. I left England as soon as I could, when I was sixteen, went to spend some time with my real mom. That was five years ago. I haven't been in contact with Laurel from that day to this. Oh, I get Christmas and birthday cards from dad every year, and there's a couple of lines about what my beloved stepsister is up to, but I don't take any notice. I doubt your name ever came up in conversation, and if it did, I wouldn't have remembered it.'

'So you're not going over to London on a family visit, then?' Roger said.

'No way. I'm homesick, but not for Laurel. I've got no intention of looking her up while I'm over there. I don't see the point.'

'That's a pity,' Roger replied. 'You see, things had become somewhat strained between Laurel and myself, too. I thought it was easier if I spent some time away, let Laurel get on with things by herself for a while. I knew it would either make her or break her.'

'Hopefully the latter,' Nina interjected.

'Just the reverse. Laurel took the decision – entirely unilaterally, I might add – to concentrate on providing a service for female clients with submissive needs.' Roger parroted the information he had seen on Domination Inc. in a recent issue of a Los Angeles-based fetish magazine. 'She's making a remarkable success of it.' He took a deep breath, aware that he had to phrase the tale of events in a way which showed him in a favourable light. 'I'm going back to London to take a more hands-on approach to the agency.'

'Meaning?' Nina asked.

'Successful as she's been, I don't think Laurel's the right person to take the business on to the next stage. I think we should be expanding the brand globally. There are a lot of wealthy businesswomen in cities like New York, Amsterdam and Paris who would welcome the opportunity to buy the services of a discreet escort who'll pander to their secret sexual needs.' This had been the thrust of the article Roger had read, but he was happy to let Nina think it was his own opinion. 'I intend to relieve Laurel of her day-to-day duties, and work towards that global expansion.'

'In other words, you're going to give her the push,' Nina said gleefully.

'Not quite how I would have phrased it,' Roger said, 'and it's not going to be easy, given that she owns half the business. And I doubt she'll be too pleased to see me return to the office. Like I said, our relationship wasn't on the best footing when I left. But this is where you might come in.'

'Me?' Nina said. 'How?'

'Well, you'd like to get one over on your stepsister, wouldn't you?' Roger did not wait for the obvious answer. 'Have you changed at all while you've been away from London. In terms of your appearance, I mean?'

'Sure. I used to have mousy hair in a corkscrew perm, braces on my teeth and weigh thirty pounds more than I do now. Is that enough of a change for you?'

'Better than I could have hoped. You see, Nina, I want you to go down and try to get a job at the agency. Be my spy in the camp, if you like. Use a false name. Wear dark glasses to hide those lovely eyes of yours.'

'Two questions. What do I do if Laurel recognises me, and secondly, what the hell happens if I get the job? I wouldn't know how to go about servicing female clients with submissive needs, or however you put it.'

'I could teach you everything you need to know about domination and submission. I have the feeling you'd make a more than willing pupil.'

'Now this *is* a come-on,' Nina retorted, but Roger noticed she was not as bristly and defensive as she had been.

'Trust me. Once we touch down in England, I'll give you a small demonstration of what I believe your true sexuality to be. If I'm wrong, you can walk away, and I'll find someone else to help me. But if I'm right, then you have the chance to watch your stepsister lose her livelihood. And if she does recognise you, if you're half the woman I think you are, she'll be too glad to have found a top-quality escort to turn you down. Do we have a deal?'

Nina hesitated for the merest fraction of a second, then said, 'Yes, we do.'

They chinked their plastic glasses. 'To the downfall of Laurel Angell,' Roger said.

'Now that's something I'd drink to on any occasion,' Nina replied, downing the dregs of her wine.

Clearing Customs at Heathrow was a formality. Unbeknown to Nina, Roger had called in another favour, and when they left the arrivals hall they did not, as she had expected, make their way to the tube station or the taxi rank. Instead, he led her out to the airport forecourt, where a limousine with tinted windows was waiting for them. The chauffeur who took Nina's suitcase was impeccably dressed, in grey livery with a peaked cap. Despite herself, she was impressed.

Until Roger Preston had claimed his connection through to Laurel, Nina had thought he was nothing more than a creep on the make. Charming and not exactly unattractive, admittedly, but a creep nonetheless. When she had shed her braces and puppy fat, she had gained a legion of unwanted admirers, usually twice her age, who thought that simply because she was beautiful, articulate and educated, she was simply dying to let them paw her with their slimy hands, or fall into their bed. Not her. She had standards to which most of these elderly sleazeballs could not even begin to aspire. She would have tolerated Roger's attention until he had made a pass, or tried to grope her beneath her regulation airline blanket as she dozed, and then she would have kneed him in the nuts and called a stewardess. It was a crude tactic, she knew, but remarkably effective.

And then he had offered her the chance to humiliate her own stepsister. It was a chance she could not pass up. Ever since they had been forced together by her father's remarriage, the two girls had barely been able to tolerate each other. Nina had resented the fact that she had to be nice to the snivelling Laurel, whose father had been so tragically killed in a car crash. Laurel, on the other hand, seemed jealous of the fact that Nina, though four years younger and overweight, exuded a raw sensuality which she herself did not appear to possess. Nina knew that when she had lost her cherry on the night of her sixteenth birthday with an older biker boyfriend of whom her stepmother did most definitely not approve, her last act of defiance before she left for California, Laurel's virginity was still in place. For all she knew, that remained the case. Laurel had had what Nina believed to be an entirely deserved reputation as an ice maiden, and there was no reason for that to have changed. Throwing yourself into a demanding business was the typical act of a frigid bitch.

Nina, on the other hand, knew how to combine business with pleasure, which was partly what intrigued her so much about Roger's unorthodox proposal. She loved sex, and the thought of being paid for it was one of her favourite fantasies. She still wasn't sure about the domination side of the agency – as far as she was concerned, that sort of thing was for the kooks out in the Hollywood Hills – but Roger seemed to think she had the necessary qualities.

She settled herself back on the limousine's plush grey leather seat, and prepared to enjoy the ride into London. What she had not expected was for Roger to whisper in her ear, just low enough that the chauffeur could not hear, 'Not like that.'

'I'm sorry?' she replied.

'I promised you a lesson in submission,' Roger said, 'and it starts here and now. You're not correctly dressed for riding in this car.'

Nina looked down at herself. She was wearing a sweater dress in soft sage-green angora wool, opaque tights and black knee-length suede boots, and saw no problem with the outfit.

'I want you naked below the waist,' Roger told her. 'So take off your boots, your tights and your knickers.'

In other circumstances, Nina would have answered such a request with a punch to Roger's solar plexus and fled the car. However, there was something in the tone of his voice, combined with the fact that such requests might be a common occurrence if she were to be taken on at Laurel's agency, which compelled her to reach for the side zip on her boot and slide it down. The chauffeur was staring straight ahead as she began to undress, concentrating on steering a way through the early morning traffic heading for the motorway, but Nina wondered how much he might be able to see of what was happening in his rear-view mirror. As discreetly as she could, she shuffled out of her tights and lacy scarlet briefs, and placed them on the seat between herself and Roger.

'Now put your hands behind you, wrists crossed,' Roger commanded.

Nina did as she was told. Roger reached for her discarded tights and swiftly used them to tie Nina's wrists together. This was a new sensation for her, and she wriggled her hands experimentally, seeking to discover whether Roger had allowed her the opportunity to slip her wrists free. The knot seemed secure; if anything, it tightened slightly as she moved, which encouraged her to keep her hands still. She fought a flutter of panic, telling herself that Roger meant her no harm, despite the fact that the last road sign she had seen had seemed to indicate that they were heading away from London, rather than towards it.

'Would now be a good time to ask exactly where you're taking me?' Nina asked.

'Somewhere you've never been before,' Roger replied. As he spoke, he was reaching for the tie which had been loosely knotted around his neck. He stroked Nina's head gently, the caress soothing her and encouraging her to relax against him. Swiftly, he looped the tie around her eyes; it made a crude but effective blindfold, and she stiffened at the sudden deprivation of sight.

Unable to see what Roger was doing, she strained her ears, listening for clues, and was rewarded with the sound of a zip coming down. Then he took hold of her hand, guiding it towards her lap, and encouraging her to grope for his cock. Her fingers closed around the warm, semi-erect length.

'Stroke it for me, Nina,' Roger said. She did as he asked, her hand shuttling up and down the column of flesh, feeling it lengthen and grow more solid as she did so. She tried to gauge its dimensions: around six inches, she thought, with a thick vein on the underside and a foreskin that moved smoothly over the moist head as she masturbated it. It was the first uncircumcised cock she'd handled since she'd left England, and she was sorry she could not see exactly how it was reacting to her touch.

'That's good,' Roger told her. 'Now suck it.'

She had no intention of refusing to comply, but he seemed prepared to believe that she might, for his hand was on the back of her neck now, pushing her head down towards the tip of his erection. She made her mouth into an 'O' and closed it around his hot glans where it protruded from its protective sleeve of skin. He tasted of salt and expensive soap, and she sucked softly, her tongue licking away the drops of juice her actions were coaxing from the little eye at the centre.

He muttered his satisfaction, his hand twining in her silky dark hair. She was taking her time, wanting to bring him gradually to the peak of excitement, but Roger was impatient. His grip on her hair grew stronger, controlling the pace at which her head bobbed up and down on his cock. Obediently, she increased her movements, taking more and more of his length into her throat. Over the years she had perfected her repertoire when it came to giving head, learning how to let her gullet relax enough to allow most of a good-sized erection to fill her mouth without choking her. Now her nose was brushing Roger's dark pubic hair as she sucked him, and his hips were jerking beneath her.

Roger grunted, and salty gouts of semen began to flow into her mouth. He kept her head firmly against his groin, forcing her to gulp down every drop. So this was what he meant by submission, Nina thought, struggling to swallow the last of his come. She should have fought against it, refused to let him use her mouth as a receptacle, and yet she did not want to. Nina was aware that her sex was pulsing, hot excitement coursing through her belly at the thought that she had been nothing more than a vehicle for his pleasure. Back in California everything was based on complete mutuality: you practically had to sign a consent form if you wanted to take a man's cock in your mouth. Roger had been in control throughout what had just happened to her, and yet she felt liberated, rather than demeaned.

Now his touch on her hair was tender once more. 'She's excellent, Chambers,' Roger said, and Nina realised he was addressing the chauffeur. 'I recommend you sample her technique. In fact, I insist. We should be able to turn off soon. You know what to do.'

'Yes, Mr Preston,' the chauffeur replied.

Nina shuddered. It was obvious what Roger was expecting of her. At no point had he mentioned that she might be required to service the chauffeur. She'd only had a brief impression of the man as he'd taken her bags, but she remembered his dark curly hair and muscular build, hinted at by the way his uniform stretched slightly across his chest and thighs. Perhaps he would be rough with her, rougher than Roger had been. The thought excited her, and she was aware that she was growing wetter between her legs.

Within a few minutes the limousine was making a left

turn. Nina wondered where she was being taken. Perhaps they had reached their final destination, or Roger knew of some quiet woodland spot where they could act out the rest of this bizarre scenario in peace.

Her hopes were dashed as soon as the car came to a halt. The driver's window of the car had been partially wound down and Nina, whose hearing seemed to have become keener to compensate for her temporary loss of sight, was immediately aware of traffic noise and voices. Where the hell were they?

The question was answered when Roger removed the blindfold. They had parked alongside a sign reading SERVICES, and as Nina looked out of the window she saw a squat red brick building with a stream of people passing in and out of its doors, and a couple of petrol pumps beneath a free-standing awning off to the left.

She suddenly felt grateful for the tinted windows. At least if she was going to have to suck the chauffeur's cock in such a public place, the darkened glass would shield their activities from the numerous passers-by.

Roger, however, had other ideas. He reached for Nina's boots, slipping them on her feet and zipping them in place. Nina, with her hands still secured behind her, sat meekly and let him drape his overcoat around her shoulders to conceal the fact that her wrists were tied together. The chauffeur got out of the car, and came to open the door nearest to Nina.

'Out you get,' Roger said. Nina swung her legs out, knees together in an attempt to prevent the chauffeur, who would be well aware of her knickerless state, taking a glimpse up her dress.

Roger followed her out and, once the car was secured, began to lead her away from the service complex and towards a copse of low scrubby trees a hundred or so yards away. Here the noise from the motorway was still a noticeable rumble, but they had a greater degree of privacy than Nina could have hoped for given Roger's apparently capricious state of mind.

Roger took the coat from Nina's shoulders. 'On your knees,' he ordered. Nina knelt, and awaited the next instruction. She could feel cold dry grass against the skin between the tops of her boots and the hem of her dress, and smell some indefinable scent that was a mixture of damp earth and diesel oil.

The chauffeur unfastened his uniform trousers and let them drop to his knees. His cock was flaccid, but even in that state Nina could tell it was big. Her snatch moistened at the thought of what it might look like when it was erect.

'You know what to do.'

With Roger's command ringing in her ears, Nina shuffled forward and let the chauffeur present his limp dick to her lips. Like Roger, he was not circumcised, and he peeled the foreskin back with his fingers, giving Nina access to the fat, plum-coloured glans. She ran her tongue over its smooth surface experimentally, then moved down to concentrate on the groove between the head and the shaft, flicking lightly at it. The chauffeur's cock was hardening rapidly as blood rushed to fill its spongy caverns, and Nina took as much of it into her mouth as she could manage. It was a good couple of inches bigger than his employer's, and Nina wondered if he would make her deep-throat it the way Roger had.

As she laved the chauffeur's shaft, she felt Roger's hands on the hem of her sweater dress. With her wrists bound she was unable to prevent him from hiking the dress towards her waist. As she felt the cool morning air on her small, high buttocks, she was glad they were in a secluded spot, away from the bustle of the service station.

Roger held her tightly by the waist with one hand, while the other stroked over the contours of her bottom cheeks, and down between them until it was cupping her sex. She registered his sharp intake of breath as he realised that her sex was completely shaven.

She stopped sucking on the chauffeur's cock long enough to say, 'Well, it was either that, or dye it the same shade as my head hair.'

Nina felt Roger's palm smack hard against her left buttock. 'Did I say you could speak?' he asked.

Nina said nothing. She knew he wanted her to reply, but if she did, he would no doubt hit her again. No one had ever spanked her, not even as a child, and she could feel the mark of Roger's hand where it had fallen, like a fiery brand.

Now Roger's hand was between her legs again, probing everywhere. He was pressing his fingers up into her vaginal opening, stretching her as a third digit followed the second. Her juices were running freely at this unexpectedly forceful treatment, and she whimpered as he thrust roughly in and out of her.

The chauffeur was stroking his own balls languidly as Nina went back to licking his shaft. She glanced up for a moment at his face; his eyes were closed, and his features were screwed up in an ecstatic grimace. Nina knew in that moment that he was about to come, and prepared herself to take a mouthful of his spunk.

To her surprise he pulled out of her mouth, rubbing frantically at his member. Dollops of his viscous come landed in Nina's hair and on her face, like thick salty rain. As her jaw gaped wide in surprise, he aimed his cock so that the last drops fell straight into Nina's open mouth. At the same time Roger withdrew his fingers from her channel and used them to scour her clitoris. His abrasive touch was enough to trigger an orgasm that left her bucking in his arms, rainbow shards of colour dancing in front of her eyes.

There was a rustling in the undergrowth close by. Nina turned her head to see a scruffy black and white dog leaping through the long grass. A few yards behind, an elderly man was standing, stock-still, the expression on his face indicating that he had seen some, if not of all, of what had just taken place. Nina's face burned with shame as she imagined the man watching as she was made to fellate the chauffeur, while Roger's fingers toyed with her sex. She must look as sluttish as she felt, with semen glistening in her hair and on her cheeks, her hands tied behind her and her naked bottom still on display.

Roger followed her gaze, and smiled at the interloper. 'She'll suck yours, too,' he said. 'You only have to ask.'

Nina felt her humiliation was complete as she watched the play of emotions that swept over the man's face. At first he seemed to think Roger was joking, then his expression changed to one of lustful desire. Nina would never know what might have happened if, at that moment, a woman's voice had not called, 'Norman! Norman, where are you? Have you found Trixie yet?'

The man turned guiltily and whistled to the dog, which stopped its explorations and trotted back to his side. Their disappearance out of the copse was Roger's cue to haul Nina to her feet. He pulled her dress down to a respectable level once more and untied her tights.

'You'd have done it, wouldn't you?' Roger said, as they walked back to the parked limousine, Chambers the chauffeur leading the way. 'You'd have sucked that man's cock, even though you had no idea who he was.'

'I—' Nina did not know what to say. How could she tell Roger that she had been so aroused by what was happening to her that she would have gladly obeyed any order he might care to give her?

'You're perfect,' he told her. 'And when Laurel interviews you, she'll say exactly the same. Now, come on. I want you to meet the friends I'm staying with. I'll ring ahead and tell them to have a hot bath and breakfast waiting for you. How does that sound?'

Nina's grateful kiss on the tip of his nose was the only answer he needed.

Chapter Ten

The call could not have come at a better time. The agency had been going to hell in a handcart since Laurel had been struck down with flu four days ago, Joe thought. Appointments had had to be rearranged to make sure the office could be manned, and a couple of potentially lucrative assignments had been turned down, simply because no one was available to take them. Because Laurel made the administrative side of the business look so easy, Joe was apt to forget that it was, in reality, hard work. But now here was some girl by the name of Devon Rylance, all the way from California, telling him she had seen a write-up of Domination Inc. on the Internet, and was eager to work for the business while she was in England. She claimed she was submissive, which would mean she could handle Cindy's clients while Cindy took care of running the office...

He realised he was running ahead of himself. He had no way of knowing whether this mysterious Devon would be at all suitable to join the agency until he saw exactly what she was capable of. If she was punctual – and that was one of an escort's most important attributes – he would find out in exactly five minutes' time.

She was not punctual. She was early, as he realised when he opened the office door to see a tall, slim, dark-haired woman standing before him, her eyes veiled by dark glasses. Even if she had not told him in advance she was American, the sunglasses would have given it away. No Englishwoman would wear them on an overcast February morning in Soho, unless she worked in advertising, had the hangover from hell or was some minor celebrity desperate to draw attention to herself.

'Hi, you must be Joe,' she said, extending a dainty hand. Her voice was soft and appealingly husky.

'That's right,' he replied, shaking her proffered hand. 'Sit down, please.'

She settled herself on a chair, crossing her long slim legs, and removed the sunglasses to reveal a pair of the most dazzlingly green eyes Joe had ever seen.

'So, tell me about yourself,' he said. 'What makes you want to do this type of work?'

'Well, I came over to England intending to look up some family members, but it's a pretty expensive country to travel round and I wanted to get some money together first. I figured this was a more lucrative and enjoyable option than waiting tables.'

'I'm glad you said enjoyable,' Joe replied. 'We get a lot of girls wanting to work for us who think they're going to earn easy money. What they don't realise is that you have to really want to offer this kind of service, and that to be a good escort you need to be a pretty accomplished actress.'

'Oh, I have no problem with that,' Devon said, with a strange smile that Joe could not fathom.

'Good. That's excellent.' Joe was beginning to respond to his would-be employee on a physical level, and hurried on, aware that he had to take Devon on because she was suitable for the agency, and not simply because he fancied her. 'Can you tell me a bit about your fantasies, and what turns you on? I mean, you said on the phone that you were submissive...'

'That's right. I like to be spanked, and I particularly love it when there's someone watching. If I've been bad, I like to have the fact emphasised. I want to be really humiliated and put in my place, particularly if it's being done in front of strangers. And I have fantasies about being mauled by construction workers with dirty hands who are going to treat me like a piece of meat.'

'What about women?' Joe asked, his cock swelling in his pants at the images Devon's words were painting in his mind. 'You appreciate they make up the overwhelming bulk of the clients we deal with?'

'The type I'm looking forward to escorting are the ones who feel that paying for their pleasures is sordid, so they're going to treat me like I'm no better than I should be. The older and uglier they are the better, because they're going to resent me for being younger and prettier than them, and reminding them of what they don't have any more. Oh, I know it sounds cruel, but it's the sort of attitude they're going to want to beat out of me, isn't it?'

Joe scribbled some hasty notes for the file the agency kept on all their staff, hoping that Devon's talents did not include the ability to read his small, spiky handwriting upside down. 'You sound like you're going to fit in here well,' he told her, 'but there's just the small matter of the audition, as we discussed over the phone.'

Devon shrugged. 'Fine by me—'

She was about to add something further when the phone rang. 'If you'll just excuse me,' Joe said, and reached for the receiver. 'Hello, Domination Inc. How can we help you?'

Nina went to stand by the window, ostensibly so as not to eavesdrop on Joe's conversation, but in actuality so that he would not see the gleeful expression on her face. This whole interview was going better than she could ever have hoped. From the moment she had made the call to the agency, there was no indication that anyone believed her to be other than who she claimed to be – Devon Rylance, born and bred in Oakland, California. The pseudonym she had chosen for herself was suitably exotic for escort work; Rylance was her mother's maiden name, and Devon was her original place of birth, having lived in Exeter until she was twelve years old. And then her mother had come to London, met Howard Angell, and everything had turned upside down...

Dwelling on the past wasn't going to help her, she told herself. Instead, she had to concentrate on the immediate future, and on continuing to make a good impression in this interview. It was all slotting so nicely into place, and even the thought of showing off her sexual capabilities did not daunt her. Over the course of the weekend, Roger Preston and his friends had taught her more than she could have expected about the realities of submitting to another person. She was already beginning to feel that she could reach orgasm from the feel of a hand slamming down hard on her backside, and she had, for the first time in her life, brought another woman to climax with the aid of her fingers and tongue.

The fantasies she had outlined to Joe Gallagher were also close to the truth. She did indeed relish the thought of being punished – and pleasured – while being watched. She supposed it stemmed from spending time in such a self-obsessed city as Los Angeles, where appearance was all, as the parade of bodybuilders and cosmetically-enhanced gym bunnies on Venice Beach testified. Everyone there wanted to be seen as a paragon, their outward image matching what they felt to be their own inner beauty and virtue, so why not turn it around, and let yourself be seen succumbing to your basest and most wicked desires?

Add to this the fact that Joe was undeniably cute, with

his mop of red hair, the rash of gold-brown freckles across his cheeks and long, straight nose. Physically, he was her ideal type – muscular without being bulky. She couldn't help noticing that he walked with a slight limp, but that only added to his desirability, rather than detracting from it. She knew from what Roger had told her that Joe was a long-time friend of her darling stepsister, and wondered if he and Laurel actually slept together. If that was the case, then she was determined to do everything she could to split that little arrangement up.

Nina suddenly realised that Joe was saying something, and noticed as she turned away from the window that he had put the phone down. She walked back to the desk, smiling at him.

'Are you ready for me?' she asked.

'Yeah. That was just Laurel checking up on me,' Joe replied.

'Laurel's the other owner of the agency, right?' Nina said.

Joe nodded. 'She's so committed to this place, even when she's on her sick bed she keeps ringing to make sure everything's okay. I was just telling her it looks like we're going to have an extra body around the place, so she can stop worrying.'

'What's she like, this Laurel?' Nina did her best to sound casual, anxious as she was to glean Joe's impression of her stepsister.

'She's great. You're going to love working for her. She's incredibly easy to get on with, she's a good laugh. She was a mate to me when I was at my lowest point...'

'You sound like you're in love with her,' Nina commented.

She watched the blush spread across Joe's cheeks. 'We're good friends and business partners, that's all.'

'But you'd like it to go further.'

'Laurel doesn't believe in mixing business with pleasure. I think she's afraid that if we have a fling and it all goes wrong, it'll screw up our business relationship, too. She never talks about it, but I think she was badly hurt in the past by someone who told her they loved her. If anybody was to say it to her now, I don't think she'd believe them.' He sat up straight. 'Why am I telling you all this when we should be getting on with the audition?'

'I know, I know, it's cheeky of me, digging into your love life when we've only just met.' Nina did a little pirouette of joy as a thought struck her. 'Isn't it the sort of behaviour that deserves to be punished?'

'You're right there,' Joe said. 'Come here.' He stood up and reached for Nina's arm, pulling her to him. She put up a vague show of resistance, but was more than happy to be pressed close to his warm firm body. Unlike Roger Preston, Joe didn't seem to favour fancy cologne, smelling instead of soap and healthy male.

'I didn't mean it,' Nina squeaked, falling into character. 'I was only joking. Please don't spank me.'

'Oh, I'm not going to spank you,' Joe retorted, and Nina felt a shiver of fearful anticipation run down her spine as she wondered what exactly he had in mind for her.

Still holding her by one arm, he picked up the chair she had been sitting in with the other. Then he marched over to the window and put the chair underneath it.

'I want you to stand on the chair and look out of the window,' he said. Obediently, she clambered up on to the wooden seat of the chair, and realised she was looking across to another office on the other side of the narrow street. The shop beneath it was a bookstore, selling respectable paperbacks at discount prices on the main floor and erotica in the basement. The room she could see into appeared to be a dimly-lit stockroom, with boxes piled up haphazardly almost to the ceiling.

'Now turn to face me and unbutton your blouse,' Joe ordered. 'I want to see those luscious tits of yours.'

Nina hesitated, still feigning modesty. Joe stared at her impassively, arms folded, until she tugged her scarlet blouse out of the tight black leather miniskirt she was wearing. Her fingers reached for the buttons and, teasingly slowly, she unfastened them, until the blouse finally hung open and her large creamy breasts were revealed, cupped in a sheer black bra through which her dark nipples were just visible.

'Very nice,' Joe said. 'Very nice indeed. But I'd get a better look at them if you took off your bra as well, don't you think?'

'Please don't make me,' Nina said automatically, even though her sex was beginning to pulse excitedly at the thought of displaying more of her body to Joe.

'I'll get very annoyed if you don't do what I tell you,' Joe replied, 'and when I get annoyed, I tend to increase the severity of a punishment. So, Nina, your bra please.'

Nina let her blouse slip from her shoulders, then reached behind her to unclip the fastening of her bra. Keeping the garment pressed to her breasts with one hand, she used the other to pull the straps down off her shoulders and free of her arms. Finally, she allowed the bra to fall to the floor. With all the expertise of a stripper, she had not allowed Joe to see anything of her nipples at any point during her intricate manoeuvres.

'My bra's off,' she said delightedly. 'Are you getting a better view of my breasts, Joe?'

She knew she had bested him, but if he admired her trick, his expression gave nothing away.

'Both hands on your head,' he told her.

She pouted at him, but obeyed, feeling like a naughty schoolgirl as she stood on the chair, fingers clasped at the back of her head. The movement was designed to lift her breasts and show them to their best advantage. She was proud of them, and of the way they were made to seem even larger by her small waist and otherwise slim frame. Their large, ruby nipples currently stood stiffly from the surrounding aureoles, paying testimony to her growing excitement.

'Now, turn round and look out of the window again,' Joe said. 'And keep your hands where they are, or it'll be the worse for you.'

As she presented herself to the window in all her semi-clad glory, Nina wondered for the first time whether she could be seen from the street. It was unlikely, she decided, that anyone would crane their head enough to see the display she was making of herself, but the room across the way was a different matter. She was assuming it was empty, but what if there was someone inside, bending over a box of books, hunting to find something to fill a space on the shelves downstairs? Or maybe there was a member of staff skiving off from their duties, or taking a lunch break, one of the shop's racier magazines on their lap as they smoked a cigarette and pored over the salacious images spread before them. What if they looked up from the pert breasts and open pussy of a centrefold only to see Nina standing opposite them, topless, in a pose of submissive obedience?

Almost without being aware of what she was doing, she dropped her hands to her breasts and caressed her nipples, feeling them harden even further beneath her own touch. It excited her to think there were unknown eyes watching her lustfully, and perhaps a hand slipping into an open fly, to free a swelling cock and begin to stroke it to stiffness...

A hand slamming hard across her backside brought her out of her erotic reverie. She stopped what she was doing and glanced round guiltily.

'Did I tell you to play with yourself?' Joe asked.

'I'm sorry. I—' Nina stammered, flustered. She had been so wrapped in her fantasy of the anonymous voyeur in the stockroom that she had forgotten the reality of her situation.

'You've tried my patience enough, Devon,' Joe said. 'Go over to my desk. What I'm going to use to punish you is in the top drawer. Bring it to me.'

This was more humiliating than Nina could have expected. Not only was Joe going to beat her, she was going to have to find the implement with which he intended to do it. She climbed down off the chair and went to look in the drawer he had specified. Among a litter of papers, paperclips, bottles of correction fluid and loose change, she found a transparent plastic ruler, a foot long. She picked it up, unable to resist the temptation to flex it. It was thin and unyielding, and she was sure it would hurt her. Chastened, she walked back to Joe, who was sitting on the chair, waiting for her.

'Very good,' he said, as she handed the ruler to him. 'Now take your skirt off and get over my lap.'

At least he was going to allow her to keep her panties on, Nina thought, as she slid the zip down and pushed the tight skirt over her hips. She gave a little shimmy as she wriggled out of it, hoping to detract Joe from his task, but he was implacable. Meekly, she clambered onto his lap, accustoming herself to the slightly precarious position as she waited for her punishment to begin. Joe's hand was in the small of her back, keeping her in place. Her crotch was pressed against his groin, and she was aware of the hefty bulge in his jeans.

The next thing she felt was a gentle tap on her bottom as Joe measured his swing. She tensed herself, eyes closed tight, but nothing could have prepared her for the feel of the first blow as it landed. She squealed, and would have fallen from Joe's lap had he not held her tight. There was a stinging line of pain across the fullest part of her bottom, like nothing she had known. The ruler fell again, sharp and unforgiving as before. Joe was spacing the strokes carefully, so that when a third landed, and then a fourth, each was on an area of skin that had not yet been touched. She was squirming and kicking as he beat her, and her bottom felt twice its normal size and unbelievably hot. Tears of pain and shame stung her eyes, and she did nothing to blink them away.

'I'll bet your bum looks beautiful now, all pink and sore,' Joe said. 'Shall we have a look?'

Nina made no attempt to stop him as he peeled her panties down off her bottom. Joe's sharp intake of breath suggested that he had registered the fact that her sex was shaven; she knew the sight to be a powerful turn-on for most men, and Joe Gallagher seemed to be no exception.

His fingers moved over her punished backside, making her moan with a mixture of pain and anticipation.

'Oh, Devon, your arse colours so beautifully,' he murmured.

For a moment Nina hoped he would make her stand in the window again. This time, anyone glancing out of the stockroom across the road would see the marks of the ruler, blazing crimson against her alabaster skin, and know that she had been soundly punished. It was a sight to make the most hardened voyeur rub his cock until it spat out its creamy load.

'I still think it could go a little redder, though,' Joe said.

He had lulled her into a false sense of security, she realised, as the ruler fell again, more agonising than ever on her naked, sensitised flesh. His next stroke caught the soft underhang of her cheeks, and she howled. But that was nothing compared to the feel of hard plastic slicing into the tops of her thighs. She was sobbing loudly now, fat teardrops running freely down her face.

'Poor Devon,' Joe muttered, his hand now soothing her once more. 'But you know you deserve it, don't you?'

'Yes. Yes, I deserve it,' Nina replied, aware of a new sensation mingling with the pain. It was pleasure, sweet and strong, and in that moment she knew that, for her, the one could no longer exist without the other. In the past couple of days, Roger and his friends had begun her education into the world of submission, but it was Joe who would ultimately teach her just how deep her submissive streak ran. She did indeed deserve the punishment she was receiving, for it would enable her to reach a peak of ecstasy she had never yet attained.

'Have you learned your lesson?' Joe asked.

'No,' Nina said vehemently, knowing it was not the reply Joe was expecting. 'I haven't been punished enough. I need more.'

This time, it was Joe who hesitated.

'Please,' Nina whispered, and that one word was enough. Joe resumed her chastisement, the ruler now cutting into flesh which was already raised and tender. As she bucked on his lap, her legs scissoring apart, she could not prevent herself giving him glimpses of her most secret places. She could still feel him beneath her, the strength of his erection shielded from her only by a layer of material. She ached to take him inside her body, and make him hers.

She would never know what unholy impulse made her

say what she did next, but the words were at once a challenge and a supplication. 'Between my legs,' she begged.

He did not question her. The flat of the ruler slapped hard against her sex lips, pain blooming like a flower, but followed almost instantly by an orgasm of such intensity that she almost blacked out.

Joe had dropped the ruler, and his hand was stroking Nina's hair. 'Are you okay?' he asked, concerned, as he drew her into an embrace.

'Fuck me,' Nina said, clinging to him.

'Look, you've passed the audition,' Joe replied. 'You don't need to do anything else to prove you're suitable to work for us.'

'This has got nothing to do with the audition,' Nina said. 'I want you.' She pressed her mouth hard against his, feeling his lips open as he relaxed into the kiss. Her hands were plucking at his chambray shirt, working rapidly on the buttons. Joe cupped her breasts, squeezing them together and running his thumbs over her aching nipples. He was wearing no underpants beneath his jeans, and when she unzipped them his cock sprang free, so hard it was almost flat against his stomach.

Nina wasted no time in impaling herself on his erection, sinking down until Joe's pubic hair prickled against her shaven mound. Her strong inner muscles gripped him covetously as she raised herself up, kissing him hard on the mouth as his cockhead threatened to slip free from her velvet grasp, before lowering herself again. Every movement served to reawaken the dormant pain in her bottom and sex, but it only aroused her further. Joe suckled her nipples as she bounced on his shaft, and she threw her head back in delight.

How could Laurel have denied herself the pleasure of

Joe's body for so long? Nina wondered. His cock felt so good inside her, smooth and long, filling her delightfully. It would have been sweeter to fuck him if he had been Laurel's lover, but it would be easy to make this man hers, and once she did, then she could begin to poison the friendship between Joe and her stepsister. Her head filled with thoughts of revenge against Laurel, she was only subliminally aware that Joe's shaft was thickening inside her, his body pressing up against hers in readiness for his orgasm. Suddenly he was flooding her with his come, the spasms of his cock enough to trigger her second climax.

Joe was muttering something into her hair as his pleasure peaked. The smile of triumph faded from her face as she realised it was the single word, 'Laurel.'

She pulled herself off him, glaring at him as though mortally wounded.

'Devon, I'm sorry. I just—'

She waved his apology away, knowing that though a couple's bodies could melt into one at the apex of sex, their minds would always be utterly separate. 'It's okay. She means a lot to you, it's obvious.'

'It's still a cardinal sin,' Joe said. 'I wouldn't be surprised if you didn't want to work with me now. Which is a shame, because you have all the makings of a superb escort.'

'Oh, I'll still work for you,' Nina said, reaching for her discarded clothes. 'I mean, I'm curious now. I want to meet the woman who can have such an effect on you.'

'She'll want to meet you, too,' Joe told her.

I wouldn't be so sure about that, Nina thought, not when she works out who I actually am. But who cares? By that time I should have learned everything about this agency, and that'll give me all the ammunition I need to get her out of this business and out of my life. And if I can take Joe Gallagher with me, then so much the better...

Chapter Eleven

'I tell you, the two of you are really going to get on. She's fantastic,' Joe said.

Laurel pulled the collar of her towelling dressing gown more closely around her, and watched him as he placed a steaming mug down on the coffee table in front of her. Joe had been popping in see her every couple of days while she had been ill, making sure she was stocked up with essentials like milk, bread and paracetamol tablets, but he would insist on making her some dubious home remedy whenever he visited. Last time, it had been the vaporous menthol steam bath which had turned her hair into rats' tails and done nothing for her sinuses; now, it was this.

'What is that again?' she asked.

'Honey, lemon juice and whisky,' Joe told her. 'It's the best flu remedy going. Either it kills the germs or it gets them so pissed they can't remember they're supposed to be doing you harm.'

Laurel sipped at it, feeling the hot, alcoholic mixture warm her throat and stomach as it slipped down. 'So what do you know about this Devon?' she asked. 'I mean, even the name sounds false.'

'She's from California,' Joe replied, settling into the easy chair opposite Laurel. 'They all have strange names over there. And does it really matter what we know about her? She's incredible. She's even more submissive than Cindy, and I never thought I'd say that about anyone. You should have seen the way she looked up at me through this tangle of dark hair, tears in her eyes, and begged me to slap her between her legs with the ruler. It still turns me on just to think about it.'

'I hope you didn't just decide to employ her because you want to go to bed with her,' Laurel said reproachfully. Since the moment Joe had rung her following Devon's audition, he had been unable to stop talking about the girl.

'It's too late for that,' Joe replied. 'After I'd finished punishing her she asked me to fuck her. So we've got all that side of it out of the way already.' He took a swig of the coffee he had made for himself. 'I know what all this is really about. You're jealous of her.'

'I'm sorry?' Laurel said. 'What do I have to be jealous of?'

'Only the fact that she's experienced the delights of my body, and you haven't.'

Laurel tried to work out whether Joe was joking. She gave up, sniffed, and reached for a tissue. She hated having flu, and she especially hated having it this badly. Normally she was up and about within a couple of days of falling ill, but this seemed to be a particularly virulent strain of the illness, and her symptoms seemed to be showing no signs of abating. She suspected it was partly her own fault for over-exerting herself, and wondered if she should have taken a couple of days off earlier in the month, as Joe had insisted. 'You sound like you've signed up for the Warren Keating self-appreciation course,' she said finally.

'Couldn't get on it,' Joe retorted. 'Warren's taken all the places for himself. He sends his love, by the way. He says if you need vapour rub applying to your chest at any time, you're to give him a ring.'

In spite of herself, Laurel smiled.

'That's better,' Joe said. 'Look, Laurel, I know you're

worrying about how we're all managing in your absence, but we're fine. Cindy's holding the office together while the rest of us are going out on jobs, and she's loving it. Half the blokes in the sandwich bar round the corner are in love with her, and she's even revived that cheese plant that was dying on top of the filing cabinet. I wouldn't be surprised if you didn't have a job to come back to when you're better. Cindy will want to do the desk job, and you'll have to go out and have your bum spanked by strange women.'

Now he was joking, Laurel was sure of it. She smiled at Joe, and tried to ignore the nagging truth of his earlier words. Though she would never admit it, she was jealous of the attention Joe seemed to be paying this mysterious Devon. She had always thought she held a special place in his affections, and it hurt her to think that some other woman could turn his head so easily.

It was all reminding her too much of Nina. She hadn't consciously thought about her stepsister in ages, but the way Joe was talking about their new escort only made her remember how good Nina had been at attracting the men Laurel had really fancied. Only because Nina was a prick-tease, Laurel thought reproachfully. She promised them something she had no intention of giving them, and it was enough to lure them into her clutches for long enough to forget which sister they had originally been interested in. The last thing Laurel wanted was to employ a woman who might operate on Nina's level, but there was no way she could tell Joe that. He knew hardly anything about Laurel's painful relationship with Nina, and she was very happy for that to remain the case.

She wrapped her fingers around the mug, lifted it to her mouth and drank from it once more.

'How is that?' Joe asked, gesturing to the mug.

'Lovely,' Laurel replied. Joe's hot toddy was relaxing her, and she was beginning to feel a little sleepy. She put the mug down and held her arms out towards Joe. 'Come here.'

Joe went to join her on the settee, and she snuggled up to him. He stroked a hand through her hair as her eyelids drooped further. She felt safe and comforted in his embrace, and she wondered how it would feel if she was to finally lower her defences and move their relationship on to the more intimate footing Joe craved.

'I do trust you, you know that,' she told him. 'It's just that after what happened with Roger, I keep thinking that something might go wrong, and we might lose the agency.'

'What's going to go wrong?' Joe asked. 'Just concentrate on getting better, Laurel, and leave everything else in our capable hands.'

The only thing I'd like to leave in your capable hands right now is my bottom, was Laurel's last conscious thought, before her head nodded onto Joe's shoulder, and she slept.

Nina Angell knelt at Roger Preston's feet, wearing nothing except for a wide black leather collar which circled her slim neck. There was a D-ring at the front of the collar to which a length of chain could be attached, as it was now. Roger was holding the other end of the chain securely as he looked down at Nina's naked body. She was in the position he had asked her to hold, body arched and knees a little way apart so that her full, ruby-tipped breasts and naked sex were displayed prominently. The sight was enough to keep him at full hardness beneath his snug-fitting black chinos.

'So, tell me what happened,' he said. They were the first words he had spoken to her since he had ordered her to strip and present herself, the second she had walked through the front door. They were alone in the house at the moment, but even if they had not been, she would have still been required to disrobe in the hallway, where anyone could see her. The secret of making a woman truly compliant, Roger had read somewhere, was to strip her of her modesty, and her current pose and state of undress were all designed to do just that. He was still pleased and slightly surprised at how quickly Nina had embraced her submissive side. If he had known how much her eagerness to submit was due to her recent encounter with Joe Gallagher, he would not have been half so smug.

'They bought it totally,' Nina replied. 'As far as they're concerned, I'm Devon Rylance, and I'm doing escort work to pay my way up north to see my family. Of course, it helped that Laurel's not well.'

'Oh, really?' Roger said. 'I didn't know that. Nothing trivial, I hope.'

Nina failed to register Roger's sarcasm. 'Flu, I think Joe said. Anyway, what matters is that she hasn't seen me yet, and she won't for a while. Even when she's better I can get my assignments over the phone. Joe said that would be no problem, given that I'm not living in London at the moment.' She looked up at Roger. 'When are you going to get a place in London, by the way?'

'What's wrong, Nina? Aren't you enjoying being a houseguest here?'

'Well, it's certainly helped me get into my rôle, but I don't know that I want to be used by so many people all the time.'

'You know you don't have a choice in the matter,' Roger said. 'If I want to give you to my friends, I'll give you to my friends. Anyway, that's not important now. I want to know what happened at Domination Inc. How thoroughly did they vet you?'

'They're doing the checks now, apparently. They need to be sure I haven't spent any time in a correctional institute, that I'm not wanted by the police in the States and that I don't have any life-threatening diseases.'

'And what will happen when they do those checks, and they don't find any records of a Devon Rylance from Oakland?'

'Oh, but they will,' Nina replied. 'I told you I was in information technology, didn't I? Well, I have some friends who are in the same field. Friends who are a little less scrupulous when it comes to altering a computer record.'

'You mean you hang around with hackers.' Roger made the word sound like a communicable disease.

'There are a couple of people who owe me one, Roger, and if anyone looks up Devon in the records, they're going to find she's a straight-A student and a model citizen. She's never even had a parking violation.' She smiled. 'You should let me have a word with my friends. It would be so easy for them to give Laurel a record. You know, a couple of outstanding fines for streetwalking, that kind of thing. We could get her six months in prison, no problem, and that'd give you all the time you need to get your hands on the agency.'

'Nina, I may be devious, but I think we can bring Laurel and Joe down without resorting to quite such underhand tactics.'

'Hey, leave Joe out of this!' Nina exclaimed.

'My, you seem terribly fond of Joe Gallagher, given that you barely know the man,' Roger said. He caught a fistful of Nina's dark hair and jerked her head up painfully until their eyes met. 'Can I assume that you find our damaged friend attractive? I really think you should tell me more about what happened at this audition.'

'Not a great deal, really. He just got me to prove I'm submissive, and that I enjoy being beaten, that I wasn't just putting on an act.'

'What did he do? I want to know every last detail. And while you're telling me, I want you to spread your thighs as wide as they'll go. I want to see if thinking about it is getting you wet.'

Obediently, Nina parted her legs, giving Roger an even better view of the intricate folds of her sex. Already the fleshy petals were beginning to unfurl, revealing the secret places within.

'Well, first of all he got me to take my blouse and bra off, and then I had to stand in the window with my hands on my head. There's a bookstore across the road, and while I was standing there, I was imagining that someone was looking out of the window, staring at my tits and masturbating.'

'That turns you on, doesn't it,' Roger said, 'the thought that no man could resist your naked charms? I'll really have to beat such presumption out of you, you little slut. So what came next?'

'I thought he was going to spank me, but he wanted to use a plastic ruler on my ass, and I had to go to his desk and bring it to him. Then he made me take my skirt off and get on his knee. And then he slapped me with the ruler. You can't believe how much it hurt.'

'If you think that's painful, you have a lot to learn,' Roger told her. 'I'm assured that the birch is a far more evil implement. Perhaps once you've finished your little tale we should go out into the woods and pick a nice, juicy bunch of birch twigs. Imagine how that will feel as it slices across your wanton little arse.'

Nina shuddered. If that was to be her fate, she would rather not finish her story at all. She half-hoped that her hosts would return at this point, to spare her, but she suspected that Roger would simply invite them to join in his planned birch-hunting expedition. There was no punishment he could devise which could not be improved by the input of his friends, who were far more sophisticated and cruel in their pleasures. She sighed, and continued with her tale.

'After a while he pulled my panties down, and then he carried on hitting me, this time on my bare behind. God, did it sting! He really knew what he was doing. Don't even think about getting rid of him when you get rid of Laurel. He'll be a valuable asset to you.'

'Are you totally sure that this is an unbiased opinion on your part?' Roger asked. He gazed at the heart of Nina's sex, noticing how it was beginning to glisten with the oily sheen of her excitement. Talking about being punished by Joe was indeed turning her on. She was even more submissive than he had dared to believe.

'Completely,' Nina assured him. 'By this time I'd crossed the threshold between pleasure and pain. The ruler was still hurting, but I knew I needed that pain to take me all the way to orgasm. So I begged Joe to slap my snatch with it, and that's what made me come.'

Roger felt his penis lurch at the thought of the ruler being brought down sharply on Nina's shaven pussy, aroused beyond belief to think that she had requested such a severe punishment.

'And that's when he offered you the job?' Roger said.

Nina shook her head. 'Not straight away. Before he could do that, I'd climbed on top of him and screwed him. Then he offered me the job. Well, he couldn't really turn me down after that, could he?'

'You're a forward little minx, and no mistake,' Roger told her. 'Come with me.' He tugged sharply on the chain, and began to walk into the drawing room. Obediently, Nina crawled after him on her hands and knees.

Roger settled himself down on the big grey leather settee; like the rest of the furnishing in the room, it bore all the hallmarks of his hosts' understated and quietly expensive taste. He dropped Nina's chain and gestured in the direction of the drinks cabinet. 'Fix me a brandy,' he ordered.

Nina rose, flexing her slightly cramped limbs, and went to do as she had been told. She took a heavy crystal tumbler and poured into it a generous measure, before returning to Roger's side and handing him the drink.

Later, he would inform her she had used the wrong glass; a brandy of this vintage needed to be served in a balloon glass, so it could be warmed between the palms and its aromatic vapours released. It would be more instructive if he were to beat Nina's mistake into her backside, Roger thought, picturing her squirming naked on his knee while her pretty bum cheeks reddened under his palm. Perhaps he would let her have a drink herself afterwards, though she would not be using a glass of any description for that. No, he intended to see her lapping the brandy from a bowl on the ground, like a dog. It would remind her of her lowly position in this new hierarchy.

His face showed nothing of his intentions as he said, 'So, were you told anything else about the agency?'

Nina, kneeling by his side, looked up at him through her curtain of dark hair. 'The way Joe talks about them, they're more like a family than a business. They only seem to have a very few members of staff, which I suppose is why he was so grateful when I rang up looking for work. There's Warren, Chris, Cindy and Elisha.' She counted them off on her fingers as she spoke. 'Between them and Joe, apparently they can cater for just about every taste you can think of – providing it's legal, of course.'

'Of course,' Roger murmured. 'And what about the lovely Laurel? Does she offer her services for hire, too?'

'Oh, no. According to Joe, she's the glue that binds all the rest of them together. She's incredibly efficient and organised, he said. Which basically means she's just as boring as she was when I knew her.'

'Well, that's one area where I'll certainly be planning to make changes.' Roger smiled to himself. Perhaps throwing Laurel out of the agency was not the only option. Perhaps he should keep her on, and make her do escort work. He'd make a point of attracting dominant male clients, and reserve her for the ones with the most specialised tastes. The thought of the prim and proper Laurel Angell being in situations where she was forced to expose her naked body in a public setting, or to have clamps and heavy chains hung from her nipples and sex lips, or have her pretty face and body covered with mud and gooey foodstuffs, excited him greatly. She deserved to be humiliated and brought low – on that point, he was in full agreement with Nina – and this was the perfect way to do it.

He took another sip of his brandy, relishing its taste. 'We have to plan our next move very carefully, Nina,' he said. 'We shan't do anything immediately. You need to work for the agency for a week or two, until you're on a friendly footing with as many members of the staff as possible. It's vital that everyone likes you and trusts you – that way, when we strike, they won't suspect that someone within the organisation has been responsible.'

'What exactly are you planning to do?' Nina asked.

'We have to get Laurel in a position where she's on her own and vulnerable,' Roger replied. 'I envisage her being placed in a situation where she's completely helpless, and the only way in which she can save herself is by handing over the deeds of the agency to me. This is where I need your help, Nina. I know you don't want to risk blowing your cover, but I need you to find out as much as you can about her routine – where she goes, who she's friendly with, that sort of thing.'

'Oh, that's no problem,' Nina said. 'All I have to do is get closer to Joe Gallagher. He's so besotted with her he'll tell me anything I need to know. I know his type; it'll be easy to wrap him round my little finger.'

'You seem to be regarding all this as some sort of game,' Roger said, his voice taking on a sudden severity. He was tired of talking about Laurel; Nina had been naked in front of him for the best part of an hour now, her body betraying signs of her own arousal, and he was growing increasingly impatient to haul her onto his lap and give her a good spanking. 'This is deadly serious, Nina, I can assure you, and if you're not going to treat it as such, then you're going to have to suffer the consequences. Over my knee, now!'

'Oh, please, no,' Nina whimpered. 'Joe only took the ruler to my ass a couple of hours ago. It's still sore.'

'That's no excuse.' Roger caught hold of the chain and dragged her, protesting, to her feet. 'Turn round,' he ordered.

Meekly, Nina did so, giving Roger the opportunity to study her firm backside at length. It did indeed bear the signs of a recent punishment, the skin bruised and slightly raised. Roger could not help wishing he had been the one who had inflicted those marks on Nina's taut cheeks, but contented himself with the thought that a spanking on such abused and tender flesh would be all the more painful.

'You simply have to learn that when you're due a punishment, there's no point in arguing,' Roger told her, hearing Nina's indrawn breath as his fingers traced over the weals the ruler had left. 'You also have to learn that when you serve brandy, you use a balloon glass. In fact, I think we're going to have to make that point very clear.'

Roger sat down sharply, tugging at the chain around Nina's neck as she did so. Caught off-balance, Nina toppled onto his waiting lap in a tangle of lithe arms and legs. In a businesslike fashion, Roger arranged her to his satisfaction; he took one of the butter-soft leather cushions from the settee and pushed it under her body so that her bottom arched up towards him, prominent and ready to be chastised. However, Roger had not quite finished. His glass now contained only the dregs of the brandy, but what he was about to do would still be a waste, knowing how much the bottle would have cost. He paused for a moment, leaving Nina enough time to wonder what he was about to do, then picked up the glass and poured the remnants of his drink over her backside. Although the alcohol would dry quickly against her warm skin, it would sting her freshly-punished flesh, and the first couple of slaps would be all the more painful.

'Only a dozen slaps, I think,' Roger said, 'but you'll have to count each one and thank me for them. Any mistakes, and we go back to the beginning. Is that clear?' As he spoke he brought the flat of his hand firmly down on the crown of Nina's left buttock.

She stifled whatever noise of complaint she was about to make and said instead, 'One, thank you.'

'Very good,' Roger replied, treating her right buttock to a spank of the same severity. Obediently, Nina counted the stroke. Roger could feel his erection pressing hard against the cushion through his trousers, as though it might bore through the leather in its quest to reach Nina's sex. When he had finished punishing Nina he would order her to her knees and tell her to suck his cock. It was definitely her area of expertise, he had decided, and he could barely wait to feel those lips of hers closing around his glans and teasing him to a climax.

The thought of that impending pleasure took him through the next few slaps more quickly than he might otherwise have gone. By the time he realised where he was, Nina was muttering, 'Eight, thank you,' the strain in her voice increasingly evident as she fought to keep control of the situation.

'You are the most presumptuous woman I believe I've ever met,' Roger told Nina as the ninth slap fell on the fleshy crease of her buttocks, and she yelped, but did not lose track of her counting. 'You seem so determined to get one over on that sister of yours that all other considerations become utterly irrelevant. Well, I assure you they definitely are not.' The tenth and eleventh slaps landed in rapid succession on the very tops of her thighs, making her wriggle and kick her legs. It was the sight of her denuded sex, pink and glistening, that she afforded him as she fought against the pain of the penultimate slap that made Roger decide on the target for his *pièce de résistance*. Following Joe's lead, but this time unbidden by Nina, he parted her cheeks as she struggled on his lap, and let the last slap descend squarely on her juicy, pouting labia.

She bucked and shrieked with what Roger suspected was the merest ripple of orgasmic sensation. 'Twelve, thank you,' she whispered finally.

Without ceremony, Roger pushed her to the thickly-carpeted floor and unzipped his trousers, releasing his rigid erection. 'You know what to do,' he told Nina. As she took the bulbous head into her mouth, Roger entertained the thought that if his plans worked out, before very much longer it might be Laurel who knelt before him, naked and with her backside bearing the livid prints of his palm, obediently sucking him to climax. With that satisfying thought uppermost in his mind, he closed his eyes and reclined back to enjoy the wet pleasures of Nina's oral caress.

Chapter Twelve

There was a message on the answerphone when Laurel let herself into the office. She pressed the play button and listened as a smooth, deep voice filled the little room. 'This is Clive Lawson. The service you provide has been highly recommended to me, and I'd be interested in discussing some potential business with you...'

Laurel scribbled his number into her contacts book, before dialling it swiftly. The phone was picked up on the second ring, almost as if the man had been anticipating her call.

'Mr Lawson, it's Laurel Angell here. I'm ringing about the message you left for me.'

'Ah, yes.' His voice seemed to caress her ear. 'I've heard lots of very good things about your agency, and I may be able to put a substantial piece of business your way, but first I'd like to know more about what you can actually provide.'

'Well, the basic fee is—'

Lawson interrupted her. 'There's something very sordid about discussing money over the phone, don't you think? What I want to do is hire a couple of your girls for a party I'm planning to host, and I'd really like you to come down and see the house, get a feel for the ambience I'm trying to create.'

'Well, that makes sense,' Laurel replied. 'When did you have in mind for this meeting, Mr Lawson.'

'Please, call me Clive. Tell you what, I'm actually going to be throwing a small drinks party on Saturday evening.

Why don't you come down for that? I live just outside Lymington, in the New Forest. Do you know the area at all?'

Laurel hesitated. 'Yes, but it's a bit of a distance to come just for a party.'

'Don't worry about driving back the same night,' he said, brushing her immediate objections away, 'we've plenty of room for houseguests. If you arrived early in the afternoon, say half-past three, it would give you plenty of time to look round before my other guests arrive.'

Finally persuaded, Laurel took down the address of his house, Garside Hall, and details of how to reach it by road. A small voice nagged in the back of her head as she did so, reminding her of the agency's rule never to visit a client – albeit only a potential client in this case – alone at their own home. 'Would it be okay if I brought a friend with me?' she asked.

She almost sensed a moment's hesitation before Clive Lawson said, 'Yes, that should be fine. It'll round the numbers up nicely. Doesn't do to have wallflowers at a party, now does it?'

As Laurel put the phone down on Lawson, she felt that something vital had gone unsaid in the course of their conversation, but she shrugged her unease away. It would do her good to get out of London for the weekend, and if the man was simply attempting to get her into bed without paying the agency for her services, taking Joe or Warren along would keep her safe from his unwanted attentions or those of his guests.

Except that neither Joe nor Warren was free to accompany her down to the house on Saturday. Joe and Christian were booked to take a pair of submissive blonde sisters to an all-night fetish party at a warehouse in Victoria Dock, while Warren appeared to have lined up an evening with Sara, the red-haired girl he had been with when Laurel had first met him.

'Couldn't you put her off till next weekend?' Laurel had asked him, knowing in advance what the answer would be.

Warren had shaken his head. 'Any other time I'd have jumped at it like a shot. You, me, a double bed in a strange house, a pair of your stockings...' His grin was wolfish, knowing that, despite herself, Laurel would not be able to stop her imagination straying to the scenario he was creating. 'The thing is, Sara goes back to Milan the next day. She's doing her year's teaching practice over there, and I want to give her something to think about while she's trying to tell the class about the possessive form.'

Salvation had come in the form of Cindy. Laurel had caught her moping in the office later that afternoon, staring miserably out of the window at the passers-by on the street below, a cigarette burning unattended between her fingers.

'Are you okay?' she had asked, concerned to see her favourite among the agency's girls so far removed from her usual bubbly self.

'Not really,' Cindy had replied. 'Just another kick in the teeth, but I'll get over it.'

'Do you want to talk about it?'

'There isn't that much to say. You know that bloke I was seeing, Tom, and you know how he kept promising me he was going to leave his wife? Well, it turned out to be a load of crap, like it always is. He told me yesterday they're going to make a real go of the marriage for the sake of the kids, and they're going on a second honeymoon to Barbados at the end of the month.' She stubbed the remains of her cigarette out forcefully. 'I just can't believe he kept me hanging on for so long. I thought I had it sussed when it came to men, but it seems I'm just as big a fool as anyone else. And the worst part is, I deliberately turned down a couple of jobs this weekend because I thought I was going to be spending it with Tom.'

'Well, if you're not doing anything, why don't you come down to the New Forest with me?' Laurel had suggested. 'I've been invited down to a party to meet a prospective client, and I don't want to go on my own. Come on, it'll give you a chance to get glammed up and have a good time. You'll forget all about Tom, I promise you.'

Cindy had considered the offer for a moment and then shrugged. 'Yeah, why not? Thanks, Laurel. It's a date.'

Cindy had still seemed just as keen on the weekend's adventure when Laurel had collected her from the flat she rented in a converted terrace in Bow, a couple of hours earlier. Like herself, Cindy had dressed in a sexy but businesslike fashion; her damson scoop-necked crushed velvet top and tight-fitting PVC trousers contrasted with Laurel's elegant pinstriped skirt suit, under which she wore no blouse, so that the tempting contours of her breasts, cradled in a lacy white bra, were just visible.

The traffic on the South Circular was surprisingly light for a Saturday, and they had made good time in reaching the motorway. Laurel rarely drove in London, and relished the chance to take her Peugeot 306 for a spin. It felt good to put her foot down and feel the power of the car's engine responding to her demands. At the services on the M3 they stopped for coffee and toast, bought ice lollies on a childish impulse, cigarettes, and Laurel, noticing the fuel gauge was close to empty, filled the tank with petrol.

She walked back from the cash desk beneath the service station awning, humming lightly to herself. A watery sun had broken through the leaden January clouds, and she felt as though she had left all the stresses and strains of the agency far behind her.

As Laurel slipped back into the driver's seat, a coach pulled up on the tarmac beside them, its windows festooned with flags and red-and-white scarves. The predominantly male passengers on the side nearest Laurel's car stared out of the window, their obvious boredom dispelled as Cindy pulled up her top and treated them to a good view of her pert, braless breasts.

'Cindy, what are you playing at?' Laurel asked, her attention momentarily distracted from the task of fastening her seat belt.

'They must be on their way to the football,' Cindy replied. 'Rotherham are playing Portsmouth in the cup this afternoon. There was something about it on the radio while you were paying for the petrol. I thought I'd give 'em all something to remember the day by, even if their team doesn't win.' She turned to Laurel, a wicked grin on her face. 'Go on, open your jacket. Give 'em a flash too.'

'I couldn't,' Laurel replied, appalled by the suggestion. She switched on the engine and put the car into gear, pulling away rapidly from the parked coach before Cindy could repeat her impromptu show of flesh.

'Yeah, you could – if it was Warren who was asking you.' Cindy paused to peel the wrapper carefully off her strawberry Mivvi, wrapped her lips round it and sucked suggestively. 'Except he wouldn't ask, would he? He'd tell you to do it, and you'd do it. He'd have you sitting in the passenger seat, playing with your pussy in the overtaking lane for the benefit of passing lorry drivers, and you'd love it.'

Laurel concentrated on the task of rejoining the flow of traffic on the motorway, her head turned so that Cindy could not see the flush which had risen to her cheeks. 'I don't know why you're so convinced I fancy Warren.'

'Of course you do. Don't be ashamed of it. I fancy him as well. You have to admit, whatever it is that makes a good master, he's got it in spades. Just look at the women who make repeat bookings; they all ask for him.'

'You're right.' Laurel sighed. 'It's just—'

'Just what?'

For a moment, Laurel contemplated telling Cindy that however attractive she might find the infuriating Warren Keating, her feelings for Joe ran much deeper, but she simply shrugged her shoulders and indicated to overtake an elderly Vauxhall Cavalier which was idling in the nearside lane. 'It's just he's so convinced he's a complete and utter fanny magnet, and I don't want him to have the satisfaction of knowing he's right.'

They reached Garside Hall slightly earlier than Laurel had intended, Clive Lawson's directions being explicit enough to prevent them losing their way on the poorly-signposted roads that ran through the New Forest. The house was on the outskirts of the postcard-pretty town of Lymington, set well back from the road and guarded from prying eyes by a thicket of holly trees. Laurel pulled the car to a halt on the smooth stretch of gravel in front of the main entrance and checked her reflection in the driver's mirror, fluffing up her shaggy strawberry-blonde hair until she was satisfied with her appearance.

'Nice place,' Cindy commented as she clambered out of the car. 'Whoever this Mr Lawson is, he's certainly not short of a quid or two.'

'Well, as long as he's prepared to put some of it our way, I'm quite happy,' Laurel replied. She climbed the short flight of stone steps to the front door and rang the bell. After a few moments' wait, the heavy wooden door swung open. A suave-looking dark-haired man in his early forties, dressed in a black polo-necked cashmere jumper and dark, casually-cut trousers, stood before her.

'Miss Angell.' The rich, deep voice was unmistakable. This was Clive Lawson. 'And this is…?'

'My friend, Cindy Beresford,' Laurel told him. 'I hope we're not too early?'

'Not at all,' Clive replied. 'We're all ready for you. Do come in and hang your coat up. Cindy, if you'd like to go through to the drawing room, my wife Louisa will attend to you...'

There was an old-fashioned wooden coat stand in the corner by the door, and Laurel shrugged her long coat off her shoulders. She was reaching up to hang it on the stand when she suddenly felt her host come up behind her. She caught a brief scent of musky aftershave, and glimpsed a silver Rolex watch on his wrist as his hand clamped firmly over her mouth, stifling her shocked cry. His other hand caught her two wrists and expertly cuffed them together as she tried to struggle free from his surprisingly strong grip. The slamming of what Laurel presumed to be the drawing room door, followed by a high-pitched shriek, indicated that something equally unpleasant must be happening to Cindy.

Clive Lawson reached up and took a silk scarf from the coat stand, and wrapped it round Laurel's head, effectively blindfolding her. Before she could react he had dragged her a little way down the hall and pushed her through a door into an unknown room. Thick carpet muffled the tread of her heels, and the faint dry smell of old paper led her to surmise she had been taken into Lawson's library.

His hand loosed its hold round her waist and she staggered forward; with her hands cuffed behind her she was unable to prevent herself falling heavily onto the carpet. She lay for a moment, winded, then tried to right herself, unable to see what she was doing and knowing that Lawson was watching her undignified scrambling. Her knee knocked against something thick and wooden; the leg of a table, or perhaps a chair of particularly solid construction. Her second guess was confirmed when Lawson reached out and hauled her up, dumping her on the seat.

Lawson's fingers were on the front of her jacket now; she was unable to prevent him from unfastening it and pushing it off her shoulders. He gave a slight intake of breath, and she realised he must be staring at her breasts, lifted and presented to his gaze in her underwired, front-fastening bra.

'Why are you doing this?' Laurel asked, but Lawson remained silent. She was aware of him looming over her again, and then his hands were on the hem of her skirt, pushing it up towards her waist. She tried to wriggle away from him, but he pushed her firmly against the carved wooden back of the chair with one hand, while the other reached up under her skirt to tug at her black silk panties.

'Get off me!' she exclaimed, trying to lash out and catch Lawson on the shins with her high-heeled shoe, but her struggles were futile, and he tugged the little garment down and off, tearing the delicate fabric as he attempted to manoeuvre it past Laurel's squirming bottom. The next thing Laurel knew, a little wad of material was being stuffed into her protesting mouth; from the texture and the familiar feminine aroma, she knew it was her own ruined panties which were being used as a crude but effective gag.

Lawson moved away from her for a moment, and she could hear the sound of a drawer opening and something being retrieved. She thought about trying to get up from the chair and making a run for safety while he was otherwise engaged but, frightened and disorientated as she was, she had no idea where the library door was located, and she sensed that if she tried to escape, Lawson would just send her sprawling painfully to the floor once more. She prayed that, somehow, Cindy had had more luck in escaping whatever fate had befallen her, but she suspected this was far from being the case. Whoever Clive Lawson was, and whatever his reasons were for ambushing the pair of them, this bore all the hallmarks of a well-prepared trap, into which she and Cindy had walked in blithe innocence.

When Lawson returned, his first action was to grasp Laurel's right ankle, which he guided to the nearest leg of the chair and strapped securely in place. He swiftly repeated the action with her left leg, ensuring that she was effectively tethered in place. With her short skirt still hitched up towards her waist, and her legs widely spread, Laurel knew that her knickerless pussy would be all too exposed. The knowledge made her feel more vulnerable than she had done at any point over the last few minutes and yet, at the same time, the thought that Lawson could see every fold and whorl of her sex was making an unexpected pulse of arousal beat strongly between her hobbled legs.

When he reached for the handcuffs and unfastened them, Laurel was too demoralised to protest. Almost passively, she let him remove her jacket completely and strap her wrists to the arms of the chair. She hoped he might remove the scarf that covered her eyes but this, at least, seemed intended to remain in place.

'You can't begin to believe how beautiful you look, bound and helpless like that,' Lawson began. 'Truly an angel, indeed. There's just one more thing I need to do...'

As he spoke, his fingers flicked at the clasp that fastened Laurel's bra. It sprang apart, and Laurel felt her breasts fall free of the lacy cups.

'Mouth-watering,' Lawson continued. 'Though perhaps I should remove those panties from your mouth for a moment, just so you can tell me why it is that your nipples are so hard and stiff, and why I can see the merest hint of your juices glistening at the entrance to your pussy. Could it be that sitting there in bondage, with all your little secrets on display, is actually turning you on, Miss Angell?' He laughed to himself. 'I'd heard that the girls at your agency were particularly submissive, but I had no idea their boss was of the same persuasion.'

Laurel mumbled into her silken gag. She wanted to deny his accusations, but she knew he spoke the truth. Deep down, she knew she was as submissive as Cindy, and there was a part of her which had longed to be placed in this humiliating position. But whatever her sexual feelings, it was more important that she found out what Lawson wanted. When he pulled the panties out of her mouth, she spat, 'Just what do you think you're going to achieve by doing this?'

'All in good time,' Lawson replied. 'We know we owe you an explanation.'

We? Laurel thought, then heard the soft sound of feet moving over the library's plush carpet, and realised with a shock that there was a third person in the room. She had no idea from the muted footfalls whether they had been joined by a male or a female. How long had whoever it was been standing there silently – and how much had they seen? Although, Laurel conceded, that would have been nothing in comparison to what they could see now, as she sat in passive bondage with her breasts and quim uncovered. She shivered, unable to control her reaction.

'Who's with you?' she asked.

'A friend,' Lawson told her. He was moving as he spoke, and Laurel turned her head to follow him, becoming aware that he was now standing behind her. 'That's all you need to know for the moment. But it might make things a little clearer if I tell you that you have something which rightfully belongs to this friend – and they'd like it back.'

'I'm sorry, but I really don't know what you're talking about,' Laurel replied.

'Well, let's see if we can jog your memory between us...'

Laurel felt a hand flick across her nipples, the soft touch enough to make them peak almost painfully. In spite of her vulnerable position, she was growing increasingly turned on, and when the hand was joined by a second, cupping and squeezing her breasts, she could not prevent herself sighing with undisguised pleasure.

The pleasure faded as a third hand joined in the ministrations, a long index finger trailing down the cleft between her breasts, across the gentle swell of her stomach and into the soft red-gold curls that covered her mound. She had been so wrapped up in Lawson's caresses that she had forgotten about his 'friend', but now she was all too aware that the two of them were not alone. It was a man's finger, she thought frantically, as it skimmed across the slick surface of her labia; either that, or it belonged to a woman who kept her nails trimmed short. Could it be Lawson's wife? she wondered. And then she caught the merest whiff of a spicy, defiantly male cologne, and banished all thoughts of Louisa Lawson.

'Now, Laurel,' Lawson muttered. 'Let's talk about that valuable possession of yours...'

The inquisitive finger was now circling Laurel's clitoris, causing her to question exactly which possession Lawson was alluding to. The touch was sure and skilful, designed to bring her to the brink of orgasm with, it seemed, almost minimal effort. If the hands which were stroking and teasing her had belonged to Joe and Warren, as a bedazzled part of her brain could not help hoping, she would surely have climaxed at least once by now. And if those fingers had been replaced by two warm, eager mouths, one suckling at her aching nipples and the other licking every inch of her pussy... Laurel writhed in her bonds, trying to push her breasts and sex closer to the hands which fondled them.

As suddenly as they had begun, the caresses stopped. Laurel's body slumped, as she realised just how far she had been prepared to let Lawson and his accomplice go. Tension prickled between her legs.

'This is what you want, isn't it?' Lawson's voice was rich and soft in her ear. 'Here you are, tied and blindfolded, with two virtual strangers doing exactly what they want to your body, and you're so wet you're dripping like a juicy peach. It's such a beautiful picture, I'm tempted to photograph it and keep it for posterity.'

'No, please...' Laurel begged. 'Just tell me why you're doing this – or at least stop teasing me.'

'Oh, there's no teasing here. This is all deadly serious, I can assure you. I told you that you have something my friend wants – and we're going to make sure you give it to him.'

So it definitely was a man who was the silent partner in this encounter. Had that been an unintentional slip on Lawson's part, or was he trying to raise the stakes by making Laurel aware of the true extent of her predicament? Another ruthless, dominant man like Lawson could soon have Laurel begging for mercy – if that was their intention.

When the hand slipped back between her widely-parted thighs and began its explorations once more, it was obvious they intended her to beg for something. A few swift strokes of the soft pad of the man's finger across Laurel's already sensitised clit and she was back on the verge of orgasm. Lawson had talked of photographing her, and she imagined what a picture she would make at this moment. Despite the fact that she was blindfolded, it would be obvious from the way her neck arched and her mouth was open that she was being taken to the heights of ecstasy, and her pale skin would be suffused with the mottled, rosy flush that signified the approach of her climax. With the finger working busily at her little bud – and, she realised, a second and third stretching open the pouting mouth of her sex – it would be a sight to grace any collection of erotic art. A stranger was forcing her to come, controlling the depth of her reactions, and she was loving every moment of it.

Which was when the stimulation stopped again, leaving Laurel panting in frustration. The message was clear: Lawson and his friend could give pleasure, or withhold it as they chose. What she did not understand was why they were treating her in this way.

'No more games, Laurel. I think it's time I introduced you to my friend,' Lawson said. He unknotted the scarf that covered Laurel's eyes, and whisked it away. She blinked as her vision adjusted to the soft light, then her eyes widened in disbelief as she saw who was kneeling in front of her, licking his fingers thoughtfully. The moustache had gone, and the hair was a rich copper, rather than its original light brown, but there was no mistaking her erstwhile business partner, Roger Preston.

'You!' Laurel exclaimed. 'What the bloody hell are you playing at? Where have you been? Do you know what I've been through since you disappeared?'

Roger smiled, as though he was enjoying a joke he was

not prepared to share. 'Oh yes, I know exactly what you've been up to. Your fame has spread all the way to Los Angeles, would you believe? I must say, I admire your fortitude, working so hard to build the agency back up like that. Any other girl would have given up and gone bankrupt. But then you're not like other girls, are you, Laurel?' His finger went to his mouth again. 'You taste delicious, by the way. And I never thought you'd have quite such a beautiful cunt.'

'I don't want your compliments, Roger. I just want you to untie me, and let me go.'

'All in good time.' Roger stroked her hair away from her face, where it clung in sweat-dampened tendrils. 'You see, sweetheart, I never wanted to let the agency go, not really. It was just that we'd reached a stage where it was more... expedient if I bowed out of running it for a while.'

'Yes, bowing out so completely that no one would ever know you'd been involved. You were quite prepared to let me lose everything, you bastard, and now you stand there, calm as you like, and talk about expediency.' Laurel itched for her hands to be freed, so that she could slap the self-assurance from Roger's face.

'But I knew I could leave everything in your safe hands, sweetheart.' Roger's voice dripped with the charm Laurel remembered well. 'And you didn't let me down. I tell you, you're getting rave reviews on the Internet – you must have them queuing up for our services.'

'They aren't *our* services,' Laurel retorted. 'You took your name off all the deeds. You don't have a stake in the agency any more.'

'That's where you're wrong,' Roger said. 'I have copies of all the original documents. You and me, equal partners, just as it should be. Just as it will be from now on.'

Laurel shook her head. 'Joe Gallagher's my partner now.

He bailed me out when you fled.'

'Joe Gallagher?' Roger pretended to cast around in his memory for a moment. 'Ah, yes. Your old friend, PC Hopalong. How is the dear boy? Still limping his way through life?'

'Joe's fine,' Laurel snapped, stung by Roger's snide reference to Joe's accident. 'Like I said, we're partners now. We have all the deeds, drawn up in both names, so I'm afraid those documents of yours aren't worth the paper they're printed on.'

'Oh, Laurel.' Roger sighed. 'I did hope you were going to make this easy for me. After all, a few moments ago you seemed so willing.'

'Our partnership's over, Roger. It was over the day I found out you'd skipped the country and left me with a pile of debts. Why should I want anything to do with you now?'

'But we were so good together.' Roger's hand stroked down Laurel's cheek and caressed the nape of her neck. 'This is our chance to start again. To put our partnership on a whole new footing.'

Laurel shivered. What was he suggesting? That they become not only business partners once more, but lovers, too? The idea was unthinkable: even if she had felt any desire for him, too much had happened since he had walked out on the agency. She could never regard him with any affection again.

'I'm sorry, Roger. I can't do what you want,' she replied.

'Can't? Or won't?' His hand was on her breast now, stroking the nipple, which still ached from its earlier stimulation. 'Don't forget, you're not the only person who's involved here. After all, there's your little friend Cindy to think of, too. Did Clive not mention that his wife is an accomplished dominatrix? She may not charge for her services, unlike our staff…'

Laurel could not help flinching at Roger's repeated use of the word 'our'. She wanted to fight him every inch of the way to deny him access to the agency. And yet, if by holding out against him she was placing Cindy in danger, what could she do?

'It's quite simple,' Roger said. 'I want you to agree to dissolve your partnership with Joe. And I want the half of the agency which is rightfully mine. We have plenty of time to discuss this. After all, no one will be expecting to see you before Monday morning, and if someone was to ring the agency and say you were unwell and staying with friends for a few days, who knows how long we could continue your stay here.'

'And what's in it for me and Joe?' Roger's touch on her breasts was arousing Laurel in spite of herself, and she fought to clear her head as she struggled with the implications of his proposal.

Roger smiled. 'Oh, I hear Joe has more than proved his worth as an escort, so he needn't worry about being short of a job. And, judging by your reactions, I think you're wasting your time sitting behind a desk all day. I'm sure there are many men who'd pay handsomely to have that lovely mouth of yours wrapped round their cock, or to spank your arse until it's crimson and glowing.'

'I won't do it,' Laurel said firmly. 'I can't betray my friends.'

Roger shrugged. 'Ah, well, on your own head be it. Perhaps Clive and I should go and check on what progress Louisa is making with little Cindy. If you change your mind, you only need to shout, and we'll untie you. Until then, I think we should leave you with something that might help to persuade you that you'd be wiser to do as we ask. Clive, would you do the honours?'

'Certainly.' Clive reached into the drawer of a small cabinet, and took something from it. As he brought it over to where Laurel was sitting, she saw it was a sex toy, of the kind on sale in the more arcane shops in Soho. It was made of plastic and had a central, phallic-shaped protuberance about five inches in length. Around the base, which spread out in a wide circle, was a ring of tiny bumps, which Laurel quickly realised were designed to press against and stimulate the whole of a woman's vulva and her clitoris.

The two men removed the straps that fastened Laurel's legs to the chair, and made her raise her bottom slightly, so that Lawson could insert the bizarre toy. It slid easily into Laurel's wet sex, and was pushed firmly home before her legs were secured in place once more. Clive turned something in the base of the vibrator, which began to throb quickly, stimulating Laurel's already overheated nerve-endings. She bucked and writhed in her seat, unable to fight the rolling tide of orgasm which threatened to engulf her. The last thing she wanted was for Roger and Clive to watch her in the throes of climax, and yet there was nothing she could do to prevent it.

'You bastards!' she sobbed, as she shuddered and came.

'They're not new batteries,' Clive said, almost conversationally, 'but I reckon they could power that thing for at least an hour. You still have the choice, Laurel. Agree to Roger's demands, and we'll switch that thing off. Refuse, and – how many orgasms do you think a woman could have in an hour, Roger?'

Roger Preston glanced at Laurel's resolute face. She was biting her lip as she tried to fight the sensations that were building relentlessly in her once more. 'I don't know, Clive, but I think we're about to find out.'

Chapter Thirteen

Some sixth sense had warned Cindy she was in trouble as soon as she walked into Clive Lawson's drawing room, but when the door had been swiftly shut and locked behind her, it had been too late to act on her instincts.

Cindy turned round to find herself confronted by a woman who stood almost six feet tall in her highly polished riding boots. She had chestnut hair coiled on her head in an immaculate French pleat, and her make-up was a perfect mask of porcelain foundation, ruby lipstick and thick black kohl, which emphasised her almond-shaped, violet eyes. She was dressed in a crisply laundered white shirt, which was tied under her small, high breasts to reveal a flat, well-toned midriff, and jodhpurs that clung to her long lean legs. In one hand she held the key to the drawing room door; with the other she tapped a riding crop nonchalantly against her thigh. Cindy glanced from the crop to the key to the woman's unsmiling face. So this was Lawson's wife, Louisa.

'And here was me expecting a cup of Lapsang Souchong and a plate of cucumber sandwiches,' Cindy said flippantly.

'I was warned you were a cocky little thing,' the woman replied, dropping the key she held into a tall vase of Oriental design before walking slowly towards Cindy.

Warned? Cindy thought to herself. By who? What kind of bizarre set-up was this? She said nothing, determined to let Louisa Lawson see nothing of her puzzlement or fear.

Louisa stopped inches away from Cindy, towering over the little blonde. She put the tip of her riding crop beneath the point of Cindy's chin, and used it to raise her head until their eyes met. 'Before you leave here,' she said, 'I'll have taken great pleasure in beating that cockiness out of you.'

'That's what you think,' Cindy muttered, defiance shining in her blue eyes.

'Silence!' The crop whistled ominously through the air. Cindy suppressed a shudder; this was probably her least favourite punishment implement, and she suspected that whoever had provided Louisa Lawson with her character assessment had informed her of this, too. Her heart sank as she realised that she and Laurel must have been betrayed by someone at Domination Inc.

'That's better,' Louisa said, 'but I don't want to have to tell you again.' She walked in a slow circle around Cindy, as if assessing her. Cindy stared mutely at the locked drawing room door, trying not to think about what might be about to happen to Laurel at the hands of Clive Lawson. It was not uncommon to find couples where both husband and wife were dominant, and she was certain they had fallen into the hands of just such a couple. In other circumstances she might have enjoyed the thought of being put through her paces by someone who showed every sign of being an accomplished dominatrix, but there was a menace in Louisa's demeanour which negated any erotic potential in the situation.

Louisa was back where she had started, staring at Cindy with a look of icy hauteur. She ran the riding crop idly along her palm as she spoke. 'Undress,' she said sharply.

'No,' came Cindy's simple, instinctive reply. The crop slashed through the air once more, the tip quivering inches from Cindy's left nipple. She tried not to think how it would feel if the blow had landed.

'You'll do as you're told,' Louisa warned her, her voice a low hiss. 'I could shred the clothes from your back with this thing if I had to, but I'm not in the mood for that kind of game. I want you naked, Cindy. So undress.'

'Or I'll be punished, is that it?' Cindy was determined to spin her resistance out a little longer. 'So, how come I get the feeling that I'm going to be punished anyway? Damned if you do and damned if you don't, right?'

Louisa Lawson's other hand shot out, slapping Cindy hard on the cheek. Realising she had finally overstepped the mark, Cindy reached for the button at the waistband of her PVC trousers, kicking off her shoes as she did so. Quickly, she unfastened the trousers and let them slither down her legs, aware that the other woman was watching her impatiently.

She caught hold of the bottom hem of her top and hesitated, knowing that when she raised it she would be baring her breasts to Louisa's gaze. When she had displayed herself to the coach full of football supporters earlier in the afternoon it had been a game, teasing them with something she knew they couldn't have. Now the situation was chillingly serious, and Louisa intended to have everything Cindy had to offer. Cindy had the nasty feeling that Laurel's fate, too, was bound up in whether or not she complied, in which case there was only one thing to do. She pulled the top over her head in one smooth movement, and threw it to the floor. Now all she wore was a red lace G-string, and she suspected she would not be allowed to keep that on for much longer.

To her surprise, however, Louisa did not immediately demand that she remove it. Instead, she ordered Cindy to clasp her hands behind her head, the movement lifting the little blonde's breasts and thrusting them outwards.

The tip of the riding crop flickered over Cindy's nipples, titillating them into hardness. Damn you, you bitch, Cindy thought, you know this is starting to turn me on. Why don't you just beat me with that thing, get it over with, and then we can find out what all this is really about?

Louisa's next words startled her. 'My boots are dirty. I want you to clean them, slut – or you know what to expect. On your knees, and keep your hands where they are.'

Cindy quietly knelt at Louisa's feet, the position awkward given that her fingers were still linked behind her head, and pressed her lips to the toe of Louisa's left riding boot. There was not a scrap of dirt on the boot, nothing to suggest that it had ever been worn out of the house, and Cindy wondered whether, despite her outfit, Louisa had ever been near a horse in her life. This was not about cleanliness, however, this was about obedience, and Cindy knew she had to obey. She slicked the point of her tongue over the highly polished leather, laving and worshipping the symbol of Louisa's dominance. When she had covered every inch of the boot with her tongue, having stopped frequently to gather more saliva in her dry mouth, she was obliged to turn her attention to its twin. Her nostrils were filled with the scent of leather and polish and she was growing increasingly thirsty, but she kept on diligently with her task. Eventually, she sat back on her heels, and looked up at Louisa.

The woman glanced down at her scornfully. 'They'll do, I suppose, but you haven't finished yet.' As she spoke she was pulling down her jodhpurs. She wore no underwear beneath them, and Cindy was presented with the sight of her luxuriant chestnut bush. She moved forward, so that she was straddling Cindy's head with her legs. 'Pleasure me, slut,' Louisa ordered, parting her thighs more widely.

Cindy hurried to comply, aware that Louisa was still holding the riding crop. Her tongue snaked out and up, making contact with the soft flesh of Louisa's sex. As she licked along the length of the crimson furrow, Louisa's juices began to flow, filling Cindy's mouth with the ripe tangy taste of a sexually aroused woman. Louisa's clitoris peeked out from its protective cowl, fat and juicy, and Cindy took it between her lips, nibbling on it gently. This seemed to please the other woman, who threw her head back and moaned low in her throat. Cindy sucked harder, seeking to coax a climax from Louisa. She was soon rewarded with a guttural cry and a flood of salty liquid in her mouth as Louisa reached orgasm.

Cindy stopped her oral ministrations and sat back on her heels, aware that her mouth and chin were smeared with Louisa's sex juices. It was always exciting to bring another woman to orgasm, and Cindy was aware that the gusset of her G-string was starting to dampen with her own nectar.

'Did I please you... Mistress?' Cindy asked, the word bitter as aloes in her mouth. But she knew it was what Louisa Lawson wanted to hear.

'You did your best, I suppose, but there's only one way you can truly please me,' Louisa said. 'Stand up and go over to that chair.' She indicated a low-backed wooden chair with Queen Ann legs and a padded seat covered with slightly faded damson velvet. Cindy did as she was told. 'Now bend over it.'

Cindy shuddered, but placed herself in the required position. Everything was building up to the inevitable moment when Louisa beat her.

She was aware of the other woman coming to stand behind her. 'Spread your legs,' Louisa ordered. As she did so, Cindy was aware of the G-string slipping between her bulging labia, cradling the secret places between them more closely. She knew now why Louisa had not asked her to remove the little garment: there was no real point when it already left her buttocks entirely bare. She suspected Louisa was contemplating them now, imagining how the riding crop would soon be striping their soft white skin. She felt the merest tap on her left cheek as Louisa measured the distance, and then the crop fell.

Fiery pain seared across both buttocks, and Cindy howled. A hand-spanking or a paddling she could have taken stoically almost for as long as it landed, riding the pain until it began to take on that sweet dark undercurrent of pleasure, but the crop was a more brutal, unforgiving instrument. It fell again, and again; three more stripes in quick succession that branded themselves as deeply into Cindy's consciousness as her flesh. Her limbs trembled and her knuckles whitened as she tried to steady herself against the all-consuming waves of agony.

Louisa had not finished with her yet. When the crop fell again it was aimed squarely at the underhang of Cindy's bottom, where the skin was more tender. There were tears in Cindy's eyes, now, but she dared not lessen her grip on the chair to brush them away. There was a long moment when it seemed as though the punishment was over, and then one last stroke fell, slicing across the tops of her thighs. Cindy shrieked so loudly she thought they must have heard her on the coast, but she was answered only with Louisa's low, mocking laugh.

'Stay where you are,' Louisa said, 'and keep looking straight ahead.' Cindy did as she was told, hearing what sounded like a drawer being opened, and strange rustling noises. Then Louisa was behind her once more.

This time it was only the woman's long slim fingers which touched Cindy's abused buttocks, and they were covered in a cool, soothing balm. Louisa worked quickly and gently over the weals she had raised on Cindy's flesh, the cream taking some of the heat away. Her touch was assured, almost loving, and Cindy knew that if she had been required to, she would have called this woman 'Mistress' gladly, and despised herself for being broken to another's will so easily.

There was the soft, sucking sound of Louisa dipping her fingers into the pot, but no more cream was applied. Cindy wanted to turn her head and find out what was going on, but she knew that was not advisable. So she waited, and when Louisa's fingers hooked into the waistband of her soaking wet G-string and pulled it down until it was around her knees, she braced herself for whatever was about to happen.

The next thing she felt was something solid pressing at the entrance to her sex. It had the domed head of a fully erect penis, but the cool alien hardness of plastic. The greasy lubrication that was enabling it to enter so easily must have been that last dollop of cream Louisa had taken from the pot. Without a second thought, Cindy splayed her legs more widely to let the dildo slide between her pussy lips. It lodged securely within her, and then was thrust deeper, in one swift movement.

Cindy felt soft skin pressing against her sore buttocks, and realised that the phallus was strapped around Louisa's waist. No doubt there was a second, equally large dildo inserted deeply into Louisa's cunt, filling and stimulating her just as its twin was filling and stimulating Cindy.

Louisa pulled back until the phallus had almost slipped out of Cindy's sex, then slammed it in hard. She began to fuck the little blonde with power and grace, the well-lubricated dildo thrusting to the very depths of Cindy's wet channel. With every forward stroke, Louisa's groin made contact with Cindy's buttocks, pressing against the sore stripes the crop had left behind. And yet, each painful reminder of the ordeal she had undergone only seemed to arouse Cindy further, pushing her rapidly towards orgasm.

The room was silent except for Louisa's muttered oaths and Cindy's tortured breathing. Somewhere in the house a grandfather clock chimed the hour. Louisa reached round and began to play with the puckered buds of Cindy's nipples. Cindy moaned, feeling jolts of pleasure scissor down to her womb.

'Not yet,' Louisa said, sensing that Cindy was reaching a peak of excitement. 'You'll come when I tell you, and not before, or it'll be the worse for you.'

'Yes, Mistress,' Cindy replied, the word falling from her lips unbidden.

Louisa was thrusting into her harder than ever, and Cindy suspected that the other woman was close to her own orgasm. Cindy desperately wanted to come, but knew she had to time her orgasm to Louisa's command. Her resolve was shattered when Louisa slipped a hand between Cindy's legs and lightly touched her clitoris. It was enough to send her spiralling down into the orgasm her body craved so badly.

When the last ripple of pleasure had finally faded, she opened her eyes to see Louisa glaring at her. The dildo had slipped out of Cindy's body and protruded from Louisa's crotch, slick and shiny with Cindy's copious juices. More unnervingly, Louisa was holding the riding crop once more.

'Did I say you could do that?' she asked.

'I'm sorry, Mistress,' Cindy replied softly. 'I just couldn't help myself.'

'You'll have to be taught that when I give an order, I expect it to be obeyed. Do I make myself clear?

Before Cindy could answer, Louisa's arm had moved like lightning and the crop slashed down, the tip making agonising contact with Cindy's right nipple. She had no chance to recover before the crop had fallen again, on her left nipple this time. Cindy clutched at the chair, fighting to keep her balance; the pain in her tormented nipples was like nothing she had known, but it was sending messages that her confused nerve-endings were translating as pleasure, and her womb was throbbing in orgasm once more.

Unable to stand on her weak legs, Cindy sank to the floor. Louisa turned away; in contempt, Cindy suspected, at how she had reacted to the punishment. However, she was looking in the drawer from which she had produced the strap-on dildo and the lubricant, and Cindy realised that, like Pandora's Box, there was always something lurking in its deepest recesses. This time, Louisa produced a collar and a pair of wrist cuffs, together with a slim metal pole about eighteen inches long.

Cindy was unable to resist as Louisa put the collar around her neck and buckled it securely, then fastened the wrist cuffs in place. They had been designed, Cindy quickly realised, so that they could be attached to the metal pole, which ran practically the length of her spine once it was in place. She found herself forced to kneel upright, the curious bondage contraption allowing her hardly any movement. As a final insult, a cuff was strapped around her ankle and tethered securely to the leg of the library's heavy wooden writing desk.

'Get used to it,' Louisa told her, as Cindy wriggled experimentally in her bonds. 'If your boss is putting up any sort of resistance, you'll be in it for a while.' And with that, she turned and stalked haughtily out of the library, leaving Cindy alone with her increasingly worried thoughts.

Cindy woke from a dream in which someone was trying to stuff her into a very small barrel, in which she was intended to negotiate Niagara Falls. She had no idea how long she had slept, but the sun seemed to be quite high in the sky, and she assumed it was mid-morning. This was not, she thought ruefully, how she usually spent a Sunday morning. Usually she would be waking after a night's escort work, ravenous and ready for a decent breakfast and a trawl through the morning papers. She was more than ready for her breakfast, but she doubted that the Lawsons would be falling over themselves to provide bacon and eggs and a cup of freshly-brewed coffee.

She had been left in her cramped kneeling position for a couple of hours before anyone had come to check on her. This time, it had been Clive Lawson. He had not spoken a word to her, but had merely removed the metal pole before securely fastening the wrist cuffs together. He had then unzipped his trousers and presented his almost fully erect cock to Cindy's unprotesting lips. Knowing what was required of her, she had begun to lick the bulbous head, the point of her tongue flicking into the little eye to scoop out the droplets of juice which were forming there. Swiftly and efficiently she had brought him to the point of no return, at which moment he had caught hold of her head and clamped it securely to his crotch. Unable to move, Cindy had felt her mouth filling with salty gouts of his come, which she had been obliged to swallow. Then he had simply zipped himself up once more, turned on his heel and left the room.

Grateful at least that she was no longer in her restrictive bondage, even though her wrists were still tethered behind her, Cindy had curled into a little ball. From what Louisa had said, her comparative freedom meant that Laurel was doing as the Lawsons wanted. Although Cindy suspected it wasn't actually what the Lawsons wanted at all. Someone else was responsible for what was happening, she was sure of it; someone who knew plenty about both herself and Laurel, and probably everyone else at the agency. It didn't make sense. Laurel had no enemies, as far as Cindy knew: the only person who had ever caused her any problems was Roger Preston, and he was missing, presumed lost up his own fundament. Too sore and tired to devote any serious thought to the problem, Cindy had closed her eyes and given in to sleep.

And now she was wide awake once more, and aware that she was no longer the only person in the room. Quite a crowd had gathered, in fact. Clive and Louisa Lawson, as immaculately turned out as ever and giving no indication that they had a naked, bound woman in their drawing room. Laurel, head bowed submissively, wearing nothing but a pair of tattered stockings, and with her hands fastened behind her back. And there was a fourth person, who Cindy recognised immediately despite the fact that he'd dyed his hair since she'd last seen him. Roger Preston. Suddenly, things began to fall into place.

The two girls risked a glance at each other, and Cindy winked, trying to indicate to Laurel that although they might be down, they were certainly not out. She couldn't help noticing that Laurel's sex lips were flushed and swollen, and her nipples bruised, and she wondered what had happened to her boss in the time after they had been separated.

Roger strode over and looked down at Cindy where she was huddled on the floor. 'Did you sleep well?' he asked sarcastically.

'Roger!' Cindy replied. 'I'd like to say how nice it is to

see you again, except I can't. Why don't you sod off back to whatever hole it is you've crawled out of, and leave us all alone?'

'Ah, Cindy, elegant and refined as ever.' Roger sighed. 'I thought a night in bondage might have taught you the value of keeping your mouth shut, but obviously not. Perhaps I should send Louisa for one of her ball gags, and we'll see your lips stretched round that, eh?'

'Why don't you cut out all the macho crap, and tell me and Laurel what's going through that devious little mind of yours?' Cindy said. After the cropping she had received from Louisa and her uncomfortable night in the wrist cuffs, she was in the mood for a fight, and if being stroppy was getting up Roger's nose, so much the better. She had never particularly enjoyed working for him when he had been joint owner of the old agency, much preferring to deal with Laurel. If he was back on the scene, it could only mean bad news.

'Oh, Laurel knows exactly what's happening here. Why don't you tell your little friend my plans for the future, Laurel?' He caught a handful of Laurel's hair and forced her head up until her eyes met Cindy's.

'Roger wants his share of the agency back,' Laurel said quietly. 'He's pleased with the way we've been running it in his absence, and he wants to reward us for our efforts by creaming off half the profits.' A new, more defiant tone crept into her voice. 'And he can't understand why I won't agree to this arrangement.'

'I must admit, I thought we'd have broken you between us by now,' Roger said reflectively. 'Well, if not a hardened slapper like Miss Beresford here, then I thought keeping Laurel chained up for a while might have knocked some sense into her, but obviously not. I think we shall have to raise the stakes a little.' He paced round the room, hands clasped behind his back, surveying the two girls. 'I'm sure that at some point over the last few hours you must have wondered how I know so much about the two of you and your little sexual proclivities, and about the new format of the agency. I couldn't have done it all by myself, you must have realised that, and now I think it's time you met the person who's been so vital in the success of this operation up till now.'

Roger strode over to the door. When he pulled it open, Cindy almost gasped aloud in shock as she saw who stood framed there.

Laurel, too, was gaping at the figure in the doorway in disbelief. Five years had wrought substantial changes: the mousy, messy curls and the puppy fat had gone, replaced by sleek, black, waist-length locks and a svelte, sensual figure, but there was no mistaking the cold green eyes and the expression of hatred contained within them.

'Nina!' she gasped, at the same time as Cindy exclaimed, 'Devon!'

The two girls looked at each other. 'That's Devon?' Laurel asked Cindy. 'I knew it was a false name as soon as I heard it.'

'So, who is this?' Cindy asked. 'Do you two know each other?'

'You could say that,' Laurel said. 'This is Nina, my stepsister. I haven't seen her for a few years—'

'And I'm as pleased about that as you are, believe me,' Nina retorted. Laurel was struck by the pronounced American twang in her stepsister's voice. No wonder Joe, who knew nothing of the bad blood that flowed between the members of the Angell family, had been taken in so convincingly. 'You can't know how nice it is to see you trussed up like a Thanksgiving turkey, sister dearest.'

'Why have you done this?' Laurel asked. 'How could you get involved with a slimy little crook like Roger? No, forget that. It's obvious. Everyone sinks to their own level eventually.'

Nina shook her head. 'Same sanctimonious Laurel. I always hoped you'd lighten up one day, but it doesn't seem to have happened. And if you must know, Roger's made me a very good proposition. If things go to plan, I'll be sitting behind the desk in the agency while you're out servicing the clients. It sounds like a perfect arrangement to me.'

'Well, you can just forget it, because it's never going to happen,' Laurel replied passionately. 'There's no way you or Roger are getting your grubby hands on the agency.'

'It's a shame you think like that,' Nina said. 'I hoped you'd see things our way. I mean, I sincerely hoped we could all get on well, seeing as I'm going to be spending so much time with Joe and all.'

'Joe? What do you mean?'

'Let's just say that we've been spending some quality time together.' Nina's smile was witch-like. 'We pretty much hit it off the first time we met. Let me tell you, the sex in the office that day... I've never known anything like it. He thinks I'm pretty, and smart, and fun to be with. You know, I think the guy's seriously in love with me.'

Laurel felt sick to the pit of her stomach. It was all too possible to believe that Joe might have fallen for Nina, whose innate, raw sexuality was now allied to a cool, sophisticated beauty. If only she had given in to her instincts and told Joe how she really felt about him, she wouldn't be kneeling here, listening to her stepsister boast of her relationship with the only man she had ever truly loved.

'Whatever the relationship between you and Joe, it

doesn't change the way I feel about the agency,' Laurel said. 'I'm not signing it over to you and Roger.'

Nina and Roger looked at each other in obvious exasperation, then Roger said, 'There's only one thing for it. Louisa, go and fetch the clamps.'

Louisa left the room smartly, returning a few moments later with what looked like a small, blue velvet jewellery box. She handed it to Roger, who crouched down before Laurel and opened it up. Inside was what Laurel at first took to be a pair of old-fashioned screw-fastening earrings. Roger took one out and held it before her.

'I think a session with these on will help to change your mind. Nina, would you like to do the honours?'

'Certainly. Stand up, Laurel.'

Knowing she had no option but to obey, Laurel rose carefully to her feet, wondering what was coming next. She felt Nina's hand cupping her left breast, before her stepsister flicked her thumbnail over her nipple, bringing it instantly to full hardness. In that instant, Laurel knew the true purpose of the little clamps. Nina fixed one onto Laurel's protruding nipple, screwing it tightly into place. Laurel bit her lip, wanting to cry out as the clamp's metal jaws bit viciously into her tender flesh.

Nina repeated her actions on Laurel's right nipple, fastening the clamp just as tightly. She smiled at Laurel's obvious discomfort. 'Oh, yes, they hurt when they go on, but they hurt even more coming off.' Her finger travelled down the cleavage between Laurel's breasts and down over her softly curving stomach, to settle in her red-gold pubic bush. 'They make them for down here, too,' Nina informed her. 'Imagine how they'd feel, biting into those soft lips of yours...'

Nina's finger stroked the length of Laurel's moist crease, and despite herself, she moaned at the touch.

'Nina, control yourself,' Roger said. 'I think it's about time our two houseguests provided us with a little entertainment, don't you?'

'I know just the thing,' Louisa Lawson said. 'Let me go and fetch it.'

This time, when she returned, she was carrying a little bottle of olive oil and a long, phallic-shaped object, made of very old-looking leather. She held it up so that both Laurel and Cindy could see it more clearly.

'They call it an olisbos,' she announced, drizzling a copious amount of oil over the smooth leather and rubbing it in with her fingertips. 'It's just a fancy name for a double-ended dildo. And I think you know exactly where both ends are going, don't you, girls?'

Without ceremony, she thrust the oiled dildo between Laurel's thighs, pushing it deeply into her vagina. Laurel felt the phallus lodge securely inside her, stretching her tight walls. Then Cindy was hauled to her feet and brought over to where Laurel was standing. Louisa's hands reached down to part Cindy's inner lips, then she shoved the other end of the dildo into Cindy's sex.

'Release their hands,' Roger told Louisa. 'I want to see them playing with each other's tits.'

Louisa unfastened Laurel's cuffs, and she rubbed her aching wrists, before putting her arms round Cindy and hugging her close.

'You know I don't want to have to do this,' she whispered.

'Don't kid me,' Cindy replied. 'You love being made to do things just as much as I do, but you just won't admit it.' As she spoke, she jerked her hips, thrusting the end of the dildo further up into Laurel's juicy channel. A groan of pleasure escaped Laurel's lips.

'Told you,' Cindy said. She reached out and caressed

Laurel's breasts, mindful of the clamps, encouraging Laurel to fondle her own smaller ones in return. They sank to the floor together, oblivious to their audience, their pussies grinding together as they used the olisbos to bring them to the brink of climax.

Lost in a haze of bliss, Laurel was barely aware of Roger saying, 'Go and get your address book, Nina, I need to make a call.'

Nina must have made some retort, for Roger snapped, 'Do it, or I'll have you on the end of that thing, and we'll watch as Laurel makes you come.'

The last thing Laurel heard before her orgasm hit her was the sound of the drawing room door closing softly behind Nina.

Chapter Fourteen

Joe was slumped on the settee in his dressing gown and boxer shorts, trying and failing to concentrate on the Italian football match which flickered on the television screen in front of him. It had been a long and strenuous night, and he was still tired from his exertions. The sisters he and Christian had been employed to escort to the warehouse party in Victoria Dock had insisted on being taken back to the flat they shared some time after midnight, and had proved to be almost insatiable. Joe had lost count of the number of times Serena, the elder of the two, had come on his tongue as he licked and lapped at her fleshy, shaven sex, his senses overwhelmed by the musky smell and taste of her, coupled with the sounds of Christian spanking her sister, Charmaine, as the girl wriggled and squealed on his leather-clad lap. It had been a fabulous night, and well worth the wad of notes Serena had tucked into his top pocket before he left, but by the time he had arrived home it was seven in the morning, and he'd barely enough strength to have a shower and a swift breakfast before going to bed. He'd surfaced about an hour ago, but he was beginning to think that had been a mistake. What he needed more than anything was another couple of hours' sleep...

The phone rang, and he reached out to pick up the receiver on autopilot, glancing briefly at the TV screen, where Ronaldo was placing the ball on the penalty spot, having gone down faster than a Thai bar girl in the area. It was probably Laurel, calling to tell him about her own exploits down in the New Forest. 'Hello?' he muttered drowsily.

A voice he did not recognise asked, 'Is that Joe Gallagher?'

'Yes, it is.' Joe was alarmed by the speaker's faint tone of menace. 'Who is that?'

'All in good time. I thought you might want to speak to your friend first.'

There was a muffled sound, which Joe thought might have been a sob, and then Laurel was on the line, her voice barely a whisper. 'Joe – I'm so sorry.'

'Laurel!' Joe exclaimed. 'What's going on? Are you okay?'

'It was a set-up. It's Rog—' and then the receiver appeared to be snatched away from her.

'What the hell do you want?' Joe asked.

'A straight swap,' the voice replied coolly. 'I have your friends, Laurel and Cindy. You have part ownership of Domination Inc. Give me that, and I can assure you the girls will not be harmed. Refuse me, and—' There was the sound of a palm slapping hard against flesh in the background, followed by a sudden, unmistakably female cry.

'Why should I do what you're asking?' Joe said, aware that there were two very good reasons, both of whom appeared to be in imminent and obvious danger.

'Because the agency was mine before that silly little slut got you involved in running it, and I want it back. I want you to come down to Garside Hall, alone, with the deeds to the agency; give me those, and you get your friends in exchange. Don't think about involving the police, or it will be the worse for all of you. Don't forget I hold the whip hand here – quite literally, I can assure you.' The man, who Joe now realised to be Laurel's erstwhile business partner, Roger Preston, sniggered at his own pun. 'Shall I expect to see you this evening, Joe, or do you want me to treat the girls to another night of my very special hospitality?'

'You'll see me when you see me, Preston,' Joe replied.

'Don't keep me waiting too long, Joe. I'm not a very patient man, and you might not like what happens when I get impatient.' There was another slap, another soft cry, and then the line went dead.

Joe sat for a moment with his head in his hands, all traces of tiredness gone. From everything Laurel had said about Preston, he had built up a mental image of a devious interior disguised beneath a veneer of charm, but he had not believed the man could be quite so ruthless. Somehow, Laurel and Cindy had walked into a trap, and he had allowed it to happen. If only he'd sent Warren on that job the night before, and gone down to Lawson's house with Laurel...

He grabbed the phone, punching numbers almost at random. There was no answer from Chris; he was no doubt still sleeping off the combined effects of Serena and Charmaine. Devon's phone, too, rang unanswered. When he called Warren the answerphone kicked in almost immediately. Joe waited with rising impatience for the message to finish. 'Warren,' he began, unable to conceal the urgency in his tone, 'Warren, are you there? Look, if you are there, for God's sake answer the phone! It's an emergency, they've got Laurel—'

'Joe?'

'Warren, thank Christ. They've got Laurel and Cindy. I—'

'Calm down,' Warren replied. 'Who are "they"?'

'You know the bloke who owned the agency, Roger? The one who disappeared and left Laurel with all the debts? He's in league with that Clive who invited her down to his house for the weekend. They got her there to talk business, and the only business they want to do involves stealing everything we've worked for. He wants me to give up my share in the agency in return for the girls.'

'What a fucking bastard.' Warren paused for a moment, listening to a voice that Joe could hear only faintly. 'I'm sorry, Sara. Pick your clothes up and go home, love. We'll have to finish this some other time. Sorry about that, Joe,' he said, returning his attention to the conversation in hand. 'What does he want you to do to get the girls back?'

'He said I've got to go down there on my own with the agency deeds, and we'll do an exchange.'

'And you trust him?'

'What else can I do?' Unexpectedly, Joe was finding himself close to tears. 'Warren, if they hurt Laurel I'll never forgive myself.'

'They won't hurt her. But you're not to go there alone. I'm coming with you.'

'But—'

'No buts. I'm just as worried about those girls as you are, but I think I've got a plan. Meet me at the agency at six o'clock. I've got a favour to call in and it might take me a while.'

He rang off, leaving Joe staring at the phone, trying to collect his jumbled thoughts. Roger had given a clear warning of the consequences of disobeying his orders, but Warren was right; they could not trust the man to keep his word. Whatever Warren's plan involved, it had to be better than walking blindly into the lion's mouth. Praying that they were doing the right thing, Joe went to get dressed; he had a rendezvous to keep.

Challoners' was the most famous theatrical costumier in London; the shop had stood in the same street in Piccadilly for over fifty years, its windows full of outfits its team of dressmakers had created for a succession of well-known films and TV shows. On this Sunday afternoon, its front door was firmly shut to the world. Warren Keating stood on the pavement, gazing at a display of Victorian ballgowns and waiting for Helen to arrive with the key. It was a long time since he'd seen Helen Jeffreys, but she'd dropped everything at the sound of his voice, just as he had known she would. They had met when he had landed the small part of a builder in a couple of episodes of a long-running sitcom; she had been the show's costume designer, and they had enjoyed a short-lived, but very intense fling. He thought back with satisfaction to one occasion when they had been out filming on location for the show in Norfolk and he had fucked her in the bedroom of a tiny cottage as a scene was being shot in the room below. He had watched with amusement as she had fought desperately to control her cries while he powered forcefully into her from behind; he had taken a belt to her plump white backside beforehand, and with every thrust his groin slapped against the raised welts on her soft skin. When they had both been on the verge of coming, he had tangled his fingers in her bobbed brown hair and pulled hard; her shriek of agony combined with overwhelming pleasure must have been audible to the cast and crew beneath them. He had imagined their reactions, staring up at the ceiling as they registered the unmistakable sound of a woman in the throes of orgasm; he suspected the footage of that moment had turned up on the engineers' Christmas compilation tape that year, though it would never feature on any comedy out-takes show for public consumption.

He was still smiling at the memory as Helen came hurrying down the pavement towards him. She had hardly altered since the last time he had seen her; still slightly overweight, with her figure concealed by a baggy cardigan and a shapeless skirt. For someone whose life revolved around making sure people were perfectly clothed, her own dress sense had always been appalling, Warren thought. What she needed was a man who appreciated her dramatic curves, and encouraged her to wear outfits which would reveal her sensational breasts and the bottom she thought was too chubby and pear-shaped. Still, everyone in TV was so skinny, paranoid about the extra pounds the camera added to their frame, it was no wonder Helen appeared to feel unattractive in comparison.

She pushed her long fringe out of her eyes, and smiled shyly at Warren. 'It's nice to see you again,' she said, 'but I don't quite understand what we're doing here. You said there was something I could help you with?'

'That's right,' Warren replied. 'Can we go inside and talk about it?'

'Okay. Come on.' Helen opened the front door and they stepped inside. Immediately, a high-pitched alarm began to bleep rapidly. Helen punched in a series of numbers on a keypad by the door, and the alarm fell silent.

'So are you going to tell me what this is about?' Helen asked.

'Well, when I rang, I thought you were still at the BBC, and I was going to ask you to do something which might get you the sack. To be honest, it still might, but you'd do that for me, wouldn't you, Helen?'

'I don't know. Tell me what it is you want me to do.'

'I need to borrow a couple of costumes from you, but not officially. You see, I need them now, this afternoon, and if I don't get them, well, let's just say that a friend's life might hang in the balance as a result.' As he spoke, Warren hoped he was over-dramatising the situation. He seemed to have hit the right note with Helen, however, as she seemed less defensive than she had done a moment ago.

'And what sort of costumes would these be, exactly?' she asked.

'Police uniforms – the most authentic you have. The ones they use in reconstructions, not the fancy dress stuff.'

'You're in luck,' Helen told him. 'We've just had a few returned. I take it one's for you, but what about the other one? Is it a male or female friend?'

'Male,' Warren replied. 'Funny thing is, he used to be a copper at one point. He's roughly my height, but broader.'

'Okay, let's see what we can do.' Helen took him out of the main body of the shop, and into a smaller stockroom. Costumes hung in plastic sheeting; one wall seemed to be devoted to nothing but outfits belonging to the emergency services. Warren's mind wandered as he stroked a hand absently along a rack of nurses' uniforms, and he found himself picturing Laurel in a tight, short blue dress, that would strain across her full breasts, with a little apron and a watch fob clipped to the front, and a cheeky little white cap pinned in her hair. When she bent over to take a temperature, the dress would rise up to reveal that beneath it she was wearing seamed stockings, suspenders and frothy lace knickers. Showing her undies to the elderly male patients, albeit inadvertently, would be exactly the sort of behaviour which would earn her a reprimand from Matron, and if that reprimand came in the form of a spanking on her naked, squirming little bum, then so much the better...

He snapped back to the present, aware that he was supposed to be helping save Laurel, not lusting after her.

Helen had selected a couple of police uniforms from the rack, and was holding one out for Warren's inspection.

'This should be about your size,' she said.

'So you remember my measurements, do you now, Helen?' Warren replied. 'Does that include my inside leg? I seem to remember you were very insistent on making sure everything was a snug fit in that particular area.'

Helen blushed. 'You should try it on for size. It's a shame your friend's not here, too. I'm just having to guess what will fit him.'

'Ah, well, he doesn't exactly know I'm here,' Warren said. 'And he'd probably kill me if he did,' he added quietly.

'Just what are you planning here, Warren Keating?' Helen asked. 'I mean, I wouldn't put it past you to have some kind of bizarre strippogram business going, seeing as I haven't seen your name on many credits recently.'

Warren knew there was only one way to distract her from asking questions. He began to undress, letting his battered old jacket fall to the floor before slipping off his boots. He pulled his T-shirt over his head, then unfastened his jeans and stepped out of them to stand before Helen in nothing but a pair of black jersey jockey shorts. He was aware that she could not prevent her gaze from straying to his crotch, and was suddenly conscious of how the jersey material was clinging to his cock and balls, outlining them for Helen's appreciation.

He reached out and took the supposedly police issue trousers from Helen's suddenly trembling fingers. She had picked out a pair which fitted him perfectly, and when he buttoned up the crisp white shirt and the jacket with its shining silver buttons and insignia, he began to feel the adrenaline rush which always suffused him in the moments before he stepped in front of the cameras and began to act. Helen handed him the cap, and he set it smartly on his head, subtly altering his stance to that of an arresting officer.

'D'you have a mirror anywhere around here?' he asked.

'Come back through to the shop,' Helen said. He followed her out, and found himself staring at his reflection in a full-length mirror. He had not, as yet, played the part of a policeman and, as he appraised himself, he decided it was a gap on his CV which needed to be filled. There was no denying that the uniform suited him, and Helen seemed to think so, too, judging by the hungry way she was staring at him. He was beginning to understand what people meant when they talked about the aphrodisiac qualities of a man in uniform.

He would never know quite what devil took hold of him at that moment, but he turned to Helen and snapped, 'Very careless of you, wasn't it, letting a man into your shop on such a flimsy pretext?'

'I'm sorry,' she stammered. 'I don't quite know what you're—'

'He told you he was an actor, I believe you said, Miss Jeffreys. Rather strange behaviour for an actor, isn't it? Surely his costume department would organise an outfit for him, rather than him calling for it himself. Didn't it occur to you that he might have some ulterior motive?'

Helen seemed to have realised that Warren was playing a game with her, for she quickly responded, 'I honestly don't know what it could be. I mean, there's no money in the till, not on a Sunday. Although he could have taken just about anything in the shop while my back was turned.' She glanced meaningfully at Warren. 'And I mean anything. I was very distracted once he started undressing, officer. You see, he had a very good body.'

'That's quite enough of that kind of talk,' Warren replied.

'I'm supposed to be conducting an investigation here, and you're wittering on about the suspect's body.'

'But perhaps that could be it,' Helen replied. 'He might not be a thief at all. He might just get his kicks out of undressing in front of strange women. You know, like a flasher.'

'Did you actually see his penis, Miss Jeffreys?' Warren asked.

There was almost a note of regret in Helen's voice as she said, 'No, I didn't. Well, only the outline of it through his boxer shorts. He looked as though he was quite well-endowed, if that's any help.'

Warren shook his head. 'I'm afraid it isn't.' He wandered around the shop, conscious of Helen's eyes on him as he moved. 'You see, at the moment I can't see where a crime has been committed. Nothing appears to be missing from the shop, and this man didn't actually expose himself to you. You realise I could quite easily charge you with wasting police time, Miss Jeffreys.'

'Oh, please don't do that,' Helen said quickly. 'If my boss finds out I let someone into the shop on a Sunday, I'll be in terrible trouble. I could even lose my job.'

'Well, perhaps we could come to some kind of compromise,' Warren said. 'If you were to accept some kind of... physical chastisement, then I'd say no more about it.'

Helen's face flushed as she asked, 'What sort of physical chastisement?'

Warren glanced round, and saw a crook-handled cane displayed prominently alongside a headmaster's mortarboard and gowns, and a tarty-looking schoolgirl's uniform. 'I think a good old-fashioned six of the best,' he said, walking over to pick up the cane. He gestured towards the cash desk. 'I'd like you to bend over that,

Miss Jeffreys, and raise your skirt.'

'Do I have to?' Helen asked, feigning reluctance.

'I don't think you have a choice,' Warren replied. He watched as she obediently went over to the cash desk and bent over, one elbow resting on the counter top while the other reached behind her to flip her skirt up and into the small of her back. Beneath it, she was wearing functional navy blue cotton pants and tights in an unappealing tan colour.

Warren carefully tucked the hem of her skirt into the waistband, so there was no chance of it falling back into place while he caned her. Helen waited, her head resting on her folded arms. He tapped her bottom with the cane, measuring his swing, and then brought the thick bamboo down smartly on her fleshy cheeks. Though she had been expecting the stroke, she still could not prevent herself from rising up and rubbing her bottom.

'Any more of that behaviour and I'll double your punishment,' Warren warned, as Helen leaned forward over the cash desk once more. Again the cane fell, parallel to the first stroke, and this time Helen made the considerable effort to stay where she was. A third blow followed in quick succession, and then Warren paused.

'Your tights, Miss Jeffreys,' he said finally. 'Take them down. And your pants, too.'

'Are you sure this is necessary?' Helen asked. 'I mean, it's not as though I've actually done anything wrong.'

'You're currently obstructing an officer in the course of his duties,' Warren retorted. 'Now take them down or I'll be forced to do it.'

After a short pause, Helen did as she had been told. Warren's cock pulsed in his trousers at the sight of her plump, naked bottom, the marks the cane had already left a dull red against her white skin. Helen had only pulled her pants and tights down as far as the crease of her buttocks, and Warren used the tip of the cane to push them further down her thighs.

'Now, spread your legs for me, Miss Jeffreys,' he demanded.

This time, Helen did not question the order. She must have known as well as he did that as she parted her thighs he would be able to see the hair-fringed contours of her sex, pouched between her legs, and the rosy pucker of her anus.

Ruthlessly, Warren brought the cane down swiftly on Helen's arse once more, angling it so that it fell across the lines he had already imprinted on her flesh. This time, he could see the crimson mark that sprang up in its wake. Pleased with his handiwork, he added a second, crossing from the other side. As his final trick, he planted a stroke squarely at the junction of her bottom and her thighs, eliciting a howl of anguish from her.

Even though her stated punishment was over, Helen stayed where she was, her bum stuck out temptingly towards him. He was about to free his cock from his uniform trousers when he noticed the time. He had less than ten minutes before he was due to meet Joe. Choking back his frustration, he patted Helen tenderly on her caned cheeks.

'Sorry, but I'm going to have to go.'

She stood up, pouting in disappointment. 'Are you not at least going to tell me what this is all about?'

'When I bring this stuff back, I promise.' He went to pick up the second uniform, which she had placed in a suit bag for him.

'Close the front door behind you, then,' was all she said.

When he turned back after closing the door, thinking to blow her an apologetic kiss through the glass, he saw that she was sitting on the floor, back pressed against the cash desk, her fingers buried deep in her pussy as she brought herself to the climax of which Warren's precipitous departure had deprived her.

'I hope you've got a good explanation for why you're bringing the force into disrepute,' Joe said, as he climbed into the passenger seat of Warren's four-wheel drive.

'I thought it rather suited me,' Warren replied, indicating to turn out of Soho's snarled-up maze of streets and into Piccadilly Circus. 'You've got one, too. It's in the bag on the back seat.'

'You're joking.' Joe reached over and picked up the suit bag. He shook his head in disbelief as he realised what it contained. 'Please, Warren, enlighten me.'

'It's the perfect way to get into Lawson's house. We turn up, say we've had reports of a disturbance – I don't know, someone trying to break into the building – and could we check that everything's okay? He's not going to refuse what looks like a visit from two genuine members of the Old Bill, now is he?'

'I can't do it,' Joe replied. 'I can't put a uniform on again, not after what happened to me.'

'You haven't got any choice,' Warren said. 'Not if you want to make sure Laurel and Cindy get out of that place in one piece.'

Joe sighed. 'He told me specifically not to involve the police.'

'But you're not involving them. Trust me, Joe. We can make this work. Now, why don't you grab some shut-eye while I drive us down to the New Forest?'

Against his better judgement, Joe relaxed back against the seat's padded headrest and closed his eyes. Soothed by the car radio, he drifted into an uneasy sleep.

Warren brought the four-wheel drive to a halt a couple of miles down the road from Lymington, having taken the address of Lawson's house from Laurel's desk diary. He shrugged on the uniform jacket, which he'd taken off to prevent suspicion from passing motorists as he drove, and indicated to Joe that he should get into the back of the vehicle and change his own clothes.

'I'm not happy about this,' Joe said, unbuckling his seat belt reluctantly. 'Just looking at that sodding uniform brings back too many memories.'

'I know, and I'm sorry, but I can't think of any way we're going to get into the house. I mean, we could hardly turn up as jobbing painters and decorators, or Jehovah's Witnesses, not late on a Sunday evening, now could we?'

Joe quickly stripped off his jeans, denim jacket and baggy jumper, and reached for the suit bag. A shiver went down his spine as he looked at the uniform Warren had picked out for him. Instantly, he was reminded of the many mornings when he had stepped into just such an outfit before being sent out on patrol. The camaraderie of the squad room; the thrill of making an arrest; the nerve-wracking moments waiting to give evidence in court... It all came flooding back, along with the frightening sight of the tree looming up before them, seconds before the patrol car had ploughed into it.

He was aware of Warren watching him impatiently, and at that moment he could have cheerfully strangled his friend. It was a stupid thing they were about to do, and he wanted no part of it. And yet he didn't want to hand over the agency deeds which were inside a plain brown envelope in his jacket pocket. He had dealt with blackmail cases several times in his police career, and it was a nasty, cowardly crime, made even worse in this instance by the fact that Roger Preston was intent on using the safety of two helpless women as his bargaining tool.

Knowing that he had no other real choice, he began to dress. Whoever had supplied these clothes had made a fair stab at guessing his size, and though he had filled out slightly since he was invalided out of the force, everything seemed to fit well enough. This was how he had been dressed the first time he had met Laurel, and he wondered how she would react on seeing him in uniform again.

'Fantastic,' Warren said approvingly. 'Let's go.'

Navigating the last mile or so from the elderly road map Warren kept stuffed in the glove compartment, they soon found themselves at the bottom of the drive that led to Garside Hall.

'We'd better get out and walk from here,' Joe said. 'Otherwise it's going to look more than a little suspicious if two uniformed policeman are spotted getting out of a Jeep with a cartoon rhino on the spare wheel cover.'

Joe and Warren made their way up to the house, their boots crunching on the smooth gravel. Lights were burning in a couple of the windows, and Joe wondered which room Laurel and Cindy were being kept in. Well, he thought, they would find out soon enough.

Warren paused for a moment to adjust his cap before ringing the doorbell. At first, the two men thought no one had heard them, but as Warren went to ring the bell once more, the door was opened by a tall, elegant-looking woman in a black leather bustier and short, tight-fitting suede skirt. Her expression showed clear annoyance at being asked to answer the door late on a Sunday evening.

'Mrs Lawson?' Warren asked.

'Yes?'

'I'm PC Challoner, and this is my colleague, PC Jeffreys,' he improvised. 'We've had reports of a disturbance on your property.'

'A disturbance?' The woman was staring closely at them, and Joe was certain that their cover was about to be blown at any moment.

Warren continued blithely, 'Yes, apparently a motorist driving past saw someone trying to climb over the wall at the bottom of your garden. They were worried someone might be trying to break into your house. We'd like to come in and check that everything's all right.'

'We're fine. There's no one here except my husband and I. Now, if you don't mind...' Louisa Lawson tried to shut the door, at which point Joe and Warren sprang forward, pushing her into the hall.

Joe's swift hand over her mouth stifled any cry she might have made to alert the others in the house, and Warren used the handcuffs which Helen had thoughtfully provided with the uniform to secure Louisa's hands. In her panicked state, he knew it would never occur to her that these were anything other than genuine police-issue cuffs, even though they were designed to spring free without the use of keys.

'Now, show us where the girls are,' Joe hissed in Louisa's ear. He let her stumble forward into the drawing room, where they were confronted by the sight of Cindy wriggling on Clive Lawson's knee as he used a heavy rubber paddle on her backside. The red blotchy patterns that already marked her skin indicated that this punishment had been going on for some time.

By the time Lawson looked up, registering the unexpected intrusion, Warren had locked the door, preventing his and his wife's escape.

'What the hell is going on here?' he asked. Cindy took advantage of his confusion to scramble off his knee and fling herself into Warren's arms.

'Thank God you're here!' she exclaimed.

'These men are animals!' Louisa said, finally shaking off Joe's grip. 'They turned up at the door spinning some cock and bull story. They must know what's really going on here, Clive.'

As she spoke, Clive Lawson was making a break towards the French windows at the far end of the room, but Joe was quicker. He launched himself at the fleeing man and rugby-tackled him. Lawson fell heavily to the carpet, catching his head against a table leg in the process. He lay, moaning groggily, the fight knocked from him.

Joe hauled him, unprotesting, over to where his wife stood meekly, hands cuffed.

'Cindy, could you get her clothes off?' he asked.

Cindy, happy to see the rôles reversed, began to divest Louisa Lawson of her bustier and skirt. 'Strip her husband, too,' she said. 'I've got a plan.'

When the couple were naked, Cindy went rooting in the drawer from which Louisa had produced so many punishment implements over the past twenty-four hours, emerging triumphant with a couple of coils of rope and the leather olisbos with which she and Laurel had been made to pleasure each other.

She presented one end of the phallic object to Louisa's mouth, intending her to suck it, but Louisa kept her lips stubbornly clamped shut.

'Either you lick it, and lick it well, or I'll stick it where you know it's going unlubricated, and I don't think you'll enjoy that,' Cindy warned her. Reluctantly, Louisa opened her mouth, and began to apply a generous coating of her own saliva to each end of the olisbos in turn.

When Cindy was satisfied, she took the dildo. 'Now spread your legs, bitch,' she ordered Louisa. The other woman parted her thighs enough to give Cindy access to her sex. Cindy licked her finger and ran it along Louisa's furrow. 'You don't know how much I'm going to enjoy this,' she said, positioning one end of the olisbos at the entrance to Louisa's vagina and thrusting it home.

Louisa gave a groan as the saliva-slick length lodged inside her, but Cindy had not yet finished. Now she turned her attention to Clive, who was being held by Joe. 'On your hands and knees,' she told the man. 'I want to see that arse of yours sticking up in the air.'

The formerly dominant Lawson could do nothing other than obey, as Joe began to manoeuvre him into the required position. When Cindy was satisfied she again licked her finger, and used it to circle Lawson's tightly-puckered rear hole.

'Oh, you like that, don't you?' she said, as she pushed against the resistance of Lawson's muscular ring, and felt it yield. 'Maybe my two friends here should take it in turns to bugger you, eh? Maybe you should be made to lick their cocks first, so they'll enter you nice and smoothly...'

To Lawson's obvious chagrin, his cock pulsed and stiffened slightly at Cindy's words. She reached beneath him and gave his shaft a few contemptuous rubs. As he hardened and grew more excited beads of pre-come formed in the eye of his glans. Cindy scooped it up with her finger and used it to lubricate his anus.

'Concentrate on the pleasure,' she crooned, motioning to Joe, who had already worked out where the other end of the double dildo was going, and was more than happy to drag Louisa Lawson over until she was kneeling directly behind her husband. 'That way, you'll barely notice the pain.'

Joe had taken hold of the dildo where it jutted out of Louisa's crotch, and pressed it to Lawson's anal opening. Then he gave Louisa a sharp smack on her rump. She squealed and pitched forward slightly, the dildo forcing its way deep into her husband's rectum.

Warren sprang the catch on Louisa's handcuffs, and together he and Cindy worked quickly to tie the Lawsons up, so that Clive was tethered to the legs of the table, still kneeling. Louisa's hands were fastened around his waist and secured at the wrists, and their legs were tied together, Louisa's outside her husband's.

Joe reached for the phone extension and dialled rapidly. 'Hello, police? Yes, I'm calling from Garside Hall. There's been a break-in. Could you send someone over to us? Okay, brilliant, we'll see you then.'

He put the receiver down and smiled at the Lawsons, who were wriggling in their bonds. 'You might be able to free yourselves before the police turn up. I hope you do, for your sakes. I mean, you might be able to find a convincing reason for why you're naked and tied up, but I'd love to see you both explain away that little toy of Louisa's.'

He turned to Cindy. 'Get dressed,' he said, gesturing to the discarded pile of clothes on the floor, 'and then make your way down to the jeep. We've got to be away from here before the police arrive, but first of all Warren and I are going to find out what's happened to Laurel.'

Chapter Fifteen

In the master bedroom, Laurel was secured to the bed, spread-eagled, waiting for whatever Roger might choose to do to her. He had not tied her up himself, having left that task to the skilful fingers of Louisa Lawson. Louisa had used silken ropes and left Laurel with enough purchase in her bonds that she could wriggle slightly, but had no chance of freeing herself.

It seemed like a lifetime since she had spoken to Joe, though it could only have been a matter of hours. In that time, Clive had strapped Laurel's backside for the first time in her life, as she had been held fast over his wife's knee; she could still remember the feel of the heavy leather strap as it landed on her soft flesh, causing her to cry out and buck in Louisa's surprisingly strong grasp. She had only taken five strokes from the strap, but each had burned like fire, and when she was laid on the bed by Clive, even the smooth satin counterpane had chafed painfully against her sore skin. The sensation had gradually faded to a dull ache as Roger sat in a corner of the bedroom, watching her and waiting for Joe to arrive.

She had half-hoped that Joe would refuse to hand the deeds to the agency over, but when the choice was the business or the safety of herself and Cindy, it was a refusal he could never have made. At least, she supposed, it proved he still cared about her...

Laurel's mind was still in turmoil over Nina's mocking words. The thought that Joe had fallen in love with her stepsister had hurt more than any blow from Clive

Lawson's strap. Why had she never told him she loved him herself? Why had her stupid pride prevented her from getting involved with him? It was too late now: Nina had claimed him, as she had claimed anything Laurel had ever really cared about.

She forced her mind back to her present situation. Roger had risen from his seated position, and was busying himself with something on the dressing table. As Laurel watched him she realised he had lit one of the thick wax candles which were used as decoration throughout the room. He walked towards the bed, holding it and smiling.

'Relax, Laurel,' he said. 'It'll soon be over, but we still have time for one more game.'

'Why are you doing this?' Laurel asked, her eyes widening in fear as Roger took the candle out of its solid brass candlestick. He stared at the flame with almost manic intensity.

'Nina was easy,' he said. 'She gave herself to me willingly. She's a good and obedient slave, and she'll do anything I ask of her. But you, Laurel, you're a challenge. I know I haven't broken you. Whatever we've done to you, part of you is still resisting. I haven't heard you beg for mercy, and I want that so much...'

'Never,' Laurel said, her gaze riveted to the fat bead of wax that was forming as the candle burned steadily.

Roger moved so that he was standing directly beside her. He held the candle above her supine, bound body, and began to tilt it. 'You only have to say the words.'

'Go to hell,' Laurel retorted. Seconds later she felt a brief burning sensation as the droplet of wax splashed on her stomach. Despite herself, she gave a sharp cry.

'Where shall it be next?' Roger asked. 'Those beautiful breasts of yours?'

As he spoke he let another drop of candlewax fall. His

aim was accurate, and it landed squarely on her right breast, a fraction away from her pale, puckered aureole. Another blob followed, crowning her left breast. She bit her lip, forcing herself not to make another sound. She would not give him the pleasure of seeing how frightened and vulnerable she was.

His crotch was close to her face as he leaned over her, the material of his dark trousers pushed out sharply by the strength of his erection.

'I'll stop now, on the condition that you suck my cock,' he told her. 'And while you're sucking it, I want you to frig yourself with this candle. I can just see how it will look, sliding in and out of your beautiful cunt...'

'And what if I won't do it?' she asked, having absolutely no desire to fellate her erstwhile business partner.

'Then just imagine how it will feel to have hot wax falling on that pretty little pussy of yours.'

Securely bound and with her legs widely splayed, Laurel was utterly vulnerable to Roger's whims. She fought a rising tide of revulsion as he gently stroked her hair away from her face. How could she ever have believed this man to be her friend, her equal?

He passed the candle over her lower body, so close that she could feel the heat from the flame against her sensitive sex-flesh, before pulling it away and letting wax spatter her inner thighs. Still, she would not give him what he craved, and she knew it was only a matter of time before droplets of wax were daubing her crinkled pussy lips.

As she closed her eyes and prepared for the worst, the door to the bedroom burst open. She looked up to see Warren, dressed, of all things, as a policeman, doing his best to wrestle the guttering candle out of Roger's clutches.

'Put it down, man,' Warren snarled, 'or I'll have you done for resisting arrest.'

'I told that stupid friend of yours not to get the police involved!' Roger snapped at Laurel. His voice took on a new, wheedling tone. 'Look, officer, I can explain everything. You see, this is a private party...'

His words tailed off as Joe appeared in the doorway. Laurel was stunned to see that Joe, too, was wearing a police uniform.

'Private fucking party, indeed,' Joe began, moving towards the bed and beginning to untie Laurel as Roger, the extinguished candle falling from his grip, struggled in Warren's arms with renewed purpose.

'You're not the police,' Roger said, realisation dawning. 'Clive! Louisa! Come and help me deal with these idiots.'

Warren grinned. 'I'm sorry, but your friends are tied up with other things at the moment.'

'Well, they may be, but I'm not.'

Warren and Joe's heads turned at the sound of the voice behind them. Nina was standing there, brandishing the brass candlestick from the dressing table with every intention of using it as an offensive weapon.

'Fucking hell, is this turning into *Cluedo* or what?' Warren observed. 'It's Devon Rylance, in the bedroom, with the candlestick.'

This was the moment when Laurel, her left wrist now free, expected things to turn in Roger's favour. Joe had stopped unfastening the ropes that held her, and was staring at Nina as though stunned. Roger had almost broken free of Warren's grasp, and if he managed to do that it could only be a matter of time before his roster of captives rose to four. Somehow, in all the confusion she found her voice.

'It's not Devon,' she croaked. 'It's my stepsister, Nina. She's the one who betrayed us all. She's in league with Roger because she thinks if she sides with him she'll get my stake in the agency. Well, don't believe it, Nina. Join with him, and if anything goes wrong he'll dump you in it, just like he did with me.'

'You bitch...' Joe flung himself at Nina, pushing her against the doorframe. He prised the candlestick out of her clenched fist and thrust her arm up behind her, so high that it must have been painful.

'Get off me,' Nina cried, attempting to kick Joe in the shins, but she must have sensed that the balance of power was no longer in her favour, for she soon gave up.

Laurel was working on her remaining bonds, picking at the knots with her fingernails. Warren had taken the rope which had previously bound Laurel's left arm and was using it to tie Roger's hands behind his back. When a second rope was available, Joe wrapped it round Nina's wrists and fastened it securely.

'Shall we leave them here?' he asked Warren. 'I mean, the police are going to be here soon enough.'

Warren shook his head. 'I've got something better in mind for these two,' he said. 'Come with me. Laurel, bring the rest of the rope with you; we're going to need it.'

He led Roger out of the bedroom and down the stairs. Joe followed, frog-marching Nina, and Laurel brought up the rear.

'Where's Cindy?' she asked Joe anxiously.

'She's safe. She helped us inflict a suitable revenge on the Lawsons,' he replied.

They paused in the hallway. 'Stunning as you look when you're naked,' Warren said to Laurel, 'you're going to need some clothes.'

'My coat's hanging up over there,' Laurel said. 'Will that do?'

She retrieved it, along with her handbag, which was still underneath the coatstand, where she had left it. Belting the coat over her nakedness, she followed the others outside, wincing at the feel of cold sharp gravel beneath her bare feet.

'Car keys, please,' Warren said. He took them from Laurel and unlocked the rear doors of her Peugeot, depositing Roger and Nina roughly in the back of the car. Joe got in beside the two prisoners.

'Okay, you and Joe take them to the bottom of the drive and wait for me.'

He set off down the drive at a jog. Laurel slipped her feet into the scuffed but comfortable driving shoes she always kept in the footwell. She turned the key in the ignition, and heard the engine catch first time. Executing a neat turn in front of the house, she made her way to where Warren's four-wheel drive was waiting. Cindy was sitting in the passenger seat, buffing her nails with the pad of her thumb.

'What've you brought those two for?' she asked, as Warren caught up with them, barely out of breath from his run.

'We're taking them on a little adventure,' he replied. He hunted in the four-wheel drive's glove compartment and found an old torn envelope and a pen. Scrawling the words, 'Look in the copse and all will be revealed,' on the back, he tucked the envelope prominently into the wrought ironwork of the gate.

'Okay, let's go,' he said. Laurel followed Warren as he drove the five hundred yards or so down the road to a copse of twisted ash trees. Between the four of them they helped Roger and Nina out of the car, and led them into the centre of the little wood.

'This should do it,' Warren said. He untied Roger, and motioned to Joe to do the same to Nina. Laurel and Cindy looked on, wondering exactly what he had in mind. His next order gave them some indication. 'Right, you two, strip down to your underwear. And don't forget you're outnumbered two to one, so don't try to do anything smart.'

Glancing nervously at each other, Roger and Nina began to do as they had been told. Soon their clothes were in an untidy pile at their feet, and Roger stood shivering in a pair of clinging white underpants with a designer name featured prominently on the waistband, while Nina folded her arms in front of her breasts, which were cradled in a lacy red bra.

'That as well, I think,' Warren said, gesturing to Nina's bra.

'Is all this strictly necessary?' Laurel asked, unable to conceal the thrill of pleasure she felt at seeing her stepsister humiliated in this way.

'Nah, not really,' Warren replied, 'but it's fun.'

Nina had removed her bra and dropped it on top of the other clothes. Her nipples stood out prominently in the cold evening air, and Laurel found herself trying to ignore the jealous thought that Joe had already seen those nipples in a far more intimate context.

'Now go and stand against that tree trunk.' Warren gestured to a particularly gnarled old ash. Roger and Nina obeyed him, their backs pressing uncomfortably against the rough bark, and it was mere seconds before he and Joe were fastening them both to the tree with the assorted lengths of rope they had brought with them.

'Well, hopefully once the police have sorted out your friends and their little diversion, they should come looking for you,' Warren said. 'Failing that, shout loudly and I'm sure someone will hear you eventually. I'd like to say it's been nice meeting you, Roger, but my mammy told me never to lie.'

He turned to leave the copse, but Laurel halted him.

'Hang on, we haven't quite finished yet.'

If they were expecting her to make some impassioned speech, denouncing her stepsister and her former partner as the duplicitous low-lifes they undoubtedly were, they would be disappointed. There were times when actions were much more effective than words, she thought, reaching down to pluck a handful of the dark, fuzzy-leaved plants she had recognised as stinging nettles the moment she had entered the copse.

With a wicked smile she pulled the waistband of Roger's pants away from his body and stuffed a small bunch of the leaves down the front. He grimaced as she rubbed his crotch through the cotton, pressing the nettles against the skin of his cock and balls.

She took a second handful of nettles and advanced on her stepsister. The men had bound Nina so that her breasts emerged from coils of rope above and below. They were too visible and tempting a target to ignore. Laurel brushed the nettles across Nina's breasts and nipples, watching the irritated skin flushing a mottled red. Then she deposited them in Nina's lacy knickers, pushing them well in to make sure they rested snugly against the folds of Nina's sex.

'You wicked little minx,' Warren said, with a smile of obvious approval, as they observed the agonised expressions on Roger and Nina's faces.

'Now we can go,' Laurel announced.

She kept the car window open, so she could hear the howls of frustration and annoyance fading into the distance as she drove away.

'So, do you think that's the last we'll hear of the pair of them?' Joe asked, as they sat in the living room of Laurel's flat.

'I'd like to think so,' Laurel replied. 'They'd be very

foolish to try anything else, considering how we sent them both away with their tail between their legs.'

'Well, something between their legs, anyway,' Warren retorted. 'God, but that was a piece of ingenuity on your part, so it was.'

'I almost hope they freed themselves before the police turned up,' Joe said, 'if only so they could rub some dock leaves over their bits and pieces.'

'Yeah, but Laurel should have seen what we did to the Lawsons,' Cindy said. 'I'd have loved to have seen the expressions on the police's faces when they saw that snooty cow tied up and shafting her old man up the arse with a double-ended dildo.'

Cindy drained the last drops from her glass. On arriving back in London, they had stopped at an all-night convenience shop close to Laurel's flat and acquired a bottle of champagne with which to toast their victory over Roger. While Laurel and Cindy had shared a long, leisurely bath, washing their hair and spending plenty of time soaping each other's breasts and backs, Joe and Warren had busied themselves in the kitchen, cooking pasta and a rich tomato sauce to go with it. To Laurel's surprise they had managed to do so without using every pan in the place and leaving the work surfaces looking like a building site. Now, the four of them sat discussing their success in keeping the agency out of Roger and Nina's greedy hands.

Cindy did her best to suppress a yawn, but Joe noticed her drooping eyelids.

'I think it's time someone was in bed,' he said gently. 'Come on, Cindy.' He scooped her up off the settee. In the overlong night-shirt she had borrowed from Laurel, and with her petite frame, she looked like a doll in his arms. She clasped her hands round the back of his neck, and let him carry her into Laurel's bedroom.

'I suppose Joe and I should be leaving once he's tucked Cindy in,' Warren said. 'You'll be needing your rest, too.'

Laurel shook her head. 'I feel too wired to sleep,' she admitted. 'I'm still on a high from what's happened.' She reached out for her own glass, suddenly aware that, as she did so, the neck of her dressing gown was drooping open, affording Warren a perfect view of her breasts. Despite the fact that he'd seen her naked and tied to the Lawsons' bed earlier in the day, the thought that she was displaying herself to him in this way caused a quick pulse of arousal to beat between her legs.

He glanced up, making no secret of where his gaze had previously been directed. 'Well, there are two things that are guaranteed to help you get off to sleep. One's a hot milky drink, and the other's masturbation.'

She swallowed, her throat suddenly dry. 'And which of those do you recommend in my case?' she whispered, aware of Joe and Cindy's faint conversation in the adjoining room.

'Definitely the latter,' he replied. 'Preferably with an audience.'

Laurel remembered the words Cindy had spoken in the car on the way down to the New Forest: 'He'd tell you to play with your pussy, and you'd do it'. Well, now she knew that to be the truth. Still confused about what Joe really felt for her, she was at least certain that hiding her own feelings when it came to her sexual desire was no answer. At this moment, she wanted Warren to prove his dominance over her with a need so desperate it was almost painful.

'I don't think I could go that far,' she lied.

'Of course you could, and you will,' he replied, in the low, commanding voice she had first heard him use in the pub what seemed a lifetime ago.

'But what if Joe comes in?' she asked.

'Don't be stupid, Laurel. He wants to see you play with yourself just as badly as I do. To tell you the truth, he wants it more than I do. The guy's mad about you.'

'But I thought it was Nina he was in love with.'

Warren gave a contemptuous snort. 'In her dreams. Where would you get a crazy idea like that? No, don't tell me. She told you that, right? The devious cow.' He shook his head in disbelief. 'You should have given her a better going-over with those nettles.'

Laurel leaned forward again, refilling her own glass and Warren's, too. Her movements were deliberately exaggerated, and when she pushed his glass back across the table to him, her left breast fell free of the dressing gown. She hooked her legs up under herself, so that the join of her thighs was almost visible to Warren where the gown was loosely belted.

'You wanted me to touch myself,' she reminded him, her hand absent-mindedly caressing her exposed nipple.

'I know what I wanted you to do,' he replied, 'but it's typical of a little slut like you to distract me from my purpose. If you don't behave you'll be touching yourself while you're over my knee, getting a few slaps on that impudent arse of yours...'

'Who's got an impudent arse?' Joe asked, coming back into the living room. His eyes widened at the sight of Laurel in her state of undress, her fingers toying with her hard nipple.

'Who do you think?' Warren replied. 'I told her she was going to have to frig herself in front of the two of us, and she responds like the slut she is. How wet do you reckon her cunt is?'

'Oh, I think our fingers would come away soaked,' Joe replied.

Laurel squirmed in her seat. For so long she had fantasised about her two friends treating her in this fashion, and at last it seemed as though her wish was about to be granted.

'Show us your pussy, Laurel,' Warren ordered.

As if in a dream, she unfastened the belt of the dressing gown, and let the garment fall open completely. Her knees were tight together, and she slowly parted them until both men had a perfect view of her sex, with its cap of red-gold curls. Her hand found its target unerringly, snaking between her thighs to settle on the moist cleft between them. Joe was right; she was soaking wet, her excitement fuelled by the thought of what she was about to do. The fingers of her right hand continued to toy with her hardened teats as her left rubbed at her clit in the familiar pattern which was guaranteed to bring her to a swift climax.

Her breathing grew more ragged, and she threw her head back as she felt the tension growing within her. Her pelvis arched forward and her legs splayed more widely, offering her sex to the two men who sat before her, spellbound by her performance. Her middle finger skimmed across the opening of her vagina, slipping inside to fetch out more of the moisture that pooled there, to anoint her pleasure bud. She was so close to coming that she squealed in outright frustration when she felt Warren catch hold of her wrists, pulling her to her feet.

'That's quite enough of that,' he said. 'I told you to play with yourself, I didn't tell you to come.'

'But I need to,' Laurel whimpered. 'Please, Warren...'

'Not yet, darling,' he told her. 'Joe, give me a hand, would you?'

Joe took the dressing gown cord and swiftly bound Laurel's crossed wrists in front of her. She groaned, needing something to quench the fire which still burned low down in her belly, and sensing that her two friends were about to provide it.

Her suspicion was confirmed when Warren forced her down onto the floor so that she was resting on her elbows and knees, her full breasts hanging down. His hand in the small of her back pushed her lower, so that her hypersensitive nipples brushed against the pile of the carpet and her rump was raised prominently in the air. She heard a noise behind her, and turned her head to see Joe pulling his belt free of the loops in his dark trousers.

'No,' she wailed, remembering how Clive Lawson had used the leather strap on her buttocks earlier in the day. And yet, even as she recalled the pain, her arousal sparked again. This was different; this was Joe, the man she loved, and the one she could now dare to believe loved her, who was about to punish her. And he would do it aided and abetted by Warren, who knew better than anyone how to reach the submissive heart of her sexuality. Almost unaware of what she was doing, she lifted her backside higher, offering it to Joe.

'Ask for it, Laurel,' Joe said. 'Ask me to beat you.'

In a voice which did not sound like her own, she replied, 'Please, I want you to punish me. You and Warren. Punish me, and then fuck me.'

'And if we want to fuck your mouth, or your arse?' Warren asked.

Laurel's initial reply was a feral groan, at the thought of Warren sliding his cock into the untried depths of her anus. Finally, she recovered enough to say, 'If you want them, they're yours. Do whatever you want to me.'

'Very well, I'm going to give you six strokes, and then Warren will give you another six,' Joe told Laurel. 'After each one you have to thank us, or we go back to the beginning and start again. Is that understood?'

Laurel nodded, mentally readying herself for what Joe was about to do. The next thing she heard was the leather belt whistling through the air, before it landed on her backside in an explosion of pain. Conscious of Cindy sleeping in the next room, she bit back her cry of anguish, and muttered, 'One, thank you, Master.'

She knew Joe had not asked for that last refinement, but it was the natural thing to say, and she meant it. Joe's only reply was another crack of the belt on her backside, lower than the first. Fires of pain that had fallen dormant from her earlier chastisement now reawakened, and she wondered how she was going to get through this ordeal without miscounting, or earning an extension to the number of strokes in some other fashion.

Stroke after stroke fell, each one pushing her forward slightly so that her nipples scraped against the carpet. Joe was placing them so that a new area of flesh was covered every time, patterning her backside with thick, throbbing stripes. The fifth caught the fleshy crease between her bottom and her thighs, causing her to sob openly, and when the sixth caught the meat of her upper thighs she knew she would be begging for mercy before Warren had finished his half-dozen.

He gave her a brief respite before taking over, and when he unfastened her wrists she almost believed she would be allowed to forego the rest of the punishment. Instead, he ordered her to go and stand holding on to the mantelpiece, in front of the fireplace which was only for show.

His ingenuity was greater than Joe's, for in this position her whole body was available to him. Like Joe, he concentrated on her backside at first, piling pain upon pain as the belt fell on skin which had already been belted.

Still she had not lost count, and still she continued to offer her grateful thanks after every stroke.

When only two remained she thought she had escaped the worst, but Warren had a particular refinement in mind. The belt curled around her upper body; not hard, but landing on her right breast with sufficient sting to make her loosen her grip on the mantelpiece and stuff the fleshy part of her thumb into her mouth to stifle her howl of anguish.

Eventually she recovered her composure enough to say, 'Eleven, thank you, Master.'

'You did say we could do whatever we wanted, sweetheart,' Warren reminded her.

She nodded her head, miserably, and waited for the last stroke, knowing where it was bound to fall. This time it was her left breast which suffered, the end of the belt flicking against her jutting nipple. It was a pain like nothing she had known, and as she thanked Warren she could not prevent herself breaking down in tears.

Immediately he took her in his arms. 'There, there, sweetheart,' he soothed, his fingers brushing the tears from her cheeks. 'It's over now. You took it all, and we're proud of you.'

She raised her head, and did her best to smile at him. The mixture of pride and desire in his eyes caused something within her to melt, and suddenly they were kissing, her pent-up passion finally breaking free from the barriers she had raised against it.

She was aware of rustling behind her and the sound of a zip coming down, and then Joe was behind her, his hands cupping her breasts and his strong erection pressing into the cleft between her sore buttocks.

Delirious with lust, Laurel helped Warren to scramble free of his clothes, and soon the three of them were a mass of limbs and hot wet mouths. Hands fondled flesh, and no one could tell where one body ended and another began. Joe's lips caressed Laurel's nipples, while Warren's hand delved between her legs, the pad of his thumb circling her clit. She wanted to feel both of them inside her; Warren's cock buried in her soft fleshy sheath while Joe breached one of her long-held taboos and penetrated her rectum, the two men separated from each other as they moved by only the thinnest of membranes.

'So, Laurel, is this where we stop being just friends and become lovers?' Joe asked, his voice soft in her ear.

'Yes. Oh, I should have let this happen a long time ago,' Laurel replied, the words becoming increasingly difficult to form as Warren led her insistently towards her long-denied climax.

'Some things will have to change, you know,' Joe said. 'I want us to move in together, for a start.'

'What, all three of us?' Warren asked. 'Isn't it going to get a bit crowded?'

'No, you idiot. I meant me and Laurel,' Joe retorted. 'If we're going to do this, I want us to do it properly.'

'I have no problem with that,' Laurel told him, feeling his finger begin to push against the rim of her puckered anal hole at the same time as Warren's fingers slipped into the wet clasp of her vagina.

'And there'll have to be some alterations at work,' Joe continued. 'I'm not going to let you wear knickers in the office any more, Laurel, and both Warren and I will have the right to check at any time to see if you're complying with that order. If not—' He pulled her hard onto his groin, her recently-abused buttocks grinding painfully against his crisp pubic hair to illustrate what would be in store if she disobeyed.

Joe's thumbs were stretching her cheeks apart, enabling

the head of his cock to nudge at the entrance to her anus. Warren was moving, too, positioning his glans so it was almost slipping into her eagerly waiting sex. Both men were waiting for her answer.

'I'll do it,' she replied, 'on the condition that you never, ever recruit another member of staff without my say-so.'

'You've got yourself a deal,' Joe replied.

As she felt the two men penetrate her simultaneously, Laurel gave a cry of sheer joy. The agency was saved from Roger's scheming, for the time being at least, and she and Joe were about to place their relationship on the footing where it should, in truth, have been a long time ago. Before her orgasm finally claimed her she had enough time to register Warren's hopeful question.

'So, would now be a good time to ask about a pay rise?'

Exciting titles available from Chimera

1-901388-20-4	The Instruction of Olivia	*Allen*
1-901388-15-8	Captivation	*Fisher*
1-901388-01-8	Olivia and the Dulcinites	*Allen*
1-901388-02-6	Belinda: Cruel Passage West	*Caine*
1-901388-09-3	Net Asset	*Pope*
1-901388-12-3	Sold into Service	*Tanner*
1-901388-13-1	All for Her Master	*O'Connor*
1-901388-14-X	Stranger in Venice	*Beaufort*
1-901388-16-6	Innocent Corinna	*Eden*
1-901388-17-4	Out of Control	*Miller*
1-901388-18-2	Hall of Infamy	*Virosa*
1-901388-23-9	Latin Submission	*Barton*
1-901388-19-0	Destroying Angel	*Hastings*
1-901388-21-2	Dr Casswell's Student	*Fisher*
1-901388-22-0	Annabelle	*Aire*
1-901388-24-7	Total Abandon	*Anderssen*
1-901388-26-3	Selina's Submission	*Lewis*
1-901388-27-1	A Strict Seduction	*Del Rey*
1-901388-28-X	Assignment for Alison	*Pope*
1-901388-29-8	Betty Serves the Master	*Tanner*
1-901388-30-1	Perfect Slave	*Bell*
1-901388-31-X	A Kept Woman	*Grayson*
1-901388-32-8	Milady's Quest	*Beaufort*
1-901388-33-6	Slave Hunt	*Shannon*
1-901388-34-4*	Shadows of Torment	*McLachlan*
1-901388-35-2*	Star Slave	*Dere*
1-901388-37-9*	Punishment Exercise	*Benedict*
1-901388-39-5*	Susie Learns the Hard Way	*Quine*
1-901388-11-5*	Space Captive *(Sep)*	*Hughes*
1-901388-42-5*	Sophie & the Circle of Slavery *(Sep)*	*Culber*
1-901388-41-7*	Bride of the Revolution *(Oct)*	*Amber*
1-901388-44-1*	Vesta – Painworld *(Oct)*	*Pope*
1-901388-45-X*	The Slaves of New York *(Nov)*	*Hughes*
1-901388-46-8*	Rough Justice *(Nov)*	*Hastings*

All **Chimera** titles are/will be available from your local bookshop or newsagent, or direct from our mail order department. Please send your order with a cheque or postal order (made payable to *Chimera Publishing Ltd*) to: Chimera Publishing Ltd., PO Box 152, Waterlooville, Hants, PO8 9FS. If you would prefer to pay by credit card, please call our **24 hour telephone/fax credit card hotline: +44 (0)23 92 783037**.

To order, send: Title, author, ISBN number and price for each book ordered, your full name and address, cheque or postal order payable to B.B.C.S. for the total amount, and allow the following for postage and packing:

UK and BFPO: £1.00 for the first book, and 50p for each additional book to a maximum of £3.50.

Overseas and Eire: £2.00 for the first book, £1.00 for the second and 50p for each additional book.

*Titles £5.99 (US$9.95). All others £4.99 (US$7.95)

For further details of all our titles send for our free catalogue:

Chimera Publishing Ltd
Readers' Services
PO Box 152
Waterlooville
Hants
PO8 9FS

Or visit our WebShop at:
www.chimerabooks.co.uk